RAILS ✦ WEST

The Steel Roots Series
The Boxcar Baby
Crossings
Rails West

J L MULVIHILL

SEVENTH STAR PRESS

Cover art and illustrations: Anne Rosario
Cover art and illustrations in this book copyright © 2016 Anne
Rosario & Seventh Star Press, LLC.

Editor: Amanda DeBord

Published by Seventh Star Press, LLC.

ISBN Number: 978-1-941706-46-6

Seventh Star Press
www.seventhstarpress.com
info@seventhstarpress.com

Publisher's Note:
Rails West is a work of fiction. All names, characters, and places
are the product of the author's imagination, used in a fictitious
manner. Any resemblances to actual persons, places, locales,
events, etc. are purely coincidental.

Printed in the United States of America
First Edition

DEDICATION

Let ring the battle cry, this soldier stands prepared,
let ring the battle cry, he's trained and well aware.
Let ring the battle cry, this soldier will stand tall,
let ring the battle cry, this soldier will not fall.
Stand down the battle cry, this soldier homeward bound,
stand down the battle cry, then lost without a sound.
And where the mind takes you once you have seen, the things
that should not be.
And he is lost in body and mind, yet in spirit he is free.
RIP Jesse Harris

For James Powell and Logan Masterson, you both will be
greatly missed.

Hobo Signs

CHAPTER 1

$\mathcal{G}$azing out across the blue wilderness of sky, I feel small and insignificant. Looking down at the wide world below frightens me and makes me feel dizzy. I've never been seasick, but I imagine it's somewhat the same as being airsick. My stomach lurches again and I tip my head back over the bucket Dr. Clint gave me. It's funny but I didn't get sick when I rode in the balloon with the airship pirates. Dr. Clint told me that a dirigible is different than a balloon. He said a dirigible lurches and leans like a ship on the ocean but a balloon just floats on the air. I guess it's like we are sailing the sky. I don't see the difference, but I guess he would know.

I wish I could feel well enough to talk to the captain, but every time I get up to walk, I get queasy again. Dr. Clint brought me on deck thinking that it might make me feel better to be in the fresh air. I think it's just making me worse because I can see how far up we are.

"All right there, lassie? It'll pass soon enough," says a voice behind me.

"Thank you. I'm sure you're right," I say, looking up. I see another little man I've not met before and wonder if it's the captain. I've seen several of these little men on board since I've been on deck. Sky Riders is what Mr. Gunter said they call themselves.

They all look at me with curious eyes as they go about their business. I've been trying to just stay out of their way and ignore their looks. It appears that I'm the only girl on board, and I'm also three times their size, both of which make me feel a little uncomfortable.

"Here, try this," says the man, and offers me something wrapped in brown paper.

"What is it?" I ask at the risk of sounding rude.

"It's a bit of a concoction of mine own. A bit of mint, a bit of ginger and some various roots all ground up and mixed with honey. It helps with the sickness," he says. He has a strange accent I'm unfamiliar with. It doesn't sound like the any of the other's I've heard on board.

I unwrap the package and find something that looks like earwax. I figure what have I got to lose? I put it in my mouth and I'm pleasantly surprised. The taste is not bitter or anything, it kind of tastes like ginger candy with a hint of mint and honey like he said.

"Chew it up slow now, and swallow the juice it makes with your saliva. That's how it works best to soothe your stomach," he says.

"Thank you," I say between chews.

"Ai lassie, you'll be right as rain soon," he says as he bows his head to me and walks on.

I keep chewing the candy stuff, and after a while I think I'm feeling better. I'm not sure how long I've been on deck, but I notice that the sky is growing darker now. I must have been pretty much puking all day. Well that just figures. I feel worn out like I've been dragged ten miles behind a wagon.

I stand up and look around because I'm not sure what to do next. I didn't pay much attention to where we were going when Dr. Clint brought me up deck. I have no idea which way to go to get back to my cabin, not to mention what to do with a bucket of my sick.

"I'll take that, Miss Abby, and if you follow me I'll take you where you can freshen up a bit," says a familiar voice. I turn and see Dr. Clint standing behind me grabbing at the bucket in my hand.

"It's okay. I can carry it," I say. I'm a little embarrassed to have this little man carrying my bucket of puke.

"Don't be silly, Miss Abby; I know you're feeling a bit weak right now. You'll need to steady yourself with your hands as we walk. Besides, I've carried many a bucket of this, and yours is not the first. These fellas here are not as hard as they look. When we hit a good storm more than half of these men end up with their heads in a bucket. Some of them even sharing a bucket when we run out," he says, laughing.

He takes the bucket from my hands and I follow him with no more argument. He's right. I do feel unsteady on my feet. I have to grab hold of whatever is available as we walk the deck and then down some stairs and into the ship. We go down a short hall and he directs me into a small room I take for a bathroom. At least it smells like one to the point that I almost feel sick again.

"You can take care of what you need to in here. There's a water pump and a basin to wash your face. I put a fresh towel for you. We don't have a bathtub on the ship. We usually wait for landing before we bathe, but you can at least freshen up. Whatever you need to do in here, I'll watch the door till you're done. We have the one head aft and one head forward," he adds.

"It's okay," I say. "This will be fine."

I walk in the room and find I have to stoop a bit since everyone on this ship is about three feet tall. I'm a little over five feet which makes it hard to maneuver. I hear the door close behind me and feel a sense of relief at being alone for the moment.

A long bench lines the wall with several lidded holes I gather are toilets. I'm almost curious where all the stuff goes; I hope it doesn't just drop out of the sky.

On the other side is another bench a little taller with a pump and several large bowls. On the edge of the table are a couple of small towels stacked in a neat pile. I take care of the first part of business and try not to get sick while using the toilet. When I lift the lid the smell almost overpowers me. I hold my nose until I'm done and shut the lid quick.

I take one the cleanest looking bowls and fill it up with water from a pitcher. Finding a bar of soap with the towels, I wash my hands and face and arms and even wipe down my legs. It feels good to be clean; I can't remember the last time I had a real bath.

Afterward I feel much better; I think the stuff the guy on deck gave me to eat actually helped my stomach a lot. I try and fix my hair but since there is no mirror I'm not sure if I did a good enough job at it or not. I don't have a brush so I just run my fingers through my hair. I braid it to the side, tying it off with a ribbon I have wrapped around my wrist. Feeling a little more myself I open the door to find Dr. Clint standing there dutifully waiting for me.

"Well, now you do look like you feel better," he says.

"I do, thank you," I say.

"Then let's go see if we can talk with the captain now while you're still on your feet, shall we?" he asks as he marches back down the hall and up the stairs.

I follow him with no reply. I do want to talk to the captain and find out what he knows about Papa, but I'm a little nervous too. I follow Dr. Clint up onto the deck and the front of the ship. There is a big house or building built at the front of the ship, and we go through a door into this. Inside the first thing I see are all these windows that look out to the horizon ahead.

A little man sits in a leather armchair centered in front of the windows. Next to the chair is a small table with a book and a teacup. To the left of the room is a table with an oil lamp mounted on the wall above it. Maps cover the table along with some strange metal instruments; I think one instrument is a sexton. I remember reading about sailors using tools like that to chart their location by the stars. I would imagine there are a whole lot of stars up here to follow.

To the right of the room is a bed set into the wall and covered in blankets and pillows of all colors and shapes. Next to the bed is another small table. The floor is wood decorated with various rugs with intricate designs. All around the rooms against the walls on every side are stacks and stacks of books. Some of the books are small and some are so large I can't imagine that I could even pick one up.

"Captain, I present to you our passenger, Miss Abby," says Dr. Clint.

"I'm pleased to meet you, Miss Abby. I am Captain Dux of the Sky Rider ship Moon Star," he
says.

Captain Dux jumps down from the chair and walks over to

me. He appears a little taller than his men, but perhaps it's just his captain's hat. Tuffs of gray and red hair line the side of his head, and some of the hair comes down the side of his face to a matching beard. He has a stern look about him but his eyes are bright blue and hold a mixture of wisdom and mischief. He wears tan trousers tucked into brown boots that go all the way to his knees. Over a white shirt he wears a dark brown vest with several small pockets. He pulls a pocket watch and flips it open.

After checking the watch he shuts it. Then he swings the watch on the chain around once before it lands neatly back in his pocket. His eyes look deep into mine and then he smiles at me. He has a contagious smile that spreads across his entire face leaving me to feel more at ease.

"So you are Bishop Steel's daughter, my, my, my. You are every bit as pretty as he said you were," he says to me.

"So you do know my papa?" I ask.

"Yes, yes, I know him well. But please sit down. You look a little pale. Clint, clear the table and bring Miss Abby some refreshments," says Captain Dux.

Dr. Clint quickly clears some maps off a table and sets some stools alongside for the captain and me to sit on. Two other men, whom I've just now noticed, rush out of the room.

"So how do you know Papa?" I ask, eager to get to get some information.

"We met your papa on an expedition some years back in the Appalachians. We've been doing some work there for a while and he came along looking for something. We helped him find that something and he helped us with our situation," says Captain Dux.

"I don't suppose you could be a little more specific can you? I mean I have been trying to find Papa for some time now and all I get is more of a mystery. Do have any idea what my papa is doing and why he is on a wanted list by the System?" I ask.

"Your papa is a key member of the revolution," says Captain Dux.

"Revolution? What revolution?" I ask, confused.

"Your country is about to be launched into a major battle. Your government is on the verge of being overthrown," says Captain Dux.

Just then, the two men return with plates of bread, cheese, and all sorts of nuts and fruits. They set up glasses and open a bottle of something and set it down on the table. Everything looks delicious but I suddenly feel like throwing up again. This time it has nothing to do with motion sickness.

CHAPTER 2

"Are you sure you have the right person?" I ask. "Papa is an engineer. He works on trains. How could he possibly be part of a revolution?"

"Your papa is a genius and has been part of a team working on an incredible invention," says Captain Dux.

"Papa? I know he tinkers a bit, well more than a bit I guess, but I don't know what you're talking about. The biggest thing I've ever seen him make is our steamcarriage," I say.

"Yes, yes he told me about the car, but this is much bigger and it will help your country," says Captain Dux.

"No, you can't be right, you must have the wrong man," I say.

As I deny the idea over and over out loud, inside I start to feel that maybe he is right. I know Papa is good at inventing things and building things like the steamcarriage. He's also made some contraptions around the farm. Papa made the cow milker and Granny's butter churn which he built with old clock parts. All Granny has to do is wind it up and the churn pretty much does all the work.

"I assure you I know Bishop Steel, and he is your papa and the inventor I am speaking of," says Captain Dux.

"Then you know where he is?" I ask.

"I have an idea of where he is, but his actual location is top secret, even from us," he says.

"What do you mean? I thought you were working with him on all this?" I ask.

"No, you misunderstand, child. We shared some information with your papa, but we aren't working with him," he says.

"I don't understand. You're not part of this revolution?" I ask.

"No, we don't get involved with the System and the goings on with your people," he says.

"What do you mean my people? Aren't you as much a part of our society as anyone else?" I ask.

"Oh no, not really. We pretty much keep to ourselves. We mine a little gold and prosper where we see fit, but we have no ties here," says Captain Dux.

"But you live here, don't you?" I ask.

"We live in the mountains in the north and some of our clan lives overseas. But we bow no head to any king or president or government but our own," he says.

"But you come and take stuff off our land as you please, don't you?" I ask.

He looks at me for a moment as if trying to make a decision and then clears his throat. "Please, Miss Steel. You need to eat something. It will make your stomach feel better," he says, gesturing to the food on the table.

"I'm sorry. I just can't eat right now," I say.

I think about all the times I've been hungry, and here is all this food in front of me and I just can't eat a bite.

"So you what you're saying, Captain Dux, is you don't actually know where my papa is?"

"Correct, just the general area. I can show you on a map where we last suggested he go in his search but that's all the information we have," he says.

"His search?" I ask.

"Yes, your papa is working on an invention, as I said, and needed certain components for it to work. Naturally he couldn't just order the stuff from the System supply. He also couldn't buy it, because, of course, the System would become suspicious. So he has been mining and gathering the components himself," says Captain Dux.

"That explains the map," I say. I say this more to myself than the captain. I didn't mean to say it out loud, but it slips out before I can stop myself.

"The map?" questions the Captain.

Now I've done it. Old Jim told me to keep the map a secret. Now I've gone and said something about the map in front of this man. I don't know what to say, so I might as well 'fess up. I don't think I'll tell him everything, though, or show him the map.

"Yes," I say. "Papa had a map and there are markings on it where I guess he has been or is going."

"It would be a bad thing for that map to fall into the wrong hands. It might just give away your papa's whereabouts," he says.

"That would be bad if the System got ahold of it," I say.

"Or others. It isn't just the System looking for your papa. There are other countries that would pay handsomely for your papa's invention. Not to mention the people who would take your papa hostage to work for them on other inventions," he says.

"Then you'll have to help me find him before anyone else does," I say.

"We can point you in the right direction, but that is all we can do for you," says Captain Dux.

"But I thought you said you are concerned about the fact that he is missing and that the System is after him?" I ask.

"Oh, we are, I assure you, but we can't get involved," he says. He takes a drink of his tea and crams some nuts in his mouth nervously.

"Why is he missing, Captain Dux?" I ask, suspicious that he is not telling me everything.

"My dear, I would have no idea why he is missing except for what I just told you. Perhaps he is not missing but very good at hiding," he says.

"Why would he hide from his own family? Why would he let the System take everything away from us? Why would he allow the System to put Granny into an oldies home and me into a workinhouse? Why would he just disappear like that without a word?" I ask.

My voice is starting to get loud, I guess because I'm angry now. I'm mad at Captain Dux and his sky people for taking what they want with no forethought of the consequences. I'm also angry at him for keeping a secret about my papa from me. I'm angry at Papa for letting all this happen.

"Look, I know you're upset, but you must keep your head about this or you will get nowhere. We will help you as much as we can to get you headed in the right direction to your papa. Considering the mess of things, that is the best we can do at the moment," he says.

"What do you mean mess of things? What is this revolution, anyway?" I ask.

He takes a deep breath and a drink of his tea before he begins to speak. "The System is about to fall. They are losing control of the people. Some people are rebelling by living outside their grasps like the hobos. Some people are openly rebelling by confiscating what they think belongs to the people. For instance, the Sky Pirates raiding the trains. There are others who are being more secretive about it, like your papa and the people he is working with," he says.

"Who are they?" I ask.

"They call themselves the Tinkerers," says Captain Dux.

"I haven't heard of them," I say.

"No, and you probably wouldn't have. They are a small and secret group," he says.

"I don't understand the problem," I say.

"The problem is, all these different groups are rebelling and balking against the System. Yet none of them have coordinated so it's just one big mess. There is no leader or any organization. It's going to end in a bloody battle that the System will end up winning anyway," he says.

"But it can't, it just can't. I've seen how the System treats people and it has to stop. It's not right," I say.

"I know, and your papa knows, and everybody knows. Someone has to put the puzzle together to break the System so the country can have a better government. That's why we stay out of it," says Captain Dux.

"But you're a person too; don't you want to belong somewhere?" I ask.

"We do belong, up here in the sky, watching all the messes unfold below," he says, laughing.

"If there is war they fight in the sky too, you know," I say.

"True, but we keep our distance just the same," he says.

What I don't understand is why they don't want to get involved. All this is confusing to me just the same and is giving me a headache. I don't want to think about war or revolutions. I want my family back, and I want my home back. None of that is going to happen I guess until this stupid mess is cleaned up. War and revolutions are something children should not have to think about, ever.

Children shouldn't have to go to a workinhouse either, or be made to go to brothels. Everything is upside down and I can't think on how anyone can make it better. I can't even imagine any kind of invention Papa could make that can change any of this. I hope Papa knows what he is doing. I just have to find him no matter what now.

"Okay so you're going to help me get to Papa, or at least in the right direction, right?" I ask.

"Yes, we'll help you as much as we can. I can tell you your papa had his mind set to go west toward the Rockies. I'm not exactly sure where though," says Captain Dux.

"Okay, but first I have to stop in Chattanooga where I promised to meet someone," I say.

"Oh, I'm sorry, but we are well past Chattanooga," he says.

"What? Can't we turn around? I promised Oliver T. Clark I would meet him there, I gave him my word," I stammer.

"I'm sorry, we can't go back," he says.

I'm near to tears now because I promised. What do I do now? Mr. Clark will worry about me, I'm sure. He might even go back and look for me once he's through with his business in town. That's the sort of man he is and I hate to think of him looking for me in a place I'm not. I put my head in my hands wondering what I'm gonna do now.

CHAPTER 3

Mr. Gunter comes in to escort me to my quarters. I thank Captain Dux for talking with me and follow Mr. Gunter through the corridors and decks of the ship. I find out that the dirigible has two upper decks and two lower decks. The first lower deck is where the sleeping quarters and the kitchen are. Mr. Gunter tells me they call the kitchen the galley just like they do on sailing ships. I've never been on a sailing ship; I've never even seen an ocean except on maps.

So far I'm not particularly impressed. There are dirty dishes piled in several buckets on the floor. Four long tables centered in the room are also cluttered with more dishes and papers. I look around for the chairs and find them hanging in a row on the wall. I guess that's pretty ingenious, it keeps them out of the way and from falling over in a windstorm. Then I notice the large and complicated iron stove. Now that's impressive. I walk over to get a better look and almost trip over a man kneeling at the bottom of the stove.

"Oh! I'm sorry, I didn't see you there," I say.

"No worries. You must be the girl they brought on board,"

says the little man in a whiny voice.

"I guess so, I haven't seen any other girls on board," I say. "My name's Abby," I say. I extend my hand out.

"Vitals," he says, taking my hand and standing up.

"Vitals?" I ask.

"Yes, Vitals. That's my name," he says.

Vitals is the same height as Gunter. He wears the same kind of clothes too; he has on brown pants with a beige shirt and matching brown vest. The difference is the stained white apron he wears over it all. Unlike Gunter, Vitals is bald. But what he lacks on his head he makes up for in his beard. His beard is long and white and hangs in many braids with little bells tied in that tinkle when he moves his head.

"I'm pleased to meet you, Mr. Vitals," I say.

"No Mr., just Vitals," he says, nodding and smiling as his little bells jingle.

"Okay, Vitals," I say.

"You hungry?" he asks.

"No, I just wanted to get a closer look at your stove, I've never seen one like it," I say, gesturing to the big stove.

"Oh, well most all ships have them. See the holes on the top is where you place the pots. Got to put them in the holes so they don't slide off, see," he says, pointing to the three giant holes in the top of the stove.

"Yes, I see," I say.

"On the side here are the racks to bake the bread and sometimes if I'm in the mood maybe pie," he says.

"Are you in the mood today?" asks Mr. Gunter, who is still standing in the doorway rocking on his heels.

"Maybe I am, and maybe I'm not, we'll see," says Vitals.

"Where does the wood go to heat the stove Mr. . . . I mean Vitals," I ask.

"Underneath, and it ain't wood, we use coal, burns hotter," he says.

"Well, thank you Vitals for showing me the stove, it's way jiggy. I think my granny would've loved to have a big one like this for canning season," I say.

"Canning? Yeah, it'd be good for that maybe, but I got lots of mouths to feed on the ship, no time for canning," says Vitals.

"Come miss, I need to get you settled so I can get back to my post," says Gunter.

I smile apologetically to Vitals and follow Mr. Gunter out the door. I think Vitals may be a strange man but I like him. I wonder if he knows Papa.

Thinking about Papa brings me right back to my strange conversation with the captain. I can't believe Papa is part of a revolution. It's just so hard to believe. Papa never even liked to go hunting; I can hardly imagine him in a war.

Mr. Gunter leads me downstairs to the lower level. We pass a couple of doors and at the third door on the left, he opens it. Inside there are several boxes and bags arranged neat and tidy against the walls. A little round window gives a small view of the sky. Below the window is a makeshift bed on top of some large bags of flour.

"We had to move you down here. The quarters you were in upstairs are for the crew. So you see it wouldn't be fitting for you to sleep there. The captain had us make you a place of your own for now," says Mr. Gunter.

"It's fine, thank you," I say.

"It's temporary until the captain can set down somewhere to

let you off," says Mr. Gunter.

"I know. Do you have any idea where that might be?" I ask.

"Not for certain, he'll be lookin' at the maps to see where is best," says Mr. Gunter.

"Thank you, I appreciate any help I can get," I say.

"Yep, well we moved your stuff down here too, your bag and spyglass is on the bed there, see?" asks Mr. Gunter.

I walk over to the bed and see my bag and Papa's spyglass. I pick it up, wondering if the map is still inside or if these little men have gone through my things and found it. I chastise myself for thinking so ill of them. Of course they wouldn't do that. Why would they? They have been nothing but kind to me, and I should feel more grateful to them. Suddenly the thought of the map makes me remember Hot Springs. I turn to Mr. Gunter.

"Mr. Gunter, do you know where we are now?" I ask.

"Not rightly sure at the moment, but I can find out for you," says Mr. Gunter.

"The reason I ask is that I'm supposed to meet my friends in Hot Springs, Arkansas. If you could let me off somewhere near there I would be grateful," I say.

"Thought you wanted to get to your papa?" asks Mr. Gunter.

"I do, but if the captain can tell me where I need to go then I can meet up with my friends and then we can all go to my papa," I say.

"Okay, I'll talk to the captain about it," says Mr. Gunter, and he leaves closing the door behind him.

I climb up on the bed and sit there a moment, thinking. If I can meet up with Charlotte and Freckles and maybe even Lyza and Julian then I won't have to travel alone. I don't like traveling alone, I've decided. Too many scary things can happen and I miss my friends. I wipe back the tears as I check the spyglass to make sure the map is still inside. To my relief it is. I secure Papa's spyglass over my shoulder again and slump back.

A noise coming from behind some of the boxes in the far right corner startles me. I sit up in alarm and look around for a weapon. I don't see anything in this room I could use as a weapon to defend myself, and then I notice a broom. The handle of the broom would work if I have to hit something or someone. I hope there aren't any rats in here. I start to crawl across the bed to get to the broom when quick as a flash something jumps on the bed.

I jump off the bed and grab the broom, spinning around to confront my foe, to find myself face to face with a feline.

"Oh Boots, you silly cat, you scared me!" I say, setting the broom down. I climb back up on the bed. Boots climbs up on my lap, purring and loving on me, and I'm content to pet him and love him back. I guess I realize now that I haven't been alone all this time because Boots has been with me.

I must have dozed off because the next thing I know there's a knock at my door. I sit up and notice at once that the room is dark.

"Whose there?" I ask.

"I got yer supper, miss," says a voice on the other side of the door.

"Can you open the door? It's dark in here and I can't find the lantern," I say.

The door opens and I shade my eyes to the dim light projecting from the man's lantern.

"Captain says it's best you eat in your room so the men don't feel uncomfortable," says the man.

"Thank you. I guess just put it on a crate," I say, gesturing to one of the many in the room.

"I'll leave the lantern with you too, so you'll have some light," he says.

"My name's Abby," I offer. I figure since he's being so nice he ought to know my name.

"Yeah, I know. Know your pa too. He's a good man. My names Balic and you don't have to put the Mr. on it, if you don't mind," he says, and winks at me.

"Thank you, Balic," I say.

"I brought milk for the cat too," he says as he set the tray down.

"I'm sure Boots says thank you as well," I say with a laugh.

"Good, now eat and I'll be back later for the tray," he says and leaves, closing the door behind him.

Boots and I are alone again. I set the bowl of milk down for Boots who places his attention on it most vigorously. I look to see what I have to eat and find some sort of broth and some hard biscuits. I'm a little disappointed in the meal at first. I realize then that maybe the meal is so bland because of my stomach. They give me broth and bread knowing I have not kept much else down. I eat the meal, finding the broth to be exceptional and the bread very tasty when I soak it in the broth. There is also some sort of drink that tastes sweet and bitter at the same time, with a ginger flavor. I think it's quite good and I make a point to remember to ask what it's called.

After I eat and I see Boots has finished his milk, I put everything back on the tray and set it outside the door. I take out Papa's map to have another look at it. I spread it over a crate as high above it as I can to get a good look. I see all the markings where Papa wrote things and put his mark. Some of the places I have already been to. There is one in Hot Springs, Arkansas where

I'm supposed to meet everyone. There is also one in Colorado Springs, Colorado and Clifton, Arizona.

Captain Dux said Papa has gone west and these are all the only marks on the map that are west. I see some small letters, so small I hadn't noticed them before. The word is strange to me and I've no idea what it means. I look again to be sure I'm reading it right but it looks like Ormes. I wonder what that means?

CHAPTER 4

All over the map are references to Grugen and I have since learned that Grugen is a man who owns a lot of the mines. Apparently he's not a very nice man and doesn't treat his workers with kindness. But then who in the System does? I wonder if this Ormes is a word meaning something or the name of a person. I will have to remember to as Captain Dux if he knows.

An abrupt knock on the door startles me. I quickly shove the map under the blankets before I open the door. I know I told the Captain about the map but I didn't tell him where it is or if I have it. The less I say, I think, the better. At the door I find Balic again holding the tray in his hand.

"You need to come with me lassie, the captain would like to talk with you," he says.

I follow Balic through the ship and back up on deck. On the top deck it's so beautiful now. The stars are overwhelmingly bright. They look so close that I feel like I can almost touch them. It's cold though, and I wrap my arms around myself against the cold wind blowing. I can see the sails of the ship are full and I can hear the whirling of the propellers as the ship maneuvers the sky.

I'm happy that Balic brings me back to the galley where the heat of the stove from the day's cooking warms the room. Captain Dux sits at the table with Dr. Clint, Mr. Gunter and Vitals who are all talking quietly together. Balic brings a chair down from the wall for me and I sit down. I find myself sitting very low but still level with the table. I guess everything on the ship is made for the size of the men and not anyone else, which makes sense, I suppose.

"Miss Abby, Balic informs me that you want to go to Hot Springs, Arkansas. Is this true?" he asks.

"Yes sir. I'm supposed to meet my friends there." I say.

"Are these friends, trustworthy?" he asks.

"Oh, yes sir. Lyza, Freckles and Charlotte escaped with me from the workinhouse. Well, and Raine too, but she's gone now. Julian we met on the train with another hobo named Jim. They saved our lives," I say.

"So you are supposed to meet all these people then, and to what end?" he asks.

"Well, we were all traveling together but then Charlotte got hurt. She couldn't travel very well, and Freckles wanted to help Tom get the children back home. Tom is another friend of mine. Anyway so Freckles and Charlotte left with Tom to take the children back home. Tom and I rescued all the children from one of the mines," I say. I falter here a moment. How do I describe the trolls to these men, or should I? I think I'll leave that part out.

"Well, go on," says the captain.

"Okay, so our other friend Raine fell off the train into the river. We didn't know if she was dead or not so Lyza and Julian decided to go looking for her. I accidently found her later on the reservation but she didn't want to leave. Anyway that's how we all got separated and we need to get back together," I say.

"I see," says Captain Dux.

"Captain Dux, I don't mean to be disrespectful, but I don't see how it's any of your business anyway, sir. I appreciate your help, and any help you gave my papa, but you're not my papa," I say.

I say this as polite as I can. I don't understand why he is questioning who the people are that I'm meeting. I mean, after all, I am my own person. I have been taking care of myself long before he ever came along. I guess he did save my life but that doesn't make him the boss of me to tell me who I can and can't meet with.

"Don't get upset now child, I'm only looking out for your welfare as a friend of your papa's. I don't want to see you get into any more trouble than you already have. Carrying around weapons such as these is asking for trouble," he says.

He motions to the derringer and the snake venom gun that are lying on the table. I didn't notice them until now. I suppose they have been discussing them all this time and wondering why a girl my age has such weapons.

"There is also the question of you being in the company of a man trying to kill you," he says, stroking his beard.

"Captain, I thank you for saving my life but the whole reason I have the weapons is to protect myself. I guess I wasn't doing a very good job of it when you came to my rescue. You saved me, and again I thank you for that. I would like to point out that I never asked to go on this quest. If anyone has put me in danger it's been Papa for leaving. I've had to do for myself all this time and I'm doing the best I know how," I say.

"You could have just stayed in the workinhouse until your papa came for you," says Mr. Gunter.

"You have obviously never worked in a workinhouse. Have

you any idea what they do to you in there? How hard they work you? How little food and clothing you have? You have nothing of your own, you are nothing but a work animal," I say. I am trying not to cry but I feel the tears welling up in my eyes.

"I guess I never thought much about it," says Mr. Gunter.

"No, maybe not. None of you do because your sole concern is about your own self and your own people. You said so yourself," I say. I realize I am speaking a bit boldly to these men who are my elders, but they need to hear this.

"Yes we do keep to ourselves just for that purpose and more. Long ago we were shunned from the world because of our size, laughed at and humiliated. We need nothing more to do with Landers except for a very few like your papa," says the captain.

"You know, not everyone is like that, just like not all hobos and pirates are bad. There's a lot of people out there who are lost and need saving. I'm just one girl but if my papa has something that is going help, then I'm going to find him and help him. One way or another we are going to stop the System, because it's wrong," I say taking a stance.

"You sure are Bishop Steel's daughter," says Vitals, shaking his head and laughing.

"Yes, that's right, I am. So Captain Dux, do you have any idea where my papa is?" I ask.

"Might be he's in Colorado I think, but that's all I know and all he said to me about where he intended to go. I guess he thought it best not to say too much for our sake," says Captain Dux.

"That's fine. Thank you for that information. I would like it if you could please take me to Hot Springs or as close as you can. I am going to meet up with my friends and together we are going find Papa," I say.

"We will discuss it, and I will think about all this. It will require us to change course offsetting our plans, you know," he says.

"I understand," I say.

"I'll have Balic take you back to your room for now while we discuss this," says Captain Dux.

"Thank you. I would also like to have my property back," I say, pointing to the weapons.

"I'm not so sure about that. They both seem sort of dangerous for you to have them," he says.

"I assure you I have been taught to use them. Besides, the snake venom gun is not mine. I need to return it to its rightful owner or I'll be a thief," I say.

"We will discuss this, best you go back to your room now," he says.

I follow Balic back to my room, both of us in silence. I've got nothing to say right now. For some reason I'm feeling like a hostage. Even though they saved me and I am grateful. I feel like I don't have a choice about what happens to me next, and I hate that feeling. I can't wait to be a full adult when no one can tell me what to do. I never asked for any of this. I have been doing everything I know how just to stay alive. Stay at the workinhouse he says. If I had done that, I would have been dead a long time ago; I should have told him that. I always forget important things to say and then think of them later.

In my room I'm alone with Boots and my thoughts, and I try not to get angry. I must remember and understand that they have plans too. I have to be gracious in whatever they decide because at some point in time they will want me off their ship. They don't like dealing with, what was that name he said? Landers. Well at least I can find comfort in the fact that he doesn't want me here on his ship.

And who does he think he is, keeping my property? At least the derringer is mine. I do have to return the gun because I took it from Oliver T. Clark without asking. I have always planned to give it back. I hope he isn't mad at me.

While I'm waiting to hear the captain's decision I roll up the map which is still under the covers where I had hidden it. No sooner have I got the map put away back in its hiding spot then there is a knock at the door again.

I open the door and find Mr. Gunter standing there.

"Good evening, miss. Is everything alright?" he asks.

"Fine, thank you. Do you want to come in?" I ask, trying to be polite after my angry explosion earlier.

"Oh no, no thank you. I just came to see if you needed anything and to let you know the captain has made a decision," he says.

"A decision?" I ask.

"Yes, we've turned back southeast now and we will be heading to Hot Springs for you. We should be there by the wee morning hours. It takes a bit longer because of the cross winds. The captain suggests you get some sleep before we get there," says Mr. Gunter.

"Oh thank you so much! Please tell Captain Dux thank you," I say elated.

"I will. He also asked me to give you these and told me to tell you that he hopes you will use them wisely, if at all," he says.

He hands me a box. I open it up and find both the derringer and the venom gun inside. I close the lid of the box and look up and smile.

"Thank you. I will be careful. I don't like to use them either but it's nice to know that I have them in case there is danger," I say.

"Understandable. Now you get some rest while you can," he

says, and leaves without another word.

"Goodnight," I call after him. But he is already up the stairs.

I wonder if I will have time to talk to the captain again before they drop me off in Hot Springs. I hope he plans to give me more information about where Papa might be; I mean, do I go to Colorado or Arizona? The states are right next to each other but that's an awful lot of traveling. How are we supposed to get there? Are there trains going out that way? I wonder how Papa got there.

I have so many things to think about that I just don't see how I will be able to get any sleep. I crawl up in the bed which I find to be quite comfortable, better than sleeping on the floor of a boxcar. Boots curls up next to me, purring. There is a bit of a gentle rock to the ship and instead of making me feel sick I find it kind of soothing now. I wonder how my friends are, and if they remember about meeting up or if they even can? I hope so. It's nice to have Boots but it will be so nice to see Lyza, Freckles, and Charlotte. It's still too bad about Raine.

I'm glad she's not dead, but I wish she had come with me, then we would all be together again like when we started out. I hope she is happy with her husband and that her life is good with the natives. Lyza will be a little sore at her, I'm sure, and Freckles will too. I think Charlotte will be sad though. I don't think she ever gets mad at anyone. My mind is wandering all over the place when I realize I had forgotten to ask Captain Dux about Ormes.

CHAPTER 5

$\mathcal{I}$'m sitting in my tree by the pond, the one near the kitchen door. I'm looking down at the farm, but it's not just my farm, it's lots of farms. They pass below me as if the tree is floating through the air. I feel a little afraid because everything is moving so fast. I am so high up that I'm wondering if I'll be able to climb down or jump out of the tree without getting hurt. I have a sudden fear I'm going to fall so I hold tight to the branch closest to me. Someone shakes the tree. No, not the tree, someone is shaking me and calling my name.

"Miss Abby, wake up now. It's time," says a familiar voice.

I open my eyes, realizing now that I've been asleep and must have been dreaming because I'm not in a tree. I'm lying down somewhere in a bed in the dark. I sit up and rub my eyes as I try to shake the fog out of my head. There's a dim glow coming from a doorway where someone is holding a lantern. I remember now that I'm on a dirigible with the Sky Riders. I look over and see a figure in the dark that I think might be Mr. Gunter.

"Are we there? Are we in Hot Springs?" I ask.

"So to speak. Come on get yourself up and get your things together. Use the head down the hall before you come up on

31

deck, and don't forget your cat," he says.

He turns on the lantern in the room and then shuts the door behind him, giving me privacy while I get myself together. I hurry and gather my bag and Papa's spyglass and look around to see if there is anything else left out. I don't see anything but Boots.

"Well, Boots, time to go back in the bag," I say as I gently pick him up and set him inside. He growls a little, but he doesn't fight me. I can hardly blame him, though. I grab the lantern and go to the head down the hall. It's not the nicest place to go but it is better than going in the woods. When I'm done I make my way back down the hall and up the stairs to the deck. Mr. Gunter and Dr. Clint are waiting for me at the top.

"Come on then, miss, this way," says Mr. Gunter.

"You feeling alright, miss?" asks Dr. Clint as we walk.

"Yes, sir, I guess I feel okay," I say.

"Good, good, because it's going to be quite the trip down," he says. That comment gives me a funny feeling I'm not going to like whatever comes next.

Instead of going up to the top deck as before, Mr. Gunter takes a different set of stairs to the second deck. The second deck is an open deck just below the top. Here we weave our way around boxes and crates, wood piles, and what looks to be like coal. I had been wondering what this deck is for and I guess it's just for storage of items they need to get to right away. I can see near the back is some sort of boiler and machinery that must run the ship somehow, but it's dark so I can't see it all.

Mr. Gunter leads me to a small group of people standing near the side of the ship. The group includes Captain Dux as well as a few other men I've not met. They don't see us coming because their heads are bent in deep discussion. Only when we come right up on them does the captain take notice and breaks off in mid-sentence.

"Good morning, Miss Abby, how are you feeling?" he asks.

"I'm fine, I guess. Are we going to land soon?" I ask. It occurs to me the ship has not even landed, so how am I going to get off?

"No, we're not going to land. There's no place to set down without being seen," he says.

"Oh, so I'm not going to be able to go to Hot Springs?" I ask, trying not to let him hear the disappointment in my voice.

"Oh no, don't worry Miss, we are getting you down, the men are going to lower you down from the ship," says Dr. Clint.

"Lower me down?" I ask. This doesn't sound good at all.

"It's perfectly safe, I assure you," says Captain Dux.

"Yes, well safe enough, but you might get blown around a bit. We've lowered the ship as far down as we dare without hitting the treetops. But you're going to hit a small airflow we think, that might blow you about a bit," says one of the men.

"You're sure it's safe?" I ask, turning to Mr. Gunter.

"We would not put you in any danger, rest assured, my dear. Now come along. We've already packed you some provisions and put them in the basket for you," says Mr. Gunter.

Mr. Gunter brings me close to the edge of the ship. I look over and see a small basket that appears large enough for one of them to ride in. It looks a bit small for me, my bag with a cat in it, and the provision bag. Stupidly, I look past the basket to the ground. A dizzy feeling comes over me. It's dark but I can almost make out the shapes of the tops of the trees. It feels so high up still, and I know if I were to fall or if they were to drop me, I'd surely die.

"I guess we should get it over with then," I say, because I have no idea what else to say.

"Wait," says Captain Dux, grabbing my arm. "We must ask you please keep what you know of us a secret. It is important to our safety as a society that we remain unknown."

"Some people have seen you already, like Papa. I'm sure other people have seen your ship from time to time," I say.

"Yes, but they don't know who we are or where we come from. They don't know what we are, which makes us an enigma," he says.

"An enigma?" I ask, not understanding the word.

"A mystery," says Dr. Clint.

"I'm not going to ruin your secret. Besides, who would believe me anyway? I still don't believe it," I say.

"I thank you, Miss Abby. Now we are letting you down at the foot of the Ouachita Mountain range. You will have to hike about eight hours or so to get to the town," says Mr. Gunter.

"Eight hours?" I ask.

"This is as close as we can get you," says Captain Dux.

"Okay, which way am I going, and how do I know I am going in the right direction?" I ask.

"You're going to be traveling southwest, and you will be walking downhill all the way. If that changes, then you're going the wrong way. You will walk right into the town. You can't miss it," say Mr. Gunter.

"Okay," I say and take a deep breath. "Let's do this before I change my mind."

I climb over the edge of the ship, trying very hard not to look down. I get into the basket which, as I expected, comes right to my waist. Mr. Gunter hands me my bag with Boots inside. Boy, if that poor cat knew half the stuff I'd put him through, he probably would have gone and left me long ago.

"I suggest maybe you sit down in the basket, Miss Abby," says Captain Dux.

"I told you she would be too big for it," says another man.

I sit down inside the basket and put my bag on my lap and the food bag to my side. I have to pull my knees up, but other than that it's not that uncomfortable. Well, except for the fact that I know I am hundreds of feet up in the air. I'll try not to think about that and hope that the wind doesn't blow me around too much. I look up at the tiny little man faces staring down at me.

"Thank you for everything," I say.

"You're most welcome, Miss Abby. Now remember you need to head west as soon as you can to Colorado. I think you know where. If I were you I would keep a very low profile, too. You're probably wanted by the System same as your papa now," say Captain Dux.

"I am," I say blandly.

"You got everything? Is there anything else you need?" asks Dr. Clint.

"Yes," I say looking up at him. "Don't drop me, please."

Without another word they release the basket from the ship and start to lower me down. At first it's not so bad and I try and think about other things like where Papa might be and how I'm going to get there. I wonder if there's a train in Hot Springs. I haven't a clue how we're going to get to Colorado. My other concern is my friends. Will they all be in Hot Springs when I get there? Are they waiting for me, I wonder?

A sudden breeze hits the basket and then it's not a breeze but a wind. Not a strong wind but enough to start making the basket sway back and forth a lot. All I can do is close my eyes and hope they don't let the rope go or I don't hit anything. My thought is interrupted as the basket hits something hard and jolts me.

It sways out again and starts to spin out of control. I look through the slats of the basket to see if there is anything I can do to make it stop. Maybe I can grab onto something like a tree branch, but everything is spinning so fast. There's nothing I can do so I close my eyes. I feel sick and scared and before I know it the basket hits something again. I open my eyes to see tree branches and pine needles everywhere, and the basket spins away from the tree. Now I am spinning in the air.

Again, the basket hits a tree and then swings back out into the air. It's too dark for me to have any idea how far I am from the ground now. Maybe I'm close enough to jump. The basket is filled with pine needles and I think maybe a pinecone or two. I close my eyes and hope it will stop soon. Just as I think the spinning will never end, the bottom the basket hits the ground.

CHAPTER 6

I peer out to be sure I'm on the ground. The basket has tilted on its side so as I reach out my hands touch cool grass between layers of pine needles. I scoot Boots' bag out in front of me onto the ground and then crawl out. Turning, I take the satchel of supplies out and then notice there is a blanket at the bottom of the basket. I must have been sitting on it. I take that as well. Making sure I have taken everything out of the basket I give the rope a couple of tugs to let them know I'm out.

I watch the basket recede back up into the air and into the darkness above. I can barely make out the shape of the ship against the dark sky. I look back down around me and see that it's even darker down here on the ground. There appears to be no moon tonight. Even though the stars are so bright in the sky, they don't give me enough light here in the forest.

I ease myself up though my legs feel wobbly. I guess from either fear from my ordeal or from being on the flying ship for so long. I don't feel so good right now, and walking doesn't seem like a good idea. It's much too dark to see where I'm going anyway. I sit back down and scoot myself up against a tree and spread the blanket over me. I open the bag and reach in to pet Boots.

"You can come out if you want, Boots, but I wouldn't suggest it," I say to him.

My voice seems to cut through the dark night like an intrusion. All around me the crickets stop singing. I hadn't even noticed they were singing until they stopped. Boots comes crawling out of the bag, looking around. Cats can see in the dark just fine and nothing seems to bother him as he moves around the area. I can see his glowing eyes when he looks back at me, but not much else.

"Just don't go far! I don't want to have to go looking for you when I'm ready to leave," I say.

He blinks at me and I take that as his answer of understanding. I'm a little afraid, I don't mind admitting. After all, there might be mountain lions or bears out in these woods and I'm here all alone in the dark. Most of those animals can see in the dark, and I can't. I guess I'll just try not to think about it.

It's a bit cold so I pull the blanket up close around me. The crickets start to sing again, which eases my mind. If there is any danger near, the crickets wouldn't be making noise. I remember Papa telling me they were nature's alarm. Even though they are singing again, every little sound I hear makes me jump. My heart is pounding in my chest, which adds to the noise in my head.

How silly of me! I have weapons to protect myself. I grab the bag with supplies in it and open it up, feeling inside since I can't see anyway. I feel several small packages and then my hand wraps around the gun. I pull it out, thinking it's the derringer, but it's the snake venom gun I got from Mr. Clark's wagon. I shake it next to my ear and I hear liquid, so that means it's still loaded.

Having the gun in my hands makes me feel a little calmer

than before. I still don't like being alone in the dark but it's not too long before Boots comes back and crawls up onto my lap purring. The ground may be cold and hard under my butt, and it's dark all around, but my cat warms my lap and my heart. Content for now, I relax and try to listen to the sounds around me in a different way. Maybe all the strange noises I hear are little creatures going about their normal night time business.

I remember on the farm there were mice in the barn. Sometimes Papa would be out there late at night and Granny would send me to fetch him in. It would be dark except for the light peeking through the bottom of the door of Papa's work room. I could hear the mice running around the barn doing whatever it is mice do at night, making all kinds of strange sounds. I also remember the odd chemical smells permeating from Papa's work room. I wonder if whatever he had been working on then has something to do with his disappearance now.

I must have fallen asleep thinking about Papa and the barn at home because I open my eyes and it's daylight. I'm shivering too; I guess the temperature has dropped even more. Boots isn't on my lap anymore, but I'm sure he's around close by. Rummaging through the supplies to see what I have now, I find a brick of cheese wrapped in paper. I also find a small cloth bag of already-cracked nuts, two jars of peaches, a jar of preserves, a small tin of crackers, and some meat jerky wrapped in wax paper.

I break off a piece of cheese and eat it with a couple of crackers and then pack up. I hold some meat back for Boots when I find him. After I relive myself in the woods, I start to look for Boots, calling for him softly. Finally after about ten minutes or so he comes bounding out of some bushes and rubs up against my leg. I give him the meat and wait for him to wolf it down.

"Come then, if you're ready," I say.

We head southwest like the Sky Riders told me to do, making our way down the mountain. I'm glad for the walk because it's warming me up. It occurs to me that I'm still in a skirt; maybe I ought to change back into my disguise as a boy before I get into town. I'm still wanted by the System, and I would hate to have come this far and get caught.

I stop long enough to change into my breeches, which are much warmer anyway. I put on my hat and tuck all my hair up into it. Boots sits and watches me with interest as I change my appearance. I'm guessing it will look funny if someone were to see a boy carrying this flowery carpet bag. I take the satchel the Sky Riders gave me with the supplies and put it over the carpet bag. It has a longer strap anyway and I can carry it over my shoulder along with my other satchel. I'm a bit weighed down, but I guess I will manage alright. So I start back down toward the town, I hope.

It's a long day and I find myself stopping often to rest. You would think going downhill would be easier, but at times it's harder. Sometimes the ground gets pretty steep and it's all I can do to keep from falling down the hill head first. I try to make the day go by faster by planning things out in my head. I get frustrated because there are a lot of things I just don't know.

I wonder if anyone has made it to Hot Springs besides me. What will I do if they're not there? If none of my friends have made it to town yet, then should I leave right away? And how? Is there a train station or will I need to find another way to travel?

I know I'm taking too long to get down the mountain because now it's starting to get dark again. I guess that's a good thing though, since I don't want anyone to see my face. Even though I am in disguise, I can't be too careful.

The air is feeling a bit chillier and something cold hits my nose. I look up and see that it's beginning to snow. I hope I don't have to sleep outside again, because it's going to be a cold and wet sleep if I do.

The trees start to thin out to where I can see lights ahead of me not too far away. I didn't realize Hot Springs would be such a big town and they would have so many lights. As I get closer I find a muddy road and follow it down into the lights.

Abruptly, a large building looms up to my right. At the end I can see it's well-lit, and parked out front are lots of carriages, both steam and horse-drawn. There seems to be a lot of bustling about and people talking and laughing.

I try to avoid this by going to the left side of the road which is darker and has less people walking about. I pass by one spot and stop because I can hear running water like a little waterfall. I'm awfully thirsty so I follow the sound to a little stream that opens up to a pool of water. I stop and bend down to put my hand in it to catch a drink and find the water is hot. Well that explains the name of the town, I suppose. I guess I won't be drinking this water.

I look down to make sure Boots is still with me and he looks up at me with a look of "What do we do now?" So I press on, going away from the busy part, or at least I think so. There seems to be a lot of people walking about on either side of the street. Wooden planks make do for sidewalks that line up along rows of wooden framed and canvas buildings. Steam rises from the tops of these buildings. I can't begin to imagine what is going on in these places.

I move quickly over to the other side of the street where there are less people. Some of the stores are still open and ladies and gents go in and out of them. I pass by restaurants and the smell of food makes my stomach growl. I have no idea where I'm going. When Lyza, Freckles, Charlotte and I planned this meeting, we agreed to meet at the post office. We figured every town had one. But this time of night, which I think is dinner time, the post office is most likely closed.

Boots and I keep walking and the snow keeps falling. I look at all the signs on the buildings reading the names as we walk by. I discover the buildings across the street with steam coming out of them are bath houses. Some of them have wooden signs on the outside with names, while some just have numbers. I'm guessing people are taking baths in the hot water that comes up out of the ground here. That sounds real nice about now. If I have enough money left, I could use a bed to sleep in and a nice meal and a hot bath.

I finally reach what I think is the edge of the main part of town; at least it's quieter here anyway. It's darker too, with a couple of gas lights burning, one on each side of the road on the corner. Across the street I see a tiny little building and at last the postal sign recognizable by the System flag hanging outside.

I stare at the flag a moment and study the large white star on a blue background in the middle. The big S centered in the star representing the System and the A dangling from the bottom of the S representing America. Around the edge of the flag is the border of red and white representing the wall around America keeping out the rest of the world. The more I look at the flag, the more I see a symbol of dominance over its people.

The building is dark, but I cross over to make sure it's closed. As I do I am stunned by the enormous building behind it looming like a monster on the hill. The building looks bigger than the other one I passed earlier when I first got into town. This building rises up from the hill about twelve stories high. It has elaborate decorations cut into the stone all around it. A great archway and beveled edges mark the entrance.

Tearing my eyes from the larger building, I cross and reach the post office. I'm not surprised when I find the door closed and locked. I look around to make sure no one is watching me. I have no idea what to do now or where to go. I'm not even sure if there is a train station here or not. I'm just standing here wondering what to do when I hear a "Psst." I look around but there doesn't seem to be anyone about. Then I hear it again coming from the bushes toward the large building up on the hill. Guardedly, I move toward the sound, hoping this is not a mistake.

CHAPTER 7

"Abby, is that you?" I hear a male voice ask from the dark.

"Who is that?" I ask.

By now it's full on night and the snow is falling much faster and heavier. I can't imagine who is hiding in the bushes this time of night, and in this weather, unless maybe it's Julian.

"It's me, Tom," says the voice.

A tall lanky teenage boy climbs out of the bushes looking around as he does before he walks toward me. I recognize Tom at once. Surprised and elated at the same time I rush to him throwing my arms about him in a big hug. I break away, embarrassed at my reaction to seeing him.

"Hey Tom, it's good to see you," I say, trying to cover up the awkward moment.

"I'm glad it's you and that you're finally here," he says. He laughs quietly.

"How did you know it was me?" I ask.

"I wasn't sure at first but you don't walk like a boy and not too many people have a cat following them," he says.

"You hear that Boots, you're a dead giveaway," I say.

"We need to get out of public view, come on," he says.

I follow him with Boots at my heels, as we head to the big scary building on the hill. When we get there, he turns to me and puts his fingers to his lips in a gesture to be quiet. I grab Boots, who is not happy as he has just discovered something interesting in the bushes. I don't want to get caught or get separated from him so I think it best to put him in the bag for now. Tom takes the bag from me without a word and motions me to follow him.

We duck down behind the bushes as some men walk by. I realize they are guards. I'm nearly frozen with fear; these are System guards, and we are so close to them that if they see us we are done for. Tom waits until they pass and then motions me to follow. We walk the opposite direction of the guards going around to the back of the building. Here I see a long line of windows near to the ground. I'm guessing this is the basement.

Tom goes to one of these windows and lifts it up, motioning me to climb through. I'm not keen on this idea but I guess he knows what he is doing. I climb through the window and find myself standing on some boxes in a dark hallway. Tom hands me the bag with Boots in it and I manage to climb down the boxes to make room for Tom as he climbs through the window.

"This way," he whispers in my ear.

Tom climbs down to the floor heading down the hallway. Despite my unease I follow him, barely able to see his form ahead of me in the dark. Finally he stops in front of a doorway and opens up the door and we go inside. We walk a little further until we come to some stairs going down. The stairs seem to travel down a long time until at last we are at the bottom in full dark. I hear Tom fiddling with something and then I'm blinded by candlelight.

"Come on, we're nearly there," he says in a low voice.

We keep walking farther down another hallway until we come to another door where he stops. He then taps on the door three times before opening it and walking in. To my delight, the door opens to a lantern-lit room which appears to be a storage area. There sitting on the floor in a circle are Lyza, Julian, Freckles, and Charlotte. They all look up at me at once and smiles light their faces.

"You're alive!" says Charlotte, being the first to get up and throw her arms around me.

"I can't believe you made it at last," says Lyza, hugging me.

"You're okay, but why are you dressed like a boy?" asks Freckles. She gives me a hug as well and then holds me at arms-length to look at me.

"Hey Abby girl, you made it," says Julian shyly, and then giving me a quick hug.

"Oh Boots!" exclaims Charlotte. I turn and see that Tom has let Boots out who is now reaping the benefit of the reunion as well. The girls all crowd in to pet and love on him.

"Yes, I made it at last. How long have you all been here and what are you down in this place?" I ask, looking around the storage room.

"It is the best we could think of at the time. None of us have any money to stay at any of the hotels or inns, and besides, it would look suspicious," says Tom.

"But how did you know to come here?" I ask.

"Kind of a wild guess I suppose. Tom and I had to scout it out. I came up with the idea, knowing some of these hospitals have storage in the bottom levels," says Julian.

"Yeah, they both had to sneak in one night. They had to

get past the guards and look around the place until they found this room," says Freckles.

"But isn't it dangerous to be so close to the guards? I mean what if they hear us or find us by accident?" I ask.

"Well they won't hear us down here, and the only way they will see us is when we go in or out. We just have to be careful," says Tom.

"Sit down, Abby, and tell us where you've been and what's happened? Did you find your papa?" asks Charlotte.

"No, but I have a better idea of where he is now," I say.

We all sit down and for the next hour I tell them everything that's happened to me since we parted ways. I tell them about being trapped in the saltpeter mine and the dead girl I saw. I explain how I and the other people escaped and then I almost got captured again on a train by a man from Africa. I tell them about meeting Mandy Moon and the airship pirates. I also tell them about meeting Oliver T. Clark and going to the reservation where I found Raine alive.

"You mean she's alive?" asks Charlotte.

"Yes she's alive, and she didn't try to find us to tell us. She told me she didn't think it was important," I say. I still feel bitter over the conversation I had with her.

"What do you mean? Julian and me went a long ways and nearly got caught several times just trying to find her body," says Lyza.

"I know, and she didn't want to come back with me. Says she is getting married to the chief's son," I say.

"Well fine then. Forget her. Some loyalty to friends," says Lyza, clearly she's as angry as I am about it.

To change the subject, I tell them about how I helped the

kids escape from the workinhouse. I explain how I blew it up by accident too. I tell them about the Cajun man, Mr. Bisket or whatever his name is, and how he tried to kill me.

"Oh my goodness, what did you do?" asks Charlotte.

"I shot him with this gun that Mr. Clark invented that shoots snake venom," I say, taking the gun out of my bag to show them.

"Wow, look at that," says Tom, taking the gun from me to examine. Afterwards he hands it to Julian who examines it in turn.

"So then how did you get here?" asks Freckles.

Now it comes to it, I didn't promise Captain Dux I wouldn't tell my friends about the Sky Riders. I just said I would keep their secret so they wouldn't get found out. So I tell the story about the Sky Riders and their dirigible.

"Now you must promise to never tell anyone about them, because they want to remain a secret," I say.

"I don't believe you anyway," says Freckles. "That is just too impossible to be real."

"Really? Well, believe what you want, that's what happened," I say. I feel a little hurt that she doesn't believe me.

"Hey, I wouldn't have believed in trolls if they hadn't captured me and all those kids," says Tom.

I know he has a hard time talking about the death of his brother so for him to come to my rescue with this is pretty nice of him. Freckles just gives him a sort of weird look. I haven't a clue what's going on between them so I will ignore it.

"Hey, we all just got back together, okay, so we shouldn't fight," says Charlotte.

"I agree. I'm glad to be back with all of you, and I hated traveling alone. Well not alone but you know, without you," I say.

"So you missed us then?" asks Lyza.

"Of course I did!" I say.

"Well I think we all missed you too," says Lyza.

"So tell me what happened to you and how did you get here?" I ask.

"Well," says Charlotte, "I thought we were going to get caught for sure."

CHAPTER 8

$\mathcal{I}$ listened while Charlotte, Tom, and Freckles took turns telling me about their adventures. They had set out to take the children we rescued from the mine back home. It seems they had a long frightening journey. They had to hide from System soldiers and Crushers. At one point they crossed paths with bandits who tried to rob them of all their supplies. Had it not been for Tom's quick thinking they might all be dead or in the workinhouse again.

They almost lost the wagon in some rough waters. They also had to find lost children who wandered off in the woods. They did manage to get everyone back to the hovel safe and sound but when they got there they found that a lot had changed. Fortunately, they found most of the children's families. They found good homes for the children whose families were gone or missing.

Lyza and Julian had a harrowing adventure as well. They told me about their travels down the river looking for Raine. How they met up with not-so-friendly natives and faced raging white rapids on the river. They too told of how they were almost picked up by the Crushers on several occasions. With Julian's help,

Lyza explained how Julian stood up to a bear to protect her.

I look around at my friends with a new found respect and admiration. Any of them could have kept going or stayed where they were, but they chose to come back here to see this through with me. Well, except for Raine, of course, but then she has other priorities. I guess I can't really blame her if she found a family and a home. Charlotte, Freckles and Tom could have stayed and made a home if they had wanted to. Lyza has been in the System too long and I don't think she knows how to stay and make a home anywhere.

I hope that when we do find Papa we can put all this mess behind us. We can find a secret place out of the way somewhere and make a home for all of us.

"Is anyone hungry?" I ask.

"Yeah, I could eat," say Julian.

"You can always eat," says Lyza, giggling.

"I've got some boiled peanuts," says Tom.

"Oh yum, I love boiled peanuts," says Charlotte.

"I have peaches and cheese and jerky," I say, grabbing the food from my bag.

"Jiggy! We'll eat good tonight," says Freckles.

We all settle down, dividing out the food. Lyza has some bread that is a little stale but I still have some preserves that make the bread not taste so bad. I don't ask them where they got the food. I'm afraid they'll tell me they stole from the hospital trash or something. I'm too hungry to even want to know. For now we sit around sharing the food while I get the nerve up to tell them about Papa. Julian promptly pulls out a jug from behind some barrels.

"What's that?" I ask.

"Applejack," he says taking a swig.

"Let me try some," says Charlotte.

"Where did you get that?" asks Tom.

"The guards. I nicked it when they weren't looking," says Julian.

"Oh gosh, Julian, what if they miss it?" asks Charlotte.

"They won't. There were a bunch of them in a wagon. Besides, aren't we supposed to be celebrating a birthday?" asks Julian.

"You better be careful or you'll get caught, and if you get caught, we all might get caught," says Freckles.

"Can it, Freckles. Julian knows what he is doing. Besides, Julian is right, we should celebrate Charlotte's birthday. Happy birthday, Charlotte dear," says Lyza. "Hand it over, and let me have some."

Julian hands the jug to Lyza who takes a drink and then hands it off to me. I take the jug and tip it to my lips letting the liquid pour down my throat slowly before I swallow. For a moment it's okay and it just tastes like apples. Then the burn hits my mouth and throat about the same time and I nearly start to cough.

"That's it, take another so you'll stop coughing," says Julian.

I take another drink but this time a little bigger, and I still feel the burn but not as bad, and the apple taste is so good. I take one more drink and pass it over to Freckles. She sniffs it and wrinkles up her nose but she drinks it anyway and nearly coughs it up. She takes another drink and passes it to Tom. We go on drinking and passing it around for a while before I feel a warm fuzzy feeling.

I know applejack is liquor, so I knew it would do something to me, I just didn't know what. I've had alcohol twice before. Once when Papa had some home brew ale someone gave him, and he let me have a taste. Another time, when Granny celebrated her birthday and had a bottle of port wine. She had been saving it for a long time and brought it out on her seventieth birthday. We both had one glass. The time I had the ale it had been just one sip and I didn't feel much about it though it tasted good. The time I drank that port wine with Granny, it sure made me feel warm all over and sort of comfortable too.

The next day, I had a harsh awakening when I had the worst headache I ever felt. I swore I would never drink liquor as long as I lived if that's what is does to you. But tonight I figure I'll give it another try, After all, I never tried applejack before. Everyone else is drinking it, so it must be good.

"So, happy birthday, Charlotte," I say.

"Yeah Charlotte, happy birthday," says Tom.

"Happy birthday, Charlotte," says Freckles.

"Thanks. You know y'all are my family now," she says.

"Now don't get all sappy on us," says Julian.

"I'm not," says Charlotte.

I watch as she wipes her eyes. Freckles moves over to her and gives her a hug. Maybe it's time to change the subject before Charlotte gets more teary-eyed. Right now everyone is feeling pretty good so I guess this is as good a time as any to tell everyone about Papa.

"I need to tell you what I found out about Papa," I say out of the blue. Everyone gets real quiet and still, so still I swear I can hear the goings-on in the upstairs of the hospital.

"The captain of the dirigible, Captain Dux, told me that my papa is part of a revolution," I say.

"A what?" asks Charlotte.

"A revolution against the System. The Captain said Papa is part of a group of people called the Tinkerers. He said Papa has been developing some sort of machine that is going to help the fight against the System," I say.

"Tarnation, that's a heap of trouble," says Tom.

"Thomas! Language," says Freckles.

"But it's true. Do you realize we could all go to jail, just being here with Abby?" says Tom.

"Well, you can leave if you want, Tom, or any of you. I understand and I'm sorry you've all come this way to find this out. I certainly had no idea until the other day. I'm still not sure I believe it, but look," I say. I rummage through my bag to find the newspaper that had the story about Papa and me. I had thrown out the rest of the paper but kept that part folded up. I take it out and hand it to Freckles.

"I didn't mean I would leave you, Abby, I just meant that. . ." Tom's voice trails off as he clearly doesn't know what to say.

"Tom, my good fella, they are going to throw you in the slammer anyways just 'cause you escaped them. Don't think that you are free and clear. If you get caught, you're in a heap of trouble. We all are. In fact anyone living out of the System is in trouble. They don't like that," says Julian.

"Julian's right. The System wants to keep the people of America under their thumb and controlled at all times. The fact that there are a few hobos running around has never been a real problem before, but now there are more and more of them," says Lyza.

"Don't forget the Sky Pirates. There is a whole town in the mountains that I saw, filled with people hiding from the System. They've been robbing System supplies from trains," I say.

"Oh, like that's not going to get their attention," says Lyza.

"What are you saying?" asks Charlotte.

"Charlotte dear, you really can be a dope sometimes. We're

about to go to war in our own country."

"They shouldn't have put that in the paper," says Freckles, as she hands the article over to Lyza and Julian.

"Why?" I ask.

"Because they just made you a revolutionist. Freeing the workers from the workinhouse, and then blowing them up makes you look like a revolutionist," says Freckles.

"But the first one blew up on its own, and not everyone got out, just us. You know that," I say.

"I know, but the other one looks like you meant to do it," says Freckles.

"Yeah, Abby, either that or you're going around killing innocent workers and destroying the System. Either way is bad for them," says Lyza.

"Let me see the article, please," says Charlotte.

"Maybe we should do a little more damage to the System," says Tom.

"What are you talking about? " I ask.

"We could free some more workers and blow up some more workinhouses," says Tom.

"Yeah, it makes a statement. It would help the revolution," says Julian.

"You're all crazy. I just want to find Papa," I say.

"But they're right, Abby. You're Bishop Steel's daughter, a symbol of hope to a lot of the hobos," says Lyza.

"Abby, we could make a difference, and instead of a ditsy rich girl who is poor now, I could be part of something important. I can get even with them for taking it all away," says Charlotte.

We all look at Charlotte who has just put the article down from reading it. I have never heard Charlotte talk about getting even before. I've heard her cry and complain about the things she used to have and regret that she has to work now. I had no idea there is more to her, but then I guess I never tried to look before.

"All this talk is making me lose my edge. Pass me that jug. We can save the world tomorrow," says Julian.

Save the world? I never wanted to save the world. I just wanted to get my life and my family back. I had no idea my path would lead me to this. I wonder what my real parents would think of this, whoever they are and wherever they are. Is that what happened to them? Did the System catch them or did they escape? I'm not feeling so good anymore. I can't tell if it's the applejack or the fact that my friends want me to help save the world.

CHAPTER 9

$\mathcal{I}$ wake with a start. I think I heard a sound so I listen close. I'm not sure if I actually heard anything at all or if I dreamed it. Now I can't remember what the dream had been about. My heart is beating so fast and hard I feel it in my throat; I must have heard something. I lie still for a long time it feels, listening to the sounds around me.

I can hear everyone in the room breathing. I can almost tell them apart by the different sounds they make when they breathe; I can especially pick out Charlotte because she snores. I can even hear Boots breathing, which is kind of funny. There's another noise off in the distance, a humming and whirling. I guess that sound must be the furnace or something. Yet there's a sound above all that, and closer, which is distinctly the sound of muffled voices.

I wonder if that's the sound that woke me up. I listen intently, concentrating on that sound. It seems to me that maybe they are so loud that I should not be hearing them. I know sound carries but if these people are that loud, maybe that means they are people near our hiding place. This thought causes my heart to beat even faster and I can't seem to move for fear of making a sound they will hear. But I have to warn the others in case I'm right.

"Lyza," I whisper. I figure she has a cooler head than the rest of us and will know what to do. I hear no reply.

"Lyza," I whisper again a little louder.

"What?" comes a sleepy response from the other side of the room.

"I think there are people nearby, I can hear them talking," I say.

There is stillness in the room, a deafening quiet that had not been there before. All the rhythmic breathing and snoring has stopped. I must have woken everybody up saying that and they are all listening now as I have been. Then I hear the sound again but a bit louder now and accompanied with the sound of footfall.

"You're right, there are people nearby," whispers Lyza.

"Everybody quietly get up grab your things and go to the back of the room behind the boxes," whispers Julian.

"How? We can't see anything," whispers Charlotte.

"Wait a minute. I have an idea," whispers Tom. I hear a bit of shuffling around and then the striking of a match, and then there's light.

Tom has shoved his blanket up against the bottom of the door to hide any light and then lit a candle for us to see by. It's still very dim but enough for us to see to gather our things hastily and pack. I'm concerned because I don't see Boots anywhere but he has to be in the room somewhere. I hope he stays hidden if someone comes in.

Without a word we gather all our things and clean up any trace of our being here. Freckles gathers all the packages and jars from our meal and shoves them in her bag. Tom helps Charlotte roll up her bedding as well as Freckles' and his own. Lyza and Julian are taking care of their own things. I get my stuff packed while looking around for Boots. We all stay quiet, straining to hear anyone approaching.

We all move back behind the boxes as far back in the corner of the room as we can. I hate being back in the corner like this because there is no place to go if we get caught. I feel that we don't have a choice though, as we hear the sound of voices and footsteps coming even closer now. I see Tom go to his blanket and blow out the candle as he is reaching down. That is the last thing I see before darkness. I scoot back as far as I can until I feel my back against a wall. My heart is pounding so loud that I'm sure someone will hear it. The voices now sound like they are on the other side of the door.

"I suppose there will be plenty of room down here for your men, Sergeant. There is not much else but storage," says a very stern sounding woman's voice.

"This will do fine ma'am the boys just need someplace to go out of the weather," answers a man's voice with a southern drawl.

"Well just don't let your men mess with any of our supplies, please. They're few and far between," says the woman.

"Oh, don't you worry, ma'am, I'll keep them in line. What's in this here room?" asks the man, and the door opens.

"That's just some old medical equipment and some System boxes we're holding in storage," says the woman.

"Holding in storage?" questions the man.

"Yes, yes. When a patient passes away we are required to hold their belongings until the System sends someone to go through them. They determine if the items are suitable to return to the families," explains the woman.

"Very good. We won't be bothering anything in here. Perhaps we can store some of our own precious cargo in here out the way and sight of the men," says the Sargent.

"Whatever you need to do, just don't disturb the other boxes or get them mixed up with yours," she says haughtily.

"Smells like candles have been burning in here not long ago," comments the Sargent.

"Yes it does, perhaps one of the staff has been down here recently. You know sometimes I catch them napping while on duty and in the oddest places," says the woman.

"Hard to find good help, is it?" asks the sergeant.

"Yes, well sometimes the System sends me derelicts and hobos to work when the rehabilitation center is full up. They tell me it sort of puts their minds at ease anyway, making them less disagreeable before going into the center," says the woman.

"Is that so? I never heard that before," says the sergeant.

"Yes, it helps to calm them, making them feel like maybe they were wrong in leaving the System. Gives them a sense that it's not so bad after all to work for one's keep," she says.

"And then Bam! They yank them up and throw them in the rehabilitation center and teach them what for, eh?" laughs the Sargent.

"Well, it is so unfortunate, and sometimes you do feel sorry for them, but they do deserve it," she says.

"Yes indeed, we must abide by the laws. That's what keeps our society running smoothly," agrees the sergeant.

"I appreciate you and your men being here and on watch what with all the excitement and everything," she says.

"Just doing my duty, ma'am. You know if there is anything else I can do you for you, just say the word," says the sergeant.

The woman giggles a little and I can hear them leave and close the door behind them. We wait a while and listen as their footsteps and their voices recede. Still, we don't move for a long while. I'm almost afraid to even breathe. In fact, I think I might have been holding my breath the whole time they were in the room.

"Oh my goodness, that was close," whispers Charlotte.

"Yeah, we gotta get outa here," says Freckles.

"How?" asks Charlotte.

"Yes, but how without anyone seeing us?" I ask.

"Does anyone know what time it is?" asks Tom.

"I have a watch, but I can't see it in the dark," says Julian.

"It must be morning by now. It's more dangerous to go out in the daytime," says Tom.

"Yes, but if we don't leave soon there is going to be an entire troop of soldiers in here with us and then we'll never be able to leave," I say.

"You're absolutely right, Abby, Tom and I will check it out and see what's going on," says Julian.

"Be careful Tom," says Freckles.

"Don't worry boss, I got it covered," says Tom.

It's still dark without the candle lit but I think I hear a kiss somewhere in the dark. I could be mistaken, but then again Freckles can't keep her eyes off of Tom, and Lyza seems to be hanging all over Julian. I'm kind of disappointed, though I guess I should have expected it. After all, Lyza has been traveling alone with Julian for a while; it stands to reason they would become close. As for Tom and Freckles, well she had designs on him from the moment she saw him. Charlotte and I never stood a chance, even though I met him first.

I see the door open when a sliver of gray light steals in the room for a moment. Then both Tom and Julian leave, shutting the door behind them. Darkness folds around us once again and I try not to think about it. It seems like every time I'm in the dark bad things happen. I remember the trolls in the mine and try to wash away the horrible image of their pale blood-stained skin. I keep seeing the heaps of bones and clothing lying about the cave from the people they ate.

I get a chill and try and shake it off. All those bad things are behind us now. If we can just keep from getting caught and get to Papa soon, then everything will be okay, I just know it will. I reach out and grab a hand, I think it's Charlotte's. She squeezes my hand reassuringly, and I feel better just knowing that I'm not alone.

CHAPTER 10

We wait for what feels like forever. I'm still holding Charlotte's hand and realize her hand is cold. The poor dear must be scared out of her wits and cold at that. Funny but it does seem to be a bit colder in here than I remember. I guess the weather is getting worse outside.

"Charlotte, are you cold?" I whisper.

"I'm okay, I have a blanket on," Charlotte whispers back.

"But your hands are so cold," I whisper.

"What do you mean? Lyza and Freckles are holding my hands to keep them warm. "Where are you, Abby? You sound like you're on the other side of the room," she says, still whispering.

My heart skips a beat for a moment because I'm holding someone's hand, but whose? The hand tightens its grip on mine. I think I'm about to scream when the door opens and the gray light creeps in with Tom and Julian. I look down at my hand to see nothing and no one there. I look up and see Freckles, Lyza and Charlotte at the other end of the room.

"Come on, let's go, we have scarce little time to get out of here," says Tom, breathless.

Everyone grabs their things and head for the door. I don't even have time to even think about what just happened. I'm about out the door when I remember Boots.

"Where's Boots? I can't leave without him," I whisper.

"Well, don't take too long looking for him. We have to go. We'll wait for you by the window," says Julian.

"No!" I almost say aloud but manage to whisper it. "Please someone stay with me!" I beg.

"I'll stay," whispers Tom.

The rest leave the room, and Tom and I search, calling for Boots in low voices. I am starting to get extremely frustrated, not to mention very uneasy now about being in this room. I suddenly see Boots come crawling through a small hole in the wall. I snatch him up and grab Tom by the arm, dragging him through the door.

Tom closes the door behind us and I'm somewhat relieved. I put Boots in my bag and Tom carries it as we head to the window. Finally, after walking through all the passageways and up the stairs, we get to the window and find that everyone else has already gone out. Tom helps me up the crates and I climb out.

I look around and to make sure the area is clear. There are several bushes on either side so I'm sure no one has seen me come out of the window. It's morning but still early and the sky is gray and filled with clouds and a cold wind. I reach down and grab my bag from Tom and he crawls out behind me.

"Where did everyone go?" I whisper.

Tom puts a finger to his lips motioning me to be quiet and to follow him. We maneuver through and around trees and bushes avoiding a small troop of soldiers who are in the act of breaking camp. I can understand why they would want to set up camp inside now. It appears there is going to be a bad storm. There's already a small dusting of snow on the ground. I see a lot of footprints that have been smeared around so you can't see which direction they go.

We get to the sidewalk and Tom puts his head down against the wind and his hands in his pocket. I can't do that since I have a bag to carry but I pull my hat down over my ears and dip my head against the wind as well. I would have put my scarf on but it's very girly and I am supposed to be in disguise as a boy. The coat I'm wearing is thin and not made for winter weather.

We walk a while in silence down the main street of Hot Springs and then Tom makes a turn to the left down and alley beside a brick building. We walk along to the back where there is a small door and he knocks on it lightly. Tom checks from side to side to see if anyone is around while we wait. Then abruptly the door opens and I see Julian standing there, a clever smile on his face.

"Come on," he says, motioning us in.

We get inside and follow him through a dark hallway, up some stairs and into another door. Here we find Freckles, Lyza and Charlotte are waiting. I look around the room which is quite large and has several dressing tables with mirrors. Against one wall are racks of clothes and trunks. On the opposite wall is a pile of wooden signs, painted windows, furniture, and other strange items that make no sense.

"Where are we?" I ask in a whisper.

"No need to whisper, just don't yell or anything like that. We are in the theater," says Julian, holding his arms out wide.

"The theater? But won't people come here?" I ask.

"No, it's closed for the winter. Besides, no one would come here when there is a storm coming anyway," says Julian.

"Seriously? How did you find out about this place?" I ask.

"Tom and I have been scouting around for a while. I overheard some people, actors I guess, discussing the theater being closed for a few months so I just found out where it is," says Julian.

"Well why didn't you bring us here in the first place?" asked Lyza.

"I had to be sure no one is here, I planned on check it out further, today actually, but as it is we are here," he says.

"Well I think this is just fine," say Charlotte. She walks over to the racks of clothes and starts perusing through them.

"Boots will want out, I'm sure," I say. I set my bag down and open it up for him to come and check out the new place.

"I'm sure he'll find some mice around here, that will make him happy," says Tom.

"There better not be any mice or rats," says Freckles.

"Of course there are. It's an old building; they thrive in places like this," says Lyza.

"What about us? What are we going to thrive on?" asks Julian.

"Oh my goodness, you're always hungry," says Lyza.

"Me too," says Charlotte.

"We can go out and scrounge some food from somewhere. I seriously doubt there is any here," says Tom.

"We don't have to scrounge for anything. I have money," I say.

"Where did you get money?" asks Lyza.

Do you remember me telling you about the people I helped out of the saltpeter mine? A lady found a box that belonged to her and her husband that the soldiers had taken. It had a false bottom the soldiers didn't know about and the money they stashed was still in there. She gave me some for helping them," I say.

"Well that's super jiggy. We could've gotten a room at the

hotel or something and got a bath," says Lyza.

"No, we can't. We can't risk getting caught. We all look like a bunch of bums, not some out-of-towners who can afford a room at the hotel," says Julian.

"Of course you're right. I just thought it would be nice to have a bath, that's all," says Lyza.

I'm stunned. I can't believe how Lyza just agrees with everything Julian says. The Lyza I knew would put up an argument on some grounds about how we could get away with it. But this Lyza is giving in way too easy. I feel a little twinge of jealousy and then remember that I once had someone too, I just didn't know it. Joey would have been a fine boyfriend. I'm sure I would've agreed with everything he said if he were here right now.

"So who of us is the least suspicious-looking and can go out and buy us some groceries?" I ask.

"Well, certainly not you," says Tom.

"Well, whoever is going better do it quick because there is a blizzard brewing out there," says Julian.

"Tom and I can go," says Freckles.

"Thanks for volunteering me," says Tom with a sigh.

"No, she's right. You look like a young couple maybe traveling or visiting your family," I say.

"I want to go," says Charlotte.

"You've been here before. Someone might recognize you," says Lyza.

"Even if someone did they wouldn't know what happened or where I've been. I need to go because they don't know anything about this town or even where the market is. If someone questions them they won't know what to say," she says.

"Charlotte has a point, you better let her go with you," I say.

"But be quick about it, if you're not back in an hour I will assume you have been caught," says Julian.

"Right then, here is some cash, how much do you think you need?" I ask.

"I have no idea," say Freckles.

"Well here is ten dollars, it should be more than enough," I say handing Freckles the money.

They bundle up for the cold, borrowing even some of the theater clothes, and we see them off at the door. Now we just play the waiting game and hope all goes well. In the mean time I need to take a look at Papa's map. I remember there being something marked here in Arkansas. Even though I know Papa isn't here, I would like to know what he had been doing here.

CHAPTER 11

$\mathcal{J}$ulian clears a table for me so I can spread Papa's map out. It doesn't take up much room but the table is cluttered with paint and paint brushes. I'm guessing the paint is for the props for the plays. I've never been to a real theater before, but I saw a play done once at school. I remember a traveling acting troop came through town and they did a play at our school house just for us kids. Later that night they did a show for adults at the saloon, I doubt they did the same play.

I think it had something to do with an old play by a guy from England about some fairies. I really tried to pay attention to the play but the actors spoke in a funny way and the all the boys in the audience kept cutting up and whispering jokes. The teachers weren't real impressed either. I remember hearing them discuss the play. They all had agreed the System shouldn't allow such nonsense. I overheard them talking about how they needed to make sure they screen the entertainment next time.

I told Papa about it when he came home the following week. Papa told me that it is called 'an expression of the arts' and that the System had no business trying to stop it. That man's name was

Shakespeare and he died a long time ago. His plays and poetry should not be forgotten just because they think it's nonsense. Papa told me that the System didn't believe that anything not real or considered fantasy is a waste of time. He said that the System is afraid of people using their imaginations.

Now that I think back on it, I realize that the System puts their foot down on any free thinking, or free action, or free anything. They don't want anyone to be free in any way, mind or body. Maybe that's why Papa has joined up with these revolution people. Someone has to stop the System from stopping us. I just don't understand how Papa is going to do this. I spread out the map and look at it again with Lyza and Julian.

"So Papa had some sort of lightning machine rigged up here in Marion," I say pointing at the map.

"What were they mining there?" asks Julian.

"Some stuff called fluorspar I think is what Tom said," I say.

"What is that good for?" asks Lyza.

"I don't remember. We'll have to ask Tom if he knows," I say.

"What else did you find?" asks Lyza.

"I found some stuff that makes dynamite in Bryson City," I say.

"Oh yeah, that's a big one," say Julian.

"I didn't do that on purpose. Anyway, I found out Papa helped the Sky Riders in the Appalachians here in Georgia. They were mining gold there," I say.

"Sounds to me like a recipe of some sort. Like he's gathering all these things," says Lyza.

"Maybe. I also found out that this man Grugen owns almost all these mines, and that he is bad business," I say.

"Wasn't that written on a piece of newspaper that old hobo

lady gave you?" asks Lyza.

"Yeah it was. I don't know why though," I say. I sigh heavily.

"It's a big mystery," says Julian.

"Tell me about it," I say.

"Did you make it down to Alabama or Georgia?" asks Lyza, pointing to a mark on the map.

"No, I didn't. I see no point now since I know Papa is in the west," I say.

"I wonder what is down there?" she says.

"I've been down that way. They have all kinds of mines that bring out aluminum and I think bauxite," says Julian.

"Geez Julian, I didn't know you were so learned," says Lyza.

"A man's got to work sometimes to eat. They don't always throw the poor folk in those mines; sometimes they hire people if they got a deadline. Well at least some say they'll hire you. They find you ain't got any papers and then they try and keep you like the rest of the slaves," he says.

"How'd you get away?" asks Lyza.

"Oh, me an old Jim we found our ways," says Julian.

"By the way, what happened to Jim?" I ask.

"Don't know for sure but I'm a bettin' he got caught," says Julian.

"Shouldn't we try and find him and help him? After all if it weren't for him I wouldn't even have this map," I say.

"No, Jim wanted you to find your papa and that's what you gotta do. Old Jim can take care of himself, don't you worry. Besides, he left Boots with you, didn't he?" asks Julian.

"Yes, I guess he did, and Boots has been with me every step of the way," I say.

I look over and see Boots curled up on a soft pillowed chair as if he were royalty. I guess he deserves that after sleeping in the woods and on trains or in my bag for so long. He looks a bit dirty and could use a brushing. I think I will try and find a brush later and brush some of the leaves and burrs out of his fur. There's no need for him to look like an old feral cat.

I return my attention to the map. There's a small x here at Hot Springs so I am guessing this means Papa has been here too. The only thing I know about this place is that there are hot springs here. I guess lots of people come here to get cured of their ailments.

"What is here in Hot Springs beside the water?" I ask.

"Don't know," says Julian.

"Me neither, but I wish we could sneak into one of those bathhouses and have a bath," says Lyza.

"Why do we need to sneak? I have money," I say.

"Because we look suspicious, that's why," says Lyza.

"Yeah, I have to agree, a bunch of teenagers running around without parents tends to make people wonder. They don't let you in those places without your parents. We don't have any papers to prove we are anything but what we are," says Julian.

"That just stinks," I say.

"Oh, don't worry, I'll find us a way in one of those. They can't be open all the time right?" asks Julian.

"No, I suppose not. I can't risk getting caught either," I say.

Just then we hear noises out front of the theater, a lot of loud talking and laughing. We all run to the window and look out. It must be about midday now but the sky is still gray with threatening clouds high above. Light wisps of snowflakes fly by every now and again. Down on the street three carriages have pulled to a stop and several people are getting out and walking toward the theater.

"I thought you said the theater is closed?" I ask, turning to Julian.

"That's what I heard," he says.

"What do we do now?" I ask, starting to panic.

"Grab all the stuff and come on," says Lyza.

We grab everything including Boots and follow Lyza out of the dressing room. We run own stairs and through the maze of the hallways. I can hear the people coming into the theater, laughing and making jokes. We follow Lyza as she goes through a door that goes even farther down into a basement. Julian closes the door behind us and we stash all the stuff back against the far wall in the dark.

"Where are we?" I ask Lyza in a whisper.

"Under the stage, I don't think anyone will come down here," she says.

I let Boots down to wander around on his own. He's pretty good about not letting anyone see him; Boots is very good at hiding. He doesn't trust too many people, unless they are children of course. We wait listening to all the sounds when we hear the voices just above us. All of a sudden someone is stomping on the stage. I walk further in so I can hear better and find that I can peek up through the cracks of the floor and see as well.

Some of the cracks are quite large so I stay clear of those in case someone could look down and see me too. It's like the people are in the same room as us, their voices are so close and clear. I can't see much, just the ceiling above. I just hope no one comes down here for any reason.

"Oh come on then Daisy, give us a sample," I hear a man's voice say.

"Well if you insist, but I need someone up here to say my lines to me. Mari, you come up here," says the woman. Her voice is young and sweet like the voice of an angel. I imagine that one would have to have such a voice to be a stage performer.

"No ma'am, I couldn't," I hear another female voice say. This voice has a slight accent and sounds much younger and quieter, almost timid.

"Don't be silly, they're not looking at you anyway. They're looking at me. You're just a prop," says the other woman.

I hear the sound of reluctant footsteps ascend the stage and walk to the far right.

"Now you just stand there and pretend you're a proper lady's maid, and listen to me," says the actress to the young girl.

I still can't see anything but the ceiling as I peer through the different cracks of the floor. I walk around underneath trying to see what these people look like because I'm curious.

I turn to Lyza and Julian and shrug as if to say "Oh well," and try and find a comfortable place to sit here under the stage. Who knows how long these people will be here. I hope they will be gone before the others get back. Lyza sits down too but Julian whispers something in Lyza's ear and then leaves. I look at her questioningly but Lyza just shakes her head.

We wait and listen as the woman above recites her lines and walks back and forth on the stage, showing off for her friends. I wonder what life is like as an actress. Does the System pay you or do you earn your money through ticket sales? I also wonder if there are strict guidelines about what sort of plays they are allowed to perform.

"Here, take the bracelet and hold it until I say the line 'give me what you have brought," says the actress in a quiet voice.

"Oh I am so breathless over the thought of my dear Wesley," begins the actress in a louder voice. No doubt these are the words for her lines since she is reciting them in an odd sing song voice in a louder tone.

"I wonder where he could be this day?" she continues. "If I were to marry such a man I would never face the threat of poverty and burden the System."

Oh my gosh, did she just say that? I look over at Lyza.

Though it's dark down here the lighting from above gives off enough light for me to see her expression and she is just as surprised and revolted as I am. So that must mean the System has a heavy hand even in the entertainment of our country.

CHAPTER 12

"I so want to be a good citizen but I love another that is poor and may not make the status. I could never be with him. Maid, you've come, who was at the door? I see you have something in your hand. Give me what you have brought me," says the actress.

I hear footsteps cross the stage and then a sudden screech. Not a scream of fear or anguish but a screech of anger and then a loud slap; a sound that no one can mistake no matter where you are. I hear a loud thump as someone falls to the stage floor. This doesn't sound like it's part of the play.

"You stupid girl, all you had to do was hand me the bracelet and you can't even do that right. What an imbecile. Now go down under the stage and find that right now," says the actress.

"But it's dark down there," whimpers the girl.

"Now Daisy May, she's just a girl, I'm sure she didn't mean to drop it. I'll go down and get it," says a man.

"No! She will go down and get it. That's why I have her, to do things for me, but she's always ruining things for me. I should take you back to the workinhouse. Now you go down there and find my bracelet or that is exactly what I am going to do," says the actress.

Lyza and I get up and look around for a place to hide. We head toward the back wall where it's darkest when I see something shiny on the ground and stop. It's a bracelet, the one that fell through the crack of the floor I presume. It's gold with diamonds in it. I can't even imagine how much this is worth, but I can't keep it or they'll send that poor girl back to the workinhouse.

I try and think of a place to put it where she'll find it when I hear the door open. I spin around and see the girl come in. She doesn't see me yet because I'm hidden away in the dark. As she comes closer I see she's a native and not much older than ten or eleven. She scans the floor as she walks, looking for the bracelet, when she suddenly stops, aware of my presence. Slowly she looks up until our eyes meet.

I bring my finger up to my lips in a motion to be quiet. The girl stares at me and does not say a word. I smile at her and hold out my hand to her with the bracelet in it. She looks down at my hand and then looks up at me and a smile breaks out across her face that calms my fear. I thought she might scream or tell on us but that smile tells me everything I need to know.

The girl takes the bracelet and turns running out shutting the door behind her. I go to Lyza and we wait to hear what comes next. My heart starts to beat a little faster now. I don't think she'll say anything, but there's always that chance she might.

"Here is your bracelet ma'am," says the girl.

"Well, you are just lucky you found it," says the actress.

"Come on now, Daisy, finish the scene," says a man's voice.

"I just don't feel up to it now, she's ruined the moment for me," says the actress.

"I think we should get going anyway, the storm seems to be

getting worse outside," says another man.

"Well, from what I did see of it, I think you are marvelous, Daisy, and you will be fabulous," says a woman.

"Let's go hunker down at the Arlington and have some hot toddies, shall we?" asks a man.

"Yes, that sounds marvelous. Daisy? You coming?" asks the woman.

"Of course I am," says Daisy.

"What about your little maid?" asks another man.

"She can wait up in the room, I'll give her my key when we get there," says Daisy.

"Very good," says the man.

Their voices echo off the walls as we listen to their footsteps walking away. The lights turn off and Lyza and I find ourselves engulfed in darkness, darker now than it had been before. We hear a door slam from beyond and then silence. We both wait, afraid to speak, making sure no one has stayed behind. Then we hear another noise and the door to under the stage opens and a dim light reveals a tall figure squeezing through. Lyza and I clutch each other in fear, unsure of who it is.

Lyza and I are both relieved to find that it's just Julian coming through the door. For a moment I thought that maybe that little girl might have told someone we were down here. She may still but I don't see why she should.

"They're gone. I watched them drive away," says Julian.

"Thank goodness, but geez Abby, that girl might rat on us," says Lyza.

"I don't think so," I say.

"What girl?" asks Julian.

"That little girl with them, she dropped the lady's bracelet and it fell through a crack down here. The lady made her come down and get it. Abby just picks it up and hands it to her," says Lyza. She sounds a little miffed.

"Did you hear the way she talked to her? She slapped her too. She's a servant, a slave to that lady, and she doesn't care about her. I did the girl a kindness. She won't tell," I say.

"Abby, don't be so green, geeze. You can't go along trusting everyone," says Lyza.

"I don't. I just know that sometimes you gotta take a chance," I say.

"Well, what is the point of that chance, we get nowhere with that little pumquat?" says Lyza, clearly agitated.

"It's not always about getting something back you know, sometimes it's about just being nice," I say.

"Well stop being so nice to everyone when I'm around, I don't want to get caught. I'm not going back to another workinhouse, or any other place, if you get my meaning," says Lyza.

"Girls, take a cool down, we don't need to argue about this, right? All we can do is wait and see. If she's just a little kid she don't gain nuthin' by tellin' anyone about us," says Julian.

We quietly grab our things and trudge back up the stairs to the dressing room. I call for Boots, hoping he will follow, but I don't see him anywhere. I bet he's off catching mice somewhere. I'm fuming a little about Lyza getting so upset about that girl. It's kind of stupid I guess, but it bothers me.

"That storm is getting worse," says Julian, looking out the window.

I put my things down in the corner and go to the window. I hadn't realized how fast the day had gone by. It's dark out, but the sky has grown so cloudy so it's hard to tell if it's still day or evening. Large snowflakes start hurling out of the sky on an angry wind that slashes at the land sideways. I worry about Freckles, Charlotte and Tom.

"Do you think they're alright?" I ask.

"I hope so," says Julian.

"Look over there on the corner," says Lyza, pointing to the far corner across the street. I see three figures huddled close together making their way toward the theater.

"I hope it's them," I say. I look up and down the street and don't see any carriages, steam cars, or any other people anywhere.

"It must be," says Julian as he takes off down the stairs to the back door.

Lyza and I look at each other for a moment before we race after him. We run down the stairs and through the maze of hallways to the back door where Julian is already opening it. As soon as he gets the door open the cold air blows in along with a flurry of snow.

"Hold the door," he says.

Both Lyza and I strain to hold the door open against the wind with snow blowing in our faces. I would have thought the building beside us could shelter us from the wind but it doesn't and it's hard to hold the door. We watch as Julian runs out into the storm and disappears into the white wind. But just as sudden as he disappeared he reappears with three figures by his side.

Freckles, Charlotte, Tom, and Julian all rush in through the door and collapse on the floor. Lyza and I try pulling the door shut but the wind pulls it away from us, whipping it open again. We both go out and grab the door and pull with all our might. Then there is a third person next to me helping me with the door. The door slams shut after a good struggle and we lock it. I turn to thank Freckles or Charlotte whoever it is because I know it wasn't one of the boys the figure is too small. As I turn I see a little girl standing by my side smiling at me.

"You're the girl from earlier!" I exclaim.

"My name's Mari, or that's what the ma'am calls me," she says.

"What are you doing here?" I ask.

"I sneaked out when the ma'am started drinking with her friends," she says.

"Why did you do that? This is a terrible storm. Something could have happened to you. You might get into trouble too," I say.

"Abby, who's this?" asks Freckles.

"Umm, Mari," I say.

"You didn't tell anyone about us, did you?" asks Lyza.

"Oh no, I didn't. I wouldn't," says Mari.

"Why did you come here?" asks Julian.

"To thank you," says Mari.

"You risked a lot to thank someone," says Lyza.

"Hey, all this can wait. We got bigger problems, y'all," says Tom.

"What?" I ask.

"Charlotte was spotted by someone in town," says Freckles.

"What?" asks Lyza.

"What do you mean?" I ask.

"Let's get away from here and somewhere a little warmer, and we'll tell you about it," says Tom.

"Is it safe to stay here? I mean do we have to leave here right now?" I ask.

"No, I doubt anyone will do anything during the storm, but we need to be gone as soon as the storm ends," says Tom.

We all go back upstairs including little Mari. I don't know what to make of her and why she came all the way here in this storm just to say thank you. I certainly hope no one decides to come looking for her here. It sounds as though we're already in big trouble. If someone recognized Charlotte who knows what that means. We get upstairs and Lyza finds some old rags to dry off with. Freckles and Charlotte are soaked and Tom is pretty wet too though he has a big heavy coat on.

"So what happened, and did you get any food?" I ask.

"We got food," says Tom, taking a bag out of his coat and setting it on the floor.

"We were in the bakery getting some bread. They were just about to close because of the storm when a man came in," says Freckles.

"Mr. Penton. My father used to be part of the men's club here and Mr. Penton is too. He saw me and said 'Charlotte is that you?' Well I didn't know what to say. He came right up to me and grabbed my shoulder and spun me around and said 'why Charlotte it is you. I thought your family got evicted.' I said, 'No sir, I don't know what you mean.' Then I turned away and by then Freckles and Tom had the bread and we just left," says Charlotte.

"Oh geeze, what does that mean? Were you followed?" asked Lyza.

"We don't think so. We kinda took the long way around headed down some other streets and then back up again. I kept looking over my shoulder and checking but then the storm started getting bad," says Tom.

"We shouldn't take any chances, I guess," says Julian.

"No we shouldn't, but what would it mean if she is here? I mean does that man know what happened to Charlotte or that she is supposed to be in a workinhouse?" I ask.

"I don't know. I'm not even sure how he knew about what happened to my family," says Charlotte.

"Yeah well, he might be an informant for the System," says Lyza.

"Ah criminy, what are we gonna do now?" asks Freckles.

"They have no reason to look for us here, do they?" asks Lyza, looking at Mari.

"I never said anything to the ma'am, I swear," says Mari.

"I'm hungry. Let's eat something and then figure out what we're gonna do," says Julian.

"I swear Julian, you are always hungry," says Freckles, laughing.

CHAPTER 13

We all squeeze into a smaller room where there are no windows and close the door so we can light a lamp. We don't want anyone seeing any light coming from the window of the theater. I think we're in a closet but it's a pretty large closet so there is room enough for all of us to sit in a circle. Tom opens up the bag he brought and takes out all sorts of wonderful things to eat. We have fresh bread and cheese as well as some canned preserves, dried beef, salted fish, and pickled eggs. They even bought apples, sweet potatoes, crackers and a jar of molasses. At last Tom pulls out and a string of sausages.

Since we have no way of cooking the sausages we decided to keep those for another time. We dine on salt fish and pickled eggs with some cheese and crackers. For desert we dip some bread in the molasses and eat that. Tom has taken the water skins and filled them all up with fresh water. So we wash our meal down with the fresh healing waters of Hot Springs.

After we eat, we put the food away and set up our beds. I look around for Mari but I don't see her anywhere, I hope she didn't go back out into the storm to go home.

"Has anyone seen where Mari went?" I ask.

"She was just here, wasn't she?" asks Freckles.

"I don't see her anywhere," says Charlotte.

"Should we look around the theater for her?' asks Lyza.

"You don't think she left, do you?" I ask.

"I didn't see her leave," says Tom.

"I wouldn't worry; she probably just fell asleep somewhere in the theater. After all, she is more familiar with this place than we are," says Julian.

"Yeah, Julian may be right, I wouldn't worry," says Lyza.

"I guess you're right," I say.

It's getting kind of cold in here, and I wish we had a fire or something. I guess with everyone in one room our body heat should help us keep warm. I look over at Freckles who seems to be shivering. She gets up and walks over to the costumes hanging in the corner.

"Hey, how about we use some of these for warmth? There are some men's coats here," says Freckles.

"Yeah that's a good idea," says Lyza.

"We should also take turns keeping watch, in case the storm breaks. We can watch to see if anyone comes," says Julian.

"Do you think they're going to be looking for Charlotte?" asks Lyza.

"Who can say?" says Julian.

Charlotte looks worried, more so than I have ever seen her. I remember when we first met she came off a bit timid because everything had just happened to her. She used to be a rich girl. She had everything she wanted, then one day her family loses it all. The next thing she finds herself in a workinhouse and she doesn't even know where her family is. Kind of like me I guess, except we were never rich but we never needed anything either.

I miss my life and the farm. I miss Granny and Papa and our happy home but I know it will never be like that again. When I do find Papa we will just make a new home somewhere. We'll get Granny out of the oldies home even if we have to bust her out and we'll go live somewhere no one can find us. Maybe we could even sneak out of the country and live in another country. Maybe there are other governments better than ours.

Julian takes the first watch but Tom tells him to be sure and wake him when Julian gets tired. Everyone hunkers down close to each other for warmth. I still wonder where Mari went. I hope she's warm enough because it it's pretty cold in here. My mind wanders while I try and fall asleep and I think about what other countries might be like to get my mind off the cold. I soon hear the rhythmic breathing as my friends fall into their dreams. I feel myself being lulled by the steady breathing and the comfort of my family around me.

I wake up and I'm so cold that I can't go back to sleep again. I get up and wrap my blanket around me for warmth. I leave the room, careful not to step on anyone. I notice that Boots has found his way back and is curled up asleep with Charlotte, typical. I make my way out of the room and to the next where I find Tom sitting by the window with a blanket wrapped around him.

"Hey," I whisper so as not to wake the others.

"Hey," he says, looking over in my direction.

It's dark in here and hard to see but there is a street lamp outside still burning. The street lamp gives off a faint glow through the window enough to make out objects. I come to the window next to Tom and see that the snow has lightened up quite a bit. White covers the ground and the rooftops remind me of gingerbread houses with frosting. Every exposed surface is hidden in snow. Even the street has a blanket of snow an there doesn't seem to have been any sort of traffic or foot prints anywhere.

"I guess it's easy to tell if the coast is clear," I say.

"Well from here anyway, but every now and then I go check a window at the back of the hallway to be sure," says Tom.

"And?" I ask.

"All clear so far," he says.

"How long have you been up?" I ask.

"About three or four hours now. It will be daylight in a couple more hours," he says.

"What do you think we should do then?" I ask.

"Not sure. Until people start moving around it will be hard for us to go anywhere and not leave a path," says Tom. He motions to the snow outside.

"I'm not even sure where to go anyway. I mean I still haven't even figured out why Papa had this place on the map," I say.

"Oh yeah, that reminds me, I have something for you," says Tom. He digs in his coat pocket and takes something out and places it in my hand.

In my hand he has put a rock, but it isn't an ordinary rock. The rock looks to be about the size of a walnut and has long points jutting out of it. I hold it up to the window and see the points are clear like glass with angled cuts and shapes to them. The light shows through at different angles and the ends are sharp like needles.

"I've seen this before I think," I say turning the stone over in my hand.

"It's quartz crystal. It's what they mine here," says Tom.

"That's where I've seen this! In Papa's work shop at home he had a box of these," I say looking up at Tom.

"What did he do with them?" asks Tom.

"I have no idea. Some things Papa let me help with but some things he kept secret. He didn't allow me in his workshop very often, and only when he could be there with me. He always locked the door when he left," I say. I hand the rock back to Tom.

"No you keep it. It might help you figure things out," he says.

"Thank you," I say. I put the rock in my pocket.

"Charlotte and Freckles set up a chamber pot in the room across the hall if you need it," says Tom.

"Thanks," I say, a little embarrassed.

Tom goes back to watching out the window and I leave the room to venture in the dark hallway to the next room. It is so dark and creepy here I could just imagine a ghost flying around haunting the place in the night. This reminds me of the hand that held mine back in the other building. I wonder if I should tell anyone about that or not. Thinking about it gives me a chill and I shrug that scary thought off and find the chamber pot in the next room and use it. When I'm done I do a little exploring on my own.

I walk down the hallway through the dark, feeling the wall with my hand. I guess I could have gotten a candle but I know there is a window at the other end of the hallway. Finally I feel a door and feel for the knob. I turn it slow and push the door in. The door opens to complete darkness but there is warmth coming out of the room.

Maybe the boiler or furnace is in this room, but it's so dark I can't tell. Maybe I could go get a candle and find out. I mean if it's so dark then that must mean there are either no windows or they are covered up. It would be nice to warm up it's so cold in here right now. I close the door and make my way back to our room where Tom still sits by the window.

"Have you got a candle handy?" I ask.

"There's one in the room where everyone is sleeping, by the door on a shelf. Why?" asks Tom.

"I found a room that is very warm and I'm wondering if it's where the boiler or furnace is. I thought I would check it out. If it's a good room we might want to move in there instead of freezing out here," I say.

"What's going on?" says a voice behind me. I turn and see Mari rubbing her eyes.

"Where have you been, I've been worried you just disappeared?" I ask.

"Oh. I guess I fell asleep in another room," says Mari.

"We were afraid you had gone back out in the storm to go home," says Tom.

"No, I'm sure I didn't do that," she says, kind of vague. "So what are you doing?" she asks.

"Nothing, I just can't sleep in this cold and thought I would investigate a warmer room," I say.

"Oh, I can't sleep either. Can I come with you?" she asks.

"I guess so, we just need to get a candle," I say.

"I'll get it," she says and turns back to the room.

Mari comes back with the candle and Tom hands me the matches. We make our way back to the room I found and we both go inside and close the door before I light the candle. It takes a moment for our eyes to adjust after being in the dark for so long. The warmth is already making me feel better. I hold the candle up high to get a better view of the room and see there are no windows. There are just four walls and a staircase leading down.

I have a flashback of the basement in Bryson City, remembering going down the long staircase and finding the girl chained up. Though that ended well for her and the girls that came out of that workinhouse, I'm not so sure the Matrons made it out alive. I feel bad about that. I don't like the thought that I might be the cause of someone dying, even if they are mean people.

"Stay behind me, Mari," I say.

She doesn't answer but moves behind me and holds onto my jacket. Slowly we start to descend the stairs. The candle gives off a weak light so I can't tell what is at the bottom of these stairs. I do know that with each step it get warmer and the air feels more humid. There's no sound of machinery or anything of that sort, but I do hear something. The sound is almost like a gurgling which makes me pause a moment a rethink my actions here. What could be down there that makes a gurgling sound?

CHAPTER 14

$\mathcal{I}$ think Mari hears the sound too because she clutches tighter to my jacket. I'm uncertain if I should go any further. What if it's a monster? I hear myself think that in my head at the same time Mari leans close to me.

"Is that a monster?" she asks, whispering so low she is almost not audible.

"No Mari, there are no such things as monsters," I say. Why did I just tell her that knowing full well that there are monsters? I guess because that is what you are supposed to say to little kids when they are afraid to reassure them. But I know better.

I reach into my pocket with my other hand and pull out the snake venom gun just in case. I could use the derringer but it would be too loud if I have to use it. This gun makes no sound.

With slow deliberate steps we continue down, against my better judgment. I take one step at a time until I start to see a room at the end of the stairs. It looks like there is some kind of ornate tile on the wall and there is a bench across from us on the other wall. I look down and see I'm on the last step and the floor has tile as well that matches the wall. There is an oil lamp mounted on the wall beside me and I light it.

The room becomes brighter and friendlier in an instant although there are still some shadowy corners. I feel Mari relax behind me. I move to the wall to my left and light another lamp and brighten the room even more. It looks like I have found a bath room. In the center of the room is an open hole that looks like it might have water in it.

"Mari, let go a minute," I say. She lets go and I walk over to the hole in the floor. Holding my breath and with my finger on the trigger I peer in the hole.

I see it's just a large sunken round tub. It has some water in it and there are decorative brass fish surrounding the tub. One of these fish has a little water trickling out of the mouth like a faucet. On the other side is another fish that sucks up the over flow of the water which is making a gurgling sound. I breathe out a sigh of relief and motion Mari to come over. We both stare down into the large round bath big enough for five people. It's deep but the water is clear and we can see the bottom of tub has tile laid in a design like a mermaid.

I light another two lamps on the other walls and reveal the full ornate room. There are two little rooms with curtains to pull across that I am guessing are dressing rooms. There is another little room behind a screen that has a toilet but it is set in what looks like a chair. On the other side of the room is a big mirror with two wash basins and pitcher sets on a shelf. A rack of towels is lined up underneath the shelf. There are three lounge chairs set around the bath.

"I can't believe it, the theater has its own bath house," I say.

"Everybody in this town has got a bath but some just don't have the bubbling hot water," says Mari.

I put my hand in the water and find it a nice hot temperature, but not too hot.. It feels so inviting that I'm ready to get in it right now. I see next to the tub is a bowl of various scented soaps and a bottle beside that I take to be shampoo maybe.

"But when you wash, how does the dirty water drain out?" I wonder aloud.

"It drains out through the fishes mouth, see?" says Mari.

"Yeah I guess that's how it works," I say.

"Are you gonna take a bath?" she asks.

"Oh yes, but not just yet. We better tell someone about this first. Come on," I say and head back up the stairs.

I'm surprised at the temperature change as I go up and hate having to go back in the cold. When I get to the door I blow out the candle first. I'm sure the light from below won't shine up through any windows, but just in case I close the door quick after we go through. The hallway is still dark and quiet, just as we left it.

"Tom," I whisper as I go to him at the window.

"Yeah," he says yawning.

"You won't believe what we found," I say.

"What did you find?" I hear Charlotte say sleepily coming up behind me.

"The theater has its own hot spring bath," I say smiling.

"You're kidding!" I hear Freckles say from the other room.

"I thought you were all asleep," I say.

"I was, but the cold woke me up," Charlotte complained.

"Your snoring woke me up," says Lyza.

"Well since we are all awake, how about a nice hot bath?" I ask.

"Oh my gosh, that would be amazing," says Freckles.

"My dream come true," says Lyza.

"Do you think it's safe?" asks Charlotte.

"If you girls don't take too long I will keep watch with Julian and then we can have our turn," says Tom.

"Julian is still asleep," says Lyza.

"That's alright, I'm awake, but make it quick. We don't want to get caught. I think we should try and leave before day break," says Tom.

"Alright then," I say.

We all grab our bags and make our way through the dark hallway to the door. I open it and motion everyone in quick and then go in after them shutting the door. I'm hoping that small bit of light didn't come through. I doubt it though, it's so early in the morning, like maybe two or three, and most people are still asleep. We all go down the stairs and I am once again appreciating the warmth of the room.

"Gosh oh me, look at that," says Freckles.

"Jiggy," says Charlotte.

"Color me happy, we can all fit in there," says Lyza.

"Is it warm?" asks Freckles.

"Feel it," I say.

I'm not wasting any time and start stripping down as the other girls look around and test the waters. I'm amused at the sight of them looking around the room at everything like Mari and I had done moments ago. I looking around for Mari but I don't see her anywhere in the room. I wonder if maybe she didn't want to take a bath and went back upstairs.

At last Charlotte, Freckles and Lyza strip down to their skin and get in the bath with me. We all lean back and relax, taking a moment to let the hot water seep into our bodies warming us all the way through. I never thought a bath could feel so good.

"Charlotte, can you pass me some of that soap in the bowl?" I ask.

"Which one?" she asks, as she grabs the bowl from the ledge.

"It don't matter. I just want to be clean," I say.

Charlotte hands me soap and passes the bowl around for everyone. Pretty soon the whole room smells like flowers and the water is soapy frothy. We wash and giggle as the brass fish sucks up the soapy water and its partner on the other side feeds us fresh water.

"Where do you suppose it comes from?" asks Lyza.

"It's part of a natural spring that is continually bubbling up from the ground," says Charlotte.

"But why is it hot?" asks Freckles.

"I don't know, something about it coming up from the middle of the earth and it being hot at the core," says Charlotte.

"Well I don't care where it comes from, it's wonderful," I say.

"Is this for your hair?" asks Freckles sniffing the bottle that had been beside the soap.

"Maybe, I don't know," I say.

"I think it is. It looks like the stuff we had at the bathhouse we used to go to," says Charlotte.

So the bottle gets passed around for us all to wash our hair. I'm thinking about Mari and wondering how she is going to explain her absence to her ma'am in the morning. Maybe she's not planning to go back at all and if that's the case I wonder if she thinks she is coming with us? I wouldn't mind except I think we are in a lot of trouble and she would be in worse trouble being with us. She is so young it would be hard for her to be on the run like we are.

"We need to talk about where we are going and how we're getting out of here," says Lyza.

"Yeah, you're right we do," I say. My thoughts of Mari fade away to thinking about our escape plan.

"Do you have any ideas?' asks Freckles.

"Tom said that it snowed so much if we do go anywhere we're going to leave our footprints," I say.

"Yeah that's a problem," says Lyza.

"Where are we going, anyway?" asks Freckles.

"At least to the train station. I assume there is one?" I ask looking at Charlotte.

"Oh there's a train station but the train only goes two places," says Charlotte.

"Wonderful. So what are our choices, and do you have any idea when it leaves?" asks Freckles.

"The train either goes east to Little Rock or west to Fort Smith," says Charlotte.

"Where the heck is Fort Smith?" asks Freckles.

"It's on the boarder of Oklahoma," says Charlotte.

"Well at least it's west," says Lyza.

"We just need to know when the train leaves now," I say.

"One comes in every morning when the cock crows," says Mari.

I look up and see Mari sitting on a bench by the wall. I don't remember her being there before or seeing her come down into the room. Maybe she had been there the whole time and I just didn't notice. I guess she doesn't want to take a bath with us. I could ask her but then there might be a reason that is embarrassing to her. I think I'll just not say anything, if she had wanted to get in with us she would have, I guess.

"Umm Mari, when does the cock crow?" I hear Freckles ask.

"When the sun comes up silly," says Mari.

"Right, I knew that. I just forgot," says Freckles.

I actually knew that too. I could have told Freckles that. Has it been that long since I've been on the farm? I don't even know what day it is anymore. I wonder if Papa knows what day it is or if he is just as confused as I am. Does he miss the farm and Granny and me? Is Papa even still alive, I wonder? Well I guess Oklahoma is at least closer to Papa than I am now. Lyza is right, at least it is west.

CHAPTER 15

"We better finish up and let the boys come down to get cleaned up. We can figure out a plan to get to the train station while they are taking a bath," I say.

We all reluctantly get out of the bath and dry off. We put on the cleanest of our clothes and trudge back up the stairs. It's a shock to go back into the cold rooms of the theater. When we get to the room we find that Julian is awake and has rolled up all the bed rolls. He and Tom are cleaning and packing up. This is kind of interesting because I always thought boys made messes instead of cleaning them up.

"You girls finally done?" asks Tom

"What do you mean by that? We didn't take that long," says Freckles.

"It's nearly daylight, and we have to get out of here," says Julian.

"It is not," retorts Lyza.

"How do you know what time it is? You don't have a watch," says Julian.

"By the look of the sky I know it ain't almost daylight," says

Lyza.

"Pert near," say Julian.

"Whatever," says Lyza.

"Go on guys and get cleaned up. We'll finish up here," I say.

"One of you needs to keep watch out the window," says Tom.

"Right. Mari can you do that?" I ask.

"Yeah sure, no problem," she says and perches herself on the window sill.

The boys head down the hall and to the bathroom to wash. Charlotte and Freckles pack up the remaining food and look around to make sure we haven't left anything. I look out the window next to Mari and grimace at the blanket of snow covering the ground. There is no way we are going to be able to cover our tracks unless we can fly over it.

"How are we going to get anywhere without leaving tracks?" I ask aloud. Lyza, Charlotte and Freckles come to the window and look out next to me.

"Jeepers that's a lot of snow," says Freckles.

"Maybe we can get a tree branch and wipe our tracks away behind us," suggests Charlotte.

"Charlotte, that snow is at least a foot deep or more in some places, we'll sink in at each step," says Lyza.

"Maybe we could make snow shoes?" asks Charlotte.

"Out of what?" asks Freckles.

"Where's the train station anyway?" I ask.

"Down yonder," says Mari, pointing at the other end of town.

"We have to go all the way through to the other end of the town," says Charlotte.

"Well, I guess we'll just have to hope and hide," I say.

"You could use the tunnel," offers Mari.

"The tunnel?" the three of us ask in unison. We all look at Mari expectantly.

"Yeah, there's a tunnel just over there, see the bridge yonder?" she says pointing about two blocks up the road from us.

"I see it," I say.

"There's a tunnel there that goes all the way to the other end of the town," says Mari.

"How do you know that?" asks Freckles.

"When I was at the workinhouse some men came and took some of the boys away to work in town. When the boys came back they told us they worked in a tunnel cleaning the muck out from all the rain and stuff," she says.

"Charlotte, do you know anything about this?" I ask.

"I remember that archway and a stream running through it but I didn't know it was a tunnel," says Charlotte.

"Most people don't I guess on account of the water running through it," says Mari.

"How much water?" asks Freckles.

"I don't know, maybe up to your knees I guess?" says Mari.

"Charlotte? Do you remember how deep the water is that runs through the tunnel when you saw it last?" I ask.

"No, sorry I don't. I wasn't thinking about that I guess. I remember that it looks pretty," says Charlotte.

"Well it sounds like we should give it a try anyway. We know we have to go to the other side of town, so we either find the tunnel a good way to go or we just do our best not to leave tracks I guess," says Lyza.

"I'm with you on that. One way or the other we have to leave," I say.

"We should look around to see if there is anything in here we can use to hide our tracks. Maybe a broom or something," says Charlotte.

I look out the window at the snow again. I just don't see how it will matter either way. We are going to leave a lot of tracks in the snow. It might be a problem, or it might not. Maybe no one is looking for us. Maybe if we are lucky no one will even wonder or think twice about our tracks.

"Okay well everyone be sure and bundle up. If you have to take a coat or extra clothes to stay warm then so be it. Seems to me this theater belongs to the System anyway," I say.

"Yeah after hearing that monologue, I think you're right," says Lyza.

"What's a monologue?" asks Mari.

"It's like a speech in a play," says Charlotte.

"Mari? What are you planning to do? You've been gone all night; won't it be difficult to explain to your mistress where you've been?" I ask.

"I want to go with you. I'm not staying here. She beats me, and if I don't do right she'll take me back to the quartz mine and I'll have to pick through rocks all day," says Mari.

"I'm sorry, but I don't think that's such a good idea Mari. We have people after us," I say.

"We're wanted citizens," says Charlotte.

"I'm sure they don't consider us citizens anymore. I think we are rebels," says Lyza.

"Ha! More like agitators," says Julian, as he and Tom walk in the room.

"Get off it," says Lyza. "None of us intended to be on the System's hit list, it just happened that way."

"Yes because we didn't conform to the System's standards,"

says Freckles.

"Well the System stinks," I say. "Fine, Mari. You can come with us as long as you can pull your own weight and don't cause any extra trouble for us," I say. I am resigned in my decision by the mere fact that I would be dooming this girl to a fate I don't even desire. What right had I to do such a thing? She has every right to be as free as I do.

"You girls ready to get out of here?" asks Tom.

"Yes, and we have a plan too," I say.

"Okay so what is your plan?" asks Julian.

"Come and look out the window," I say. Both Tom and Julian move over to the window.

"What are we looking at besides snow?" asks Tom.

"Look down the road there toward town where that dimly glowing street lamp is. Then look straight across over to that bridge," I say pointing.

"I see it," says Tom.

"The bridge over the stream. What of it?" asks Julian.

"Mari says there's a tunnel there that goes all the way up through town and lets out on the other side. That's where we have to go to get to the train station," I say.

"Are you sure about that?" asks Tom, turning to Mari.

"I'm sure," says Mari.

"We don't know how deep the water might be, though," says Freckles.

"And we'll make an awful lot of footprints getting to the bridge," says Lyza.

"But it's better than making an awful lot of footprints to the train station isn't it?" I ask.

"If we could figure a way to cover our tracks to the bridge," chimes in Charlotte.

"Yeah it's a plan, but what if we get there and the water is too high or the tunnel doesn't go all the way through?" asks Tom.

"If you logic it out there shouldn't be much water there right now until spring," says Julian.

"If we get there and it doesn't work then we just keep going and hope for the best," says Lyza.

"Really that's all we can do," I say.

"That stream must go behind the building or the street behind us somewhere. It might be a cold walk but we could head to the stream and then walk up it to the tunnel," says Tom.

"Maybe the water is low enough that we can just walk on rocks and stuff and not have to get our feet wet," says Charlotte.

"Whatever we do we need to do it now the storm is letting up and it will be daylight soon," says Julian.

"Right then let's go," I say.

We all grab our bags and bed rolls and are about to leave when I see we are missing someone. I haven't seen Boots in a while. I wasn't worried before because I figured it wasn't a problem. I knew he would be out hunting or something. Now that we have to leave I feel frantic. I don't want to go without him. He's been by my side the whole way.

CHAPTER 16

"Boots!" I call down through the hallway as we make our way down stairs and throughout the corridors to the back door.

"Here he is," says Lyza, scooping him up in her arms. I breathe a sigh of relief as I take him from her and hold him close for a moment. He purrs and licks my nose.

"Silly cat, what would I do without you? Now I am afraid you'll get lost in the snow storm so back in the bag with you," I say as I put him in the carpetbag.

"I'll carry him for you," says Julian.

"Thanks," I say, handing Boots and bag over to Julian.

We open the door and get hit with a fist of cold and snow flurries dancing on a hard wind. I thought the theater had been cold but I had no idea how cold it is out here. Tom takes the lead with Mari close behind to help show the way. Then Freckles, Charlotte, me, Lyza, and Julian at the end as we all walk single file. I try and keep my footsteps in Charlotte's but the wind keeps blowing my balance off.

We walk between the theater and the building next door until we come out into the street at the back. The sky is dark except for an occasional light from a flickering lamp, most of which have gone out from the wind. No one is out in this weather but us and there are no lights lit in any of the windows as far as I can see. We all cross the street with haste keeping to the shadows. I turn and look behind us to see how bad our tracks are. I realize that there is so much wind we needn't worry too much about it.

We go through another alley between two more buildings and find a brief reprieve from the wind. After we pass the buildings we are back in the storm again. Tom and Mari lead us to a small hill with a line of trees, and the creek unexpectedly appears. It's dark here, and there doesn't seem to be any lamplights anywhere.

"Take my hand," says Charlotte, reaching back.

I take Charlotte's hand and reach back for Lyza's hand who in turn takes Julian's hand. Of course, I'm sure she would take any excuse to hold Julian's hand. Silly me, there's that little jealousy monster again. I push the thought back and concentrate on what we are doing.

Before I know it I'm stepping in water but it doesn't seem too deep at the moment. I hope it stays that way. It doesn't feel cold on my boots either, which I'm hoping are water proof. As we walk up the creek I notice that it's not just dark but steam is rising all around us making it even harder to see. The good thing about this is that maybe no one can see us if anyone is about. The bad thing about the steam is that Tom, who is leading us, can't see where he is going. We are all just stumbling blind through the water.

This makes me think about how I've been kind of just stumbling through this whole thing blind. I mean I have the map that old Jim gave me, but in truth I have had no idea where I'm going or even what I'm doing. I've tried to have plans and set out to do what I need to do but things never turn out the way I expect them to. I hope that all this is worth it and I find Papa. But what if I don't? What if I never do? What do I do then?

I can't let myself think about that right now, I have to think about something else. I look around trying to see through the fog and look up to see the archway looming in the gloom above us. We made it at least this far. As we enter the tunnel the fog lowers to our feet, but the tunnel is a gaping hole of dark.

"Just a little further in and I'll light the lamp," whispers Julian.

"Lamp? What lamp?" I whisper back, but I get no response.

We continue to stumble through the dark, holding hands for a while to ensure that we are far enough in. I guess that if we do light any sort of light, no one will see it. I think this might be a bit dangerous since Tom can't possibly see ahead of him, what if he falls in a hole or something? Then I realize that the water is getting a little deeper and has climbed up to my ankles.

"That's not good. Tell Tom to stop," whispers Julian.

"Tell Tom to stop," I whisper to Charlotte, who relays the message ahead until we all stop walking.

I hear Julian fiddling with something and then I'm blinded by a yellow light. After my eyes have adjusted I see that Julian is holding an oil lamp he must have taken from the theater. We all take a moment to look at our surroundings.

We're in a tunnel alright. The walls are a mixture of concrete, rocks, dirt, and the natural ground. It looks as if someone just dug a tunnel into the earth and put patches of stuff on the walls here and there to shore it up.

The darkness swallows the light leaving only the dim area directly around us. It's a good thing we are aimed in the direction we want to go; I think if we got turned around we might accidently head back the way we came. Above us are long metal pipes that follow the tunnel. At our feet is the creek bed with rocks and some concrete here and there and water above my ankles. If it goes any higher the water will be pouring into my boots.

"Right then. Hand this off to Tom, he should have it to lead the way," says Julian.

We hand the lamp down the line to Tom, and he takes it. We can stop holding hands now, but I noticed that Julian and Lyza are still holding hands. Freckles is now standing next to Tom and holding onto his belt. It is kind of spooky in here but then I think about the mine with the trolls in it. The saltpeter mine with the dead girl that had been spooky too. Now this place doesn't seem so bad.

We keep walking, none of speaking, and we try not to splash too much. As I feared though, the water is getting higher and has spilled into my boot and now I have wet feet. It doesn't bother me too much at the moment that my feet are getting wet because the water is warm. It's almost like the bathwater; I had expected it to be freezing.

It also doesn't stink down here, or at least it's not too bad. I thought it might smell like sewer or something. It smells kind of musty and old and a little like iron or some kind of metallic smell. I'm trying to remember how long the town is or how many blocks we will be walking. I have no idea of time right now. It might be daylight by the time we get out of here, assuming that we do get out of here at all.

We continue to walk on with nothing more to look at but the slimy walls and pipes above. The water is getting higher which is a concern to me, and I hope we don't to end having to swim. I wonder where all this water is coming from? A strange squeaking noise catches my attention. I notice slight movement to my left at the edge of the water, rats I bet. If I let Boots out of the bag he might enjoy himself, on the other hand, cats don't like water and there is an awful lot of it.

"It's getting a bit deep," says Charlotte.

"Yeah, I hope it doesn't get any deeper," says Freckles.

"I'm soaked to my knees," says Lyza.

"Shh, quiet ladies. There's grates above us in the street, someone might here us," says Tom.

Everyone stops' talking but the splashing about is still a bit noisy I notice. The small tunnel we are in abruptly opens into a larger room with several split off tunnels going in different directions. We all stop and Tom raises the light so that we can see better. The light doesn't help much because all we can see are just more pipes above us and the tunnels. In the center is a large pool with water bubbling up. The water here is even warmer.

"This must be one of the springs bubbling up from the ground," says Tom.

"Which way from here, you figure?" asks Julian.

"Not sure," says Tom.

"We have to go north. That's where the train station is, at the north end of town," says Charlotte.

"But which way is north from here?" asks Freckles, turning around and looking at all the tunnels.

"Shh, keep it to a whisper," says Tom.

"I have a compass in my bag," I whisper.

I reach into my satchel and rummage around until I find the small compass the old woman had given me at the hobo jungle. I hand it over to Tom. Tom holds it up to the light so he can see better and turns a bit until he is facing a tunnel.

"This way," he says, and hands me back my compass.

We continue through the new tunnel in silence except for the splashing of our feet which we try to keep to a minimum. I am glad to see the water is receding as we continue on, and at last we can see a small grey light at the end of the tunnel. After a little while Tom turns off the lamp so as not to draw attention as we near the end. I wonder where we will end up. I hope it's close to the train station. I would like nothing better than to get up into a boxcar and take my wet soggy shoes and socks off.

A brisk wind blows into the tunnel and I am reminded that it's still cold outside. Our feet are all wet, so it will be important to get dry as soon as possible so we don't freeze or get sick. I remember back home in the winter when I would get home from school. Granny would make sure to warm me up so I wouldn't get sick. Granny would say, "There's nothing worse than being cold and wet to make a body ache with fever."

Tom motions us to stay back in the shadows against the wall. He sets the lamp down and motions Julian to follow him. Julian hands me my bag with Boots in it and follows Tom out of the tunnel. I guess they are going to scout out and make sure it's all clear.

I can see that the sky is getting lighter and it will be full daylight soon. I don't see any snow falling from where we stand but that doesn't mean anything because I have no idea where we are. I feel the cold coming into the tunnel and that's not very reassuring. I don't want to be cold and wet; I don't want to be here at all. But I am here so I must do whatever I have to do to get through this and to Papa. I hear a scuffling noise and Tom and Julian suddenly jump down from above the tunnel opening.

"It's all clear for now, too early and too cold for anyone to be out just yet," whispers Tom.

"The train station is just around the corner from here and around a building. There are several boxcars sitting empty on the tracks. We can hide out in the one furthest from the round house until the train comes," says Julian.

"Everyone be quiet, stay close, and follow me," says Tom.

We do as Tom says and we follow him out into the cold morning air. Julian follows behind us to make sure no one straggles along. The air is so cold I think my lungs will freeze but I guess it just feels that way because we were so warm down in the tunnel. But there's no denying my feet are starting to feel the warm squishy water in my boots and socks turning to cold slush. I try not to think about it as we hurry along after Tom.

The snow has indeed stopped, and the sky is growing ever lighter. Gray shadows start to emerge as buildings. I can't make out what they are but I gather from all the wagons and farm equipment we are in the working part of town. This makes me nervous since this would be where most of the workinhouses are. I keep a lookout and notice some towering smoke stacks above some of the buildings. I can hardly make out the smoke rising from them.

I imagine the workers in there are just now waking up and getting ready to work for some meager meal and a bed. They get nothing more. I feel guilty that I'm out here when they're trapped in there. But there is nothing I can do about that right now. Besides, I don't even know for sure if these are workinhouses. Sometimes my brain just gets the best of me.

We come around a corner and there's the train yard with a small round house in the center and a crow's nest set atop. There's no light in the crow's nest so that must mean no one is there right now. Stealth takes us across the yard to the other side where a boxcar sits on a lone track. The door is pulled open already and we all climb in right quick before anyone sees us.

"We all gotta keep quiet and still. Don't go movin' around much. It won't do for someone to see this car wiggling' on its tracks," says Julian.

Without a word we all take off our shoes and socks, wringing them out in a corner and drying our feet the best we can. I happen to have a couple of extra pairs of socks with me; I put on one pair and wait to see who needs the other. I look about to see if Mari needs any clothes or socks. I know she didn't bring anything with her.

She isn't here, though. I look over at the door and see that it's still closed. There is no way she could have gotten out. It's dark in here so I try and tell myself that she just rolled up in someone's blanket asleep in a corner. I can't explain her absence otherwise. Well, except for maybe she didn't follow us in.

CHAPTER 17

"The train!" I say, maybe a little louder than I meant to.

We all get up and gather our things. Julian goes to the door and slides it open just a little to peek outside. I'm anxious and I can't stand waiting. I feel like shoving him aside to look myself but I'm not going to do that. Julian has been train hopping a lot longer than the rest of us so I suppose we should let him handle this.

"Okay, here is what we are going to do," says Julian.

"The train is blocking the view of the roundhouse from here and there doesn't seem to be anyone in the crow's nest. So we're going to wait a few minutes until they get all the passengers off. We'll have to wait until they unload the cars too. They might just unhitch them and put empty cars on but it's so cold and the rails are iced, so it depends on if they can move them or not," he says.

We wait as patient as we can while Julian watches out the door. While we wait I look around the room to see if I can see Mari. It's a little lighter now so I can see better. I still don't see her anywhere.

"Has anyone seen Mari?" I ask.

"No, the last time I saw her was in the tunnel," says Tom.

"No, I haven't seen her since we left the theater," says Lyza.

"What do you mean she led Tom to the tunnel," I say.

"Actually, I thought I saw her next to me or just ahead of me, but every time I tried to look at her straight on, she wasn't there," says Tom.

"But she was right in front of Freckles," I say.

"I thought she was too, but then she wasn't," says Freckles.

"She talked to us; she told us the way. Are you saying she ran back?" I ask.

"I don't know, Abby, maybe she did. Maybe she ran back to her mistress after all," says Charlotte.

"You don't suppose she's lost in the tunnels do you?" I ask.

"No, I doubt that, they all end up somewhere in or near the town. She must have changed her mind and gone back. We can't go back and look for her now, can we?" says Julian.

"No, I suppose not. I guess she did go back, I just wish she would have said something before she up and left," I say.

"Abby, you worry too much. You can't take care of everyone, you know," says Lyza. She puts her arm around me and hugs me.

I know she's right. I do tend to worry about everyone. I guess too much and that's why I'm even on this trip because I'm worried about Papa. I have to stay focused. Just like Mr. Clark said. I just hope Mari is okay and is safe, I guess that's all I can do.

After what seems like has been an hour Julian turns to us with a smile on his face. It's the sort of grin you see on a little kid who is about to steal a pie out of a neighbor's window.

"We're up," he says.

"What does that mean?" asks Charlotte.

"It means they unloaded but they haven't loaded anything or

shut the cars yet. The wind has died down so it won't hide our tracks anymore so were are going to have to walk on the rails or whatever else we can walk on that doesn't leave a footprint. Follow me, stay close, and stay low," he says.

He slides the door open and we all jump down one by one, keeping low to the ground. The small overhang of the train's roof has blocked some of the snow so there is a thin line of rocks to walk on until we get to the tracks. Then we all get up on the steel rail which is very slippery and iced over. It's hard to stay on it especially when carrying all our stuff. If I slip I try to just put my toe down and not a whole footprint.

The car we were in is parallel to the train so it's going to be a mad dash to the train. We follow Julian who zigzags through equipment and cars. We are on the back side of the train, and if we look down underneath, we cans see the feet and legs of the people on the other side.

I look back behind us and see there may be tracks but you can't really tell what they are. It just looks like a mess of dirty snow and mud now. I think it will be okay. Julian heads to the back of the train, near the caboose. I'm worried there might be someone in the caboose, but I don't see anyone through the windows, at least not from here. We get right up to the caboose and darned if he doesn't climb right up the step and inside. We all just look at each other dumbfounded. Nothing happens after a few seconds so I go right on up and inside too. Everyone follows after me and we all get inside and shut the door.

"Nobody's here," says Julian.

"Where'd they go?" asks Charlotte in a whisper.

"I watched them leave. Probably to get some breakfast or a change of shift or somethin,'" he says.

"But we can't stay here. They'll be coming back," says Freckles.

"I know that, but this is the way to the next car, so come on," he says.

We follow him through the caboose to the other door. As I'm walking through I remember the last time I had been in a caboose. I had been so scared that I didn't pay much mind to what the place looked like. I look around now and see there's a stove pipe in the center of the room; I remember the other caboose had that too. Above us is the cupola where someone can sit and watch out the top of the train. They can see the whole line of cars from there I guess. Papa had told me it's so they can see if anything is going wrong with the cars.

We walk by a pair of bunks set into the walls on either side. There are curtains in these which are open right now but if someone were sleeping in there they could pull them shut for privacy. Past those is a table and some chairs, and a couple of trunks set on the floor against the wall. The walls have a dark color of paint but there are no pictures or anything of that sort. The room is plain, unlike the ornately decorated passenger cars. But then why would they care if the workers enjoyed nice things or not? As we came in we passed two other doors. I remember those from last time; one door opened to a closet and the other a water closet.

Julian goes through the door and out to the walkway between the cars. No one has come down this way yet so no one sees us as we walk through to the next car which is a boxcar but not for supplies. This is for luggage and parcels for the System Post. There should be a guard in here but I guess he went for breakfast too. No one is in here and the room is devoid of all luggage and parcels. There is nothing but shelves against the wall and they are empty right now.

We walk through to the next car and I'm starting to get nervous because it's only a matter of time before we run into someone. I'm sure not everyone has gone to breakfast. There has to be someone around. But again we find the car empty. This car perplexes me. This car looks like the caboose with the pipe stove in the middle, but instead of two bunks in it there are several. There are bunks lined all along the walls on either side and on top of each other.

"This is the System's armed car," says Julian.

"What? Do you mean the army is on this train?" asks Freckles.

"Yep, so we gotta be real quiet the whole trip so they don't find us," he says.

"Oh jeepers," says Charlotte.

We open the door to the next car but there is no door to get in it. We can't go on the roof because someone might see. I'm wondering what's next when Julian swings around to the backside of the car and slides through an open slat. I realize then this is a livestock car. I should have caught that by the smell. There doesn't seem to be any animals in it right now so we all climb through.

"This car is for the army horses," says Julian.

"Where are the horses?" I ask.

"I watched them take them off, so either they are taking them for a walk or the army is getting off here," says Julian.

"Taking them for a walk? They're not dogs, they're horses," says Freckles.

"I don't know what they do with them, but they're not here right now are they?" he asks.

"No they're not," says Lyza, "What's your plan?" she asks.

"Come on," he says.

Julian leads us to the hay bin, kind of like where I rode once on another train. There are some long boxes like caskets up against the head of the car. I walk over and lift the lid of one of them to see what is inside. I'm not surprised when I see they have saddles, bridles, and ropes in them. I immediately understand what Julian has in mind.

"You want us to hide in these until the train sets off?" I ask.

"That's the plan. I figure they wouldn't search in here if they are looking for anyone. They are bound to search the boxcars and under for travelers," he says.

"You are crazy! I'm not getting in that box. What if it gets stuck or locked or nailed shut or something?" asks Freckles.

"I'm with Freckles. I'm not getting in that box," says Lyza.

"I don't think I can fit," says Charlotte.

"I gotta say, I'm too tall," says Tom.

"Look, this is the best we can do right now. It's only for a little bit. Once the train starts moving, you can get out," says Julian.

Reluctantly we all pick a box and climb in and try our best to fit in it. I have to arrange Boots up near the top and then slide in beside the saddles with my bags at my feet. I can't imagine how Tom is able to fit but I'm sure it's difficult because he's so tall. Julian is right though. We can't go running around to find a car to get into; we would just be leaving our tracks all over the place. It isn't long before I hear voices and someone walking around in the boxcar.

"Toss me that straw there then get up in here and help," says a gruff male voice.

"Not right next to me. Go lay the straw on the other side. I got this part," says the same voice.

I hear movement and scuffling. I guess they're laying straw

down on the floor for the horses. The next thing I hear is loud thumping and banging and people shouting orders. Then I hear whinnying and snuffling and I know they have just brought the horses on board. Then I hear the door slide shut. At this point I'm relieved because that means we'll be leaving soon. It also means the people are gone from the car. The only sounds I hear now are the shuffling of horse feet and snuffling every now and again.

The whistle blows, and the train lurches into motion. I breathe another sigh of relief. In another few minutes and we can get out of our caskets. The thought strikes me funny and I giggle a little. I cover my mouth and hope no one has heard me.

CHAPTER 18

$\mathcal{I}$ am awakened by the soothing sound of a train whistle, though louder than I am used to at home. I think maybe the wind is just blowing the sound toward the house. Then I open my eyes and remember I don't have a house. I'm in a boxcar somewhere in Arkansas on the way to Fort Smith and it's cold. I sit up fast, maybe too fast because I feel a little dizzy and my head starts to pound. I have to wait a moment before everything is right again in my head.

I look around and see everyone is still huddled together here in the stock car trying to keep warm. I remember after the train started we were able to get out of the tack boxes. I hated laying there it was like a coffin. Once we all got out though we found a little space to sit away from the horses so we wouldn't get trampled on.

We decided it would be best to settle ourselves up front in the middle of the car. That way if the train ran on a curve left or right no one would see us. The horses are kind enough to grant us space, but even with their warm bodies around it's still cold. The walls of a stock car are not solid but have wide slats that allow the wind to flow through.

I scoot closer to Charlotte, trying to warm up. This is just miserable and I can't believe that we even have to do this. We should be riding in the passenger car near the stoves where it's warm inside. I hope we don't have to go much longer because I think my legs are going numb from the cold.

The train whistle blows again and I think that means we must be coming into town. I feel like I might as well get up since I can't sleep anymore anyway. I stand up but keep the blanket wrapped around me. Boots sees me get up and he starts stretching and yawning, like he knows it's time to go.

Tom gets up too and we both walk over to the wall and peer out. I'm surprised when I stand up that it seems to feel a little warmer. Kind of odd, I think. Back down on the floor it feels cold. Above, the sky is a bright blue with just a few puffy clouds here and there. You would never have known a storm came through the day before except for the snow on the ground.

We are passing through a mountainous forest of pines wearing their new winter coats. The trees stretch out their snow covered branches in graceful display. On the ground the snow is starting to melt, but sun shines down on what remains, bedazzling the eyes with the glitter of diamonds. The wind blows past the train carrying the scent of pine, fresh snow and mud as the melted snow mingles with the earth.

I breathe in deep this euphoria and start to a little feel better about everything. There is a sense of newness and hope. We are heading west to Papa and I just know we will find him soon and everything will be alright. I turn to Tom and study his face as he scans the landscape passing by.

I can see his face has grown older. He doesn't look old, but since the time in the mine where I met a pale and frightened boy, he has become a man. He's no longer pale either from working the mines but has a healthy sunny look. I can see the attraction Freckles has for him. But he is Freckles' beau, and he isn't Joey.

I wonder what Joey is doing now? I know I'll never see him again and it just makes me want to cry to think of him. When I do, I think that if he were here, he would be my beau and I his girl. That will never happen; his mother saw to that when she turned me in to the Crushers. That stupid woman, it just makes me angry all over again. I hear Tom's voice and he is saying something to me.

"What?" I ask, "I didn't hear you, the wind is loud," I say.

"I said it's a beautiful day out, isn't it?" asks Tom.

"Yes it's lovely. Do you think we'll be getting into town soon?" I ask.

"Yes I think so. The train is slowing," says another voice behind me.

My heart jumps a beat as I'm startled to find Julian standing right behind me. I never even heard him. I turn and look at his beautiful Adonis face. There is no question why Lyza likes him. Of course I found both these guys first, but I guess that doesn't matter, the heart wants what the heart wants.

"We should get up and get ready to jump off the train before we get into town," says Julian.

"Well not too far outside town, I hope. I don't want to have to walk so much before breakfast," says Lyza.

"No my dear, we're going to the hobo jungle," says Julian rushing to Lyza's side to help her up and gather her things.

"The hobo jungle? But that was back in Missouri, surely we

haven't backtracked," I said.

"No," laughs Julian. "Hobo jungles are all over the place and they can pop up wherever they need to be."

"How do you know there's one near here?" asks Charlotte.

"There on the wall is a sign," says Julian, pointing to the back wall.

I turn and walk over to the wall where we had just been sitting. I'm joined by Lyza, Freckles and Charlotte. I'm surprised we hadn't noticed it before but there are scratches in the wood. Light markings that look like figures drawn by like a child.

First there's an x with an arrow across it. Then what looks like a little wagon with two wheels. The next symbol is a circle with a line coming up from the top. After that is a tree looking figure with a circle under it to one side. The following symbol is a circle, but it almost looks like a large Q but with the tail going the other way. The last symbol is an x with a circle on each side and a squiggly line above it.

"What does it mean?" asks Charlotte.

"Well the first two signs mean to leave the train at the crossing. The next two signs indicate that you go straight 'till you get to either a tree with a rock or some trees with nothing else there. That's a little vague. Then this Q backwards says to turn left at that point and the last signs says we will find a safe camp with fresh water," says Julian.

"You got all that from these lines and circles?" asks Freckles.

"Well there's a little train drawn here," says Tom.

"Yes and that's clearly a tree with maybe a rock. I don't get the nothing part," says Lyza.

"It's just something you learn like when you learned the alphabet. The hobos just have unified signs that give you a general idea of stuff. They leave messages like this on the trains and sometimes in the towns," says Julian.

"Hmm, don't that beat all," says Lyza.

"It's a good idea to stay there at least a day and have someone scout out the town. Maybe get a layout of the train yard and schedule before we grab the next train. Some of the other hobos may have some information for us too," says Julian.

"Yes and Abby can rally the troops," says Tom.

"What do you mean rally the troops?" I ask.

"Yes you're right, that's a great idea. She did it so well with that speech last time," says Julian.

"Only don't give our food away this time," says Freckle.

"Yeah, you don't have to always share our stuff to make friends," says Lyza.

"I think it's nice that Abby shares some things with people who have nothing. It makes people like her even more," says Charlotte.

"Charlotte dear, we are the ones who have nothing now, or did you forget?" says Lyza.

"You don't have to get ugly about it," says Charlotte.

"Hey, I am not rallying anyone for anything. It's Papa who's supposedly part of some revolution. I'm not going to start some rebellion in the trees with a bunch of hobos," I say.

"Oh Abby, you're so silly, its gone way beyond that, you know," says Freckles.

"What are you talking about?" I ask.

"Never mind, you'll see," says Lyza.

I somehow get the feeling that something has been going on that I'm not aware of, like they started a war in my name without telling me. I don't want any war with the System. I just want my family back and to go somewhere safe to live without the System, if that's even possible.

As the train slows to come through the crossing, making sure it has the all clear, we throw our bags off. Julian carries the one with Boots in it, of course. We've had to crawl through the slats of the stock car to get out so we are in a precarious situation. As soon as we throw our bags we all jump out after them.

I'm worried Charlotte might be afraid to jump because last time I saw her jump she hurt her ankle. She jumps off before me and I see she has developed a technique to where she doesn't get hurt. I guess after traveling with Tom and Freckles a while they figured it out.

I jump last, and as usual it's like a rush. Just before I jump my stomach gets all tied up in knots and I feel a little afraid. I try not to think too much about it and remember to roll when I land, and I do okay. When I get up my heart is just a pounding in my throat though. I keep running away from the train, afraid someone will see me. I grab my bag and follow everyone else.

We go straight for a while like the instructions say in the picture. Of course the drawing seems so simple. They just look like doodles to me but Julian seems to think they are a map. I see a tree with a rock beside it and Julian takes a left turn just as the instructions say. I hope he's right about this because I don't want to be walking in these woods at night.

It isn't long though before I hear music. The further we walk through the trees the louder the music gets until all of a sudden we come out into an opening. Just like the sign said, there it is, the hobo jungle. This one is much bigger than the last one we were at.

CHAPTER 19

We start to walk through the camp and I see old and young people all around. Some even have babies in their arms. I guess all these people are living as best they can without the System finding them. There are lots of makeshift tents. People have their laundry hanging and pots over fires cooking. In fact the smell of food is permeating the air and I'm starting to feel mighty hungry. I see Julian stop and he comes over to me.

"Take your hat off," says Julian.

"Why?" I ask.

"Oh Abby, just do it," says Lyza, and she pulls my hat off my head and stuffs it in my hands.

My red hair tumbles down and starts blowing in the wind. I don't understand why I gotta take my hat off but I realize now that something has changed. The camp is a bit quieter. The music has stopped and everybody is staring at us as we walk by, me especially. Oh I wish they hadn't taken my hat off. Suppose someone runs to tell the Crushers now where I am.

People are looking at me and whispering, some are nodding at me and others are smiling. I don't understand any of this. I guess they all read the paper, and they all know who I am. This could be a good thing or a bad thing. I hope Julian and Lyza know what they're doing. Some of these folk don't look too friendly and are liable to kill us all in our sleep. That, or turn us in. I don't like either of those ideas.

"Julian, my boy," I hear a voice from the crowd. I look up and see an older version of Julian walking toward us.

We stop and I watch as Julian and the other man hug each other. They converse quietly a moment and I can't hear what they're saying. It's obvious this is a relative of Julian's but I can't decide if he is an older brother or his father. The guy looks like maybe he is too young to be Julian's father, but I'm not good at judging a man's age.

Finally Julian turns to us and says, "This here's my cousin Kent."

"Hi," we all say to Kent. I would never have figured cousin though; they look so much alike they could be brothers.

"Kent says we can stay up yonder with him at his campsite," says Julian.

We all head up the hill to Kent's campsite and little by little the camp starts buzzing with commotion again. Someone starts playing a fiddle and people are talking and laughing. Kids are playing and giggling, but some are still looking at me and whispering. I wonder what they are saying and if they're talking about me. I hate to be paranoid, but I think they are.

We get to the hill and there are two other families camped beside Kent. Their tent is made up of blankets thrown over some logs. Kent doesn't have a tent, just a bedroll on the ground. After some discussion Kent, Julian and Tom decide to make a lean-to next to a tree on the other side.

The tree has a low branch about five feet high that angles up making a v where it meets the trunk. We search for a bit through the branches lying around until Julian finds a broken branch about a foot higher with a v at the end of it. Tom digs a hole about a foot deep. He puts the branch in the hole level with the tree, but wide enough so there will be room for all of us to fit under.

After the branch is in the ground we all go searching for branches and pine boughs to make the back wall. We pile the boughs on the ground and Julian and Kent weave them all together. With this they create a wall which leans far enough over that it protects like a roof. They weave it in tight so it won't blow away and even put up a side wall to help block the wind better.

While they are doing that, Tom and Freckles dig out a fire pit close by. Charlotte and I scout out for rocks for the fire pit while Lyza collects kindling and firewood. By the time we're done, we have a proper campsite and roll out our bedrolls alongside each other. Lyza and Charlotte take inventory of our food supply. I think they are making sure I stay away from it for fear I might give it away.

By the time all the work's done it's nearly dark. We all sit down around the fire and roast some sausages which we skewered on wet sticks. We still have some hard bread and cheese, along with a few preserves, and we make a meal of it. The preserves turn out to be apple butter. We spread it on the hard bread and eat it with the sausage and cheese. It's so good it's doesn't seem like we're homeless and sitting in a hobo jungle in the middle of a forest. It's almost as if we're just camping out for fun.

The night sets in with the twinkling of the stars above and a chilly breeze blowing through the tree tops. Someone in the camp plays a soft melody on a fiddle and I detect the twang of a juice harp every now and again. All around me are such delightful sounds it makes me feel like there is nothing wrong at this very moment and I'm at peace.

"Abby," I hear Julian say.

"Yes," I answer, reluctant to pull myself away from my moment of peace.

"Abby, you need to talk to these people," says Julian.

"What about?" I ask.

"You need to tell them who you are, and you need to tell them what you've seen and what you know," says Julian.

"But I don't understand. I haven't seen much of anything so I wouldn't know anything," I say.

"But you have Abby, and you do," says Lyza.

I know they are right but I don't understand why it has to be me. Why doesn't someone else say any of these things? Surely other people, these people, have witnessed more injustice in our world than I have.

"Why doesn't someone else do it? Tom, you were there in the mines, you know what it's like. You talk to them," I say.

"It ain't the same Abby, you know that. People heard about you. Stories are told about you," says Tom.

"It's got to be you, Abby," says Freckles.

"I'm not sure what to say to them," I say.

"Maybe you can start by introducing yourself. Then let them ask you some questions," suggests Kent.

I stand up and look around at the camp, there's a fire in the middle of the camp where everyone is gathering. I take a deep breath and turn and look at my friends. They have all stood too so I guess that means we are all going down to the fire. I turn and walk down the hill slowly because I am hoping something will come to me as I get there. I'm blank. Nothing comes in to my head. I have no words of wisdom or brilliant ideas or anything to say.

I get to the fire and I notice that more people have gathered. Some have followed us and others must have seen us go down and decided to see what is going on. This is not like before. Last time I spoke I did it spontaneous with hardly a thought to it. Now it seems I am under pressure to say something to these people, and I just don't know what they expect of me.

It's unexpectedly quiet except for the night sounds and the crackling of the fire. Someone coughs now and then, and the wind shakes the branches of trees causing them to creak. I look around at the faces all turned looking at me in expectation.

"I guess you're all wondering who I am," I start by saying. "I'm AB'Gale Steel, Bishop Steel's daughter," I say.

"The boxcar baby," someone shouts out.

"Yeah, I guess so," I laugh nervously.

"We know'd it was you, thars folks with red hair but none's as red as yours," says someone else from the crowd.

I run my hands through my hair feeling a bit anxious, but I smile at a little boy staring up at me. "Well I guess there's no fooling you is there, unless I dye my hair," I say.

A few people laugh at this, but it's not enough to stall for time.

"So you must know then that my papa disappeared some months ago and I have been trying to find him ever since," I say. The crowd nods and some agree verbally but no one offers me any help in my search.

"I had hoped that maybe some of you might know where he is?" I ask hopefully, but everyone just shakes their heads. I hear some people say things like "It's a shame," and "That Bishop's a goodly man," but no one knows where he is.

"Is it true you been blowin' up the workinhouses?" asks a man standing to my left. He looks like he's been without a home for a good long time and is very skinny.

"Umm, well I didn't blow the first workinhouse up," I say.

"No that one blew up on its own. It wasn't our fault. We barely got out of there alive," says Freckles, moving up next to me. She smiles at me with a reassuring look.

"The other workinhouse I'm accused of blowing up was an accident. I didn't mean for that to happen, but I got all the kids out of there before it blew up. I'm sorry that the matrons died in the explosion," I say.

"Why?" asks a woman from the crowd.

"Why did it blow up?" I ask.

"No, why are yaw sorry 'bout the matrons?" she asks.

"Well I never meant for anyone to get hurt or die. I just wanted to help get the kids out. Then I decided to blow something else up to distract the town so they could get away. I didn't know the dynamite dropped out of my bag when a hole burned in it," I say.

"Them matrons deserved to die, I'm sure," says the woman.

"You blowed up the mine too," says another man.

"No, I didn't do that. The kids did that themselves," I say.

"The System paper says you're a dangerous criminal. Says you blowin' up all the workinhouses and mines," says another woman.

"Now, who are you going to believe? The System or Abby?" asks Julian.

"I heard a story from a guy says you saved a whole town from a saltpeter mine," says a man way in the back.

"I just helped some people escape, I'm sure it wasn't the whole town," I say.

"The papers say you're a pirate," says the same woman who mentioned the paper before.

"Why you readin' that trash for Lidia? You know'd better than that!" says another woman.

"I know. I just wanna hear what she say 'bout it," says the lady called Lidia.

"I met some airship pirates on a train. I helped them throw some System boxes off the train, so I guess that's what they mean," I say.

"So you're workin' with them then?" asks a man in the crowd.

"No, I'm not working with anyone," I stammer. I suddenly feel like I'm on trial here.

"What Abby is trying to say is that she is not working with one particular group of people. She is working with everyone because that's what it's going to take for us to beat the System. We need to throw away our petty disputes and gripes about one another. We need to focus on the real enemy, the System," says Lyza.

I look at her for a moment because I can't believe what she is implying. Then I realize, she's right, this is what needs to be done. These people need to hear this, and I'm the one who has to tell them.

CHAPTER 20

"Listen to me. I spent some time talking with the leader of the Airship Pirates. His name is Cinder. He had no idea that the hobos were fighting, or rather living, for the same thing. They have hidden villages just like you have the hobo jungles. They rob the trains for supplies to feed their people and they take only from the System. They're not bad people just like you're not bad people. They want the same thing and that is freedom from the tyranny of the System," I say.

"Well, why don't they share?" asks a woman from the crowd.

"Maybe because there are some people who call themselves hobos who have given hobos a bad name. They steel and cheat and cause trouble. These people make the pirates think that all hobos are like that. The pirates believe the hobos don't want to help and are leaches and thieves," I say.

"We're not thieves," says one lady.

"I work when I can, but the System makes it hard to work without papers," says a man in the crowd.

"I know this, and I told the pirates this. I told them to give you a chance, that we were all fighting for the same thing and we just need to work together," I say.

"But they have airships and villages, we got nothin'," says the man to my right.

"You have the trains, you can control them. You know where they run, when they run. If you wanted to you could all work together and take control of the trains," I say.

"Steal the trains?" asks the woman to my left.

"Well, I guess we could coordinate a massive train abduction. Only if there were enough people working together," I say.

"So that's what you came to tell us?" asks a man from the back.

"I came to tell you that it's time to make a change. We can't continue to let the System control our lives. My papa worked hard for everything we had. I went to school; we had a house and a farm. Papa helped a lot of you with work and food. The System took all that away in a single day. I'm still looking for my papa. Maybe the System has him or maybe he's hiding working on something to help us break free. I just know that I can't sit around and waste away in a workinhouse, not when I could do something to help myself and maybe help others too," I say.

"Down with the System!" shouts Lyza.

"Down with the System!" shouts Freckles and Charlotte.

"Down with the System!" shouts Kent, Tom and Julian together.

"Down with the System!" the crowd starts to chant, and everyone cheers.

"I knew you had it in you," whispers Julian in my ear.

Someone picks me up on their shoulders and they carry me through the crowd as they chant. Someone starts to sing a song and then they all start to sing

Rise up and walk away,

Rise up today's the day,
We stand tall, won't let our brothers fall,
Rise up and count the ways,
We stand and face the day.

Finally the commotion dies down and I'm placed on my feet again. Charlotte, Lyza, Freckles and I make our way back up to the campsite but the boys remain at the fire. I guess they are going to make plans or something. I have no idea what just happened but I think I just set my own revolution in motion.

Right now I'm just tired and I'm more than happy to lie down on my bed roll and pull the blankets tight around me. There may not be snow on the ground but is sure is cold. The four of us cuddle up to stay warm and I listen to the murmurs of the people talking in camp. I think about Mari and I'm still wondering what happened to her. It's odd that she would just take off like that without telling us. It's strange that she would disappear and then all of a sudden reappear again.

It kind of worries me a bit, like maybe she is a spy or something. Could she have been reporting back everything she heard us say to a System agent? If so they'll know we are heading west. It won't be hard for the System to figure out what train we're on. They might even know we're here now. This disturbs me and frightens me a little. I would hate to see any of these people get hurt or captured and thrown back into workinhouses, or worse.

I wake up startled by something. I must have fallen asleep to the drone of the voices but how long ago was that? The camp is quiet now but something woke me up. I look down and see Boots has made his way back to us after hunting. He's curled up asleep in the blankets between Charlotte and me. So if Boots didn't wake me up then what did?

I look around and see everyone is here asleep in the camp. Tom is asleep next to Freckles and Lyza is curled up in Julian's arms fast asleep. Kent is on the opposite side of the fire away from the lean to but appears to be asleep as well. The fire is still burning low with mostly embers but it's giving off warmth. I scan the camp but all appears quiet. I guess maybe that's what woke me is that it's too quiet here.

I get out of bed, trying not to disturb Boots or Charlotte. I step over Freckles and Tom and walk over to the edge of our camp to get a better view of everything. A cold breeze blows across my bare arms and face, making me shiver. I reach over and grab one of my blankets and wrap it around me like a shawl, careful not to drag it through the fire.

In silence I walk the perimeter of our area looking around and over the camp below. I wonder if they post anyone to watch at night while everyone sleeps. I don't see anyone walking around or sitting at the edge of the camp watching. Something just doesn't feel right and I'm not sure what it is. I'm tempted to wake Julian or Tom to ask them. It's the stillness of everything that makes me feel so uneasy.

I want to walk down in the camp and look around but I'm afraid. Usually I can swallow my fear and face it but right now something has me frozen. Memories of the trolls in the mine flash in my head and my heart quickens. It couldn't be something like that could it? I mean we aren't in a mine or a cave, we are above ground. But it's dark and quiet with only the wind moving.

I see some movement out of the corner of my eye and turn to see old Jim standing several feet away from me. I didn't even know he was here. I start to walk toward him to speak to him but no matter how much I walk to him he still remains the same distance away from me. I can see he isn't moving. He's just standing there.

"Jim? Is that you?" I ask.

I see his mouth moving as he speaks to me but I don't hear what he is saying. I can't understand why I don't hear him or why I can't get any closer to him. I stop walking and watch him as his mouth moves soundlessly. Then he points behind me so I turn to look where he's pointing.

Down in the camp there are Crushers coming. It looks like an entire army of them, there are so many. They have torches in their hands, and as they approach the camp they start to light the tents and makeshift covers on fire. People start running out of the tents screaming but I can't hear them.

The Crushers fire their guns into the crowd of hobos and I watch as they fall lifeless to the ground. I turn back to Jim and start to run to my tent but my legs are frozen in place and I can't move. Jim shakes his head and smiles a sad smile at me as the wind blows his image away.

I turn back around and the camp is silent and still once more. There are no fires, no Crushers, and no one is dead on the ground. I try my legs again and I find that I can move. I look around as the night sounds slowly come back to me as if they had been there all along. I can't understand what just happened.

Am I dreaming? I pinch myself and it hurts, so therefore I'm not dreaming. I'm wide awake, so I just had a look'in. Granny told me about those. She told me that some of her kin had the gift of these. To be able to look into the future. If that is what I just had, then it wasn't a very nice one and something very bad is going to happen.

I walk back to the tent and crawl back under the covers trying my best to forget what I just saw. But it won't go away. The vision replays over and over in my mind and I can't stop it. I will have to warn everyone about this in the morning. I hope I have at least until then because suddenly I feel exhausted like I haven't slept for days and I can hardly keep my eyes open.

CHAPTER 21

The sunlight wakes me to a cold still morning. I'm loath to get up out of my blankets, but I remember last night and the chill inside me outweighs the chill in the air. I get up and quickly begin to gather up my things and put them away. I see that Julian and Tom are not around and Lyza and Freckles are preparing some food with Kent. Only Charlotte and Boots remain snuggling under the blankets.

"Come on, sleepy heads it's time to get up," I say. I shake Charlotte a little until she groans a complaint and Boots jumps up, agitated.

"We're having journey cakes for breakfast," announces Freckles.

"Journey cakes? What is that?" asks Charlotte.

"Kent is showing us how to make them. You cook cornmeal in a frypan," says Lyza.

"Yeah, it's somethin' I picked up in the north. You mix cornmeal and water and add some salt and sugar and whatever you got and cook it up in a little grease over some hot coals," says Kent.

I walk over to the fire and see that they have a frypan nestled in the hot coals. Inside is a gooey substance bubbling and frothing in the heat. It looks kind of like dirty glue but it smells wonderful and my stomach is growling. I notice there is a coffee pot on the coals as well and the aroma of coffee permeates the air.

"You have coffee as well?" I ask.

"Yep, I got some sugar for it too, but I only got the one cup," says Kent.

"I have a cup," says Lyza.

"So do I," says Freckles.

"I think I might have one too," says Charlotte.

"Well look at that, everyone is prepared but me," I say. It's kind of funny, I have three kinds of weapons, a cat, and all other sorts of things but the one thing I don't have is a cup. I guess I need to get one to keep with me.

"You can use the can from the preserves, just wash it out," says Freckles.

"Hmm, good idea," I say.

"There's a creek yonder past those trees you can freshen up there too, all the ladies have gone up there by now," says Kent.

"That's a good idea," says Lyza.

"I did snag a towel from the theater; did anyone else think to do that?" I ask.

"Yes!" said all three girls in unison.

"Well, aren't we smart cookies," I say.

We grab our towels and I get the can from our meal last night and we walk to the direction where Kent pointed. I want to tell the girls about what happened last night but I'm afraid of what they will say. I think maybe I better tell them though, because it might be important.

"Hey where are the boys?" asks Charlotte.

"Julian and Tom went into town early this morning to scope it out," says Lyza.

"Geeze, how early did they leave?" I ask.

"I dunno, it was still dark," says Freckles.

"Do you know when they'll be back?" I ask.

"I dunno," says Freckles.

"Well I hope soon," says Lyza.

"Yeah me too. I gotta tell you what happened last night," I say.

"What?" ask Charlotte.

"Did someone try and hurt you?" asks Lyza.

"No, it's not like that. It's like a dream but more like, I think a look'in," I say.

"A look'in? What the heck is that?" asks Freckles.

"Are you serious?" asks Lyza.

"What is it?" asks Charlotte.

"Oh, okay," I say and stop walking. "A look'in, my granny said, is when you see ahead in a dream state you look in to what's going to happen to you," I say.

"Ohhh," says Charlotte.

"Okay," says Freckles.

"So what did you see?" asks Charlotte.

I tell the girls everything that happened last night as we walk up to the creek. By the time I'm done we find ourselves at the creek and surrounded by quite a few women from the camp. They're all busy talking with each other and washing clothes, dishes, and themselves as they chat away. A few stop briefly to nod at us and then continue. None of this looks very sanitary to me. I don't relish the idea of washing my tin can for coffee downstream from someone washing their clothes or their person.

"Let's go up a bit maybe," I say in a low tone.

"Agreed," says Freckles.

We walk as if just taking it all in so as not to appear that we are trying to get away from everyone. The women and girls smile and nod and we do the same. There are so many of them here and I find myself wondering how they all manage to live and keep their families together while they're constantly on the run. At least the pirates have a place to live but these people are always on the move. Every day there's the fear of getting caught.

I guess I'm not much different except that I don't have children to take care of or feed. I'm tired of being on the road all the time and I think it would be wonderful to sleep in a bed again under a roof. The bed on the dirigible had been nice even if it had been on top of sacks.

We find a spot by the creek above everyone where the water looks clear, and we wash and primp ourselves. The bushes suffice as a place to relieve ourselves, though a bathroom is another thing I miss having. No one talks about what happened to me last night; I guess we just don't want anyone else to hear. Maybe I'm crazy and I dreamed it. It's just that it seemed so real and I have a funny feeling in my gut like something bad is going to happen.

We walk back to the camp and still no one has said anything to me about what I told them. I guess my friends think I'm nuts now. I wonder if I should have said anything at all to them. But these are my friends and if I can't talk to them about stuff like this, who can I talk to?

"Abby, I think we should pack up and leave as soon as the boys are back," says Lyza.

"Do we even have that much time?" asks Charlotte.

"What do you mean?" I ask.

"Could you determine any sort of time frame all that is going to happen?" asks Freckles.

"I think today, soon. Not morning, it felt like night time but then it had been dark already when I saw it all so I'm not sure," I say. I'm relieved. They are listening to me and believe me.

"Look, they're back," announces Freckles. She runs the rest of the way to the camp.

"Ahh, love," I say.

"What do you mean by that?" asks Lyza.

"You should know. You're smitten too," I say.

"Ha ha, yeah," Charlotte laughs.

"Okay you're right, but you're not mad are you?" asks Lyza.

"No, why should I be? I'm happy for you," I say.

"What about me? Aren't you worried I'd be mad?" asks Charlotte.

"Oh, are you?" asks Lyza.

"No, but you better find me a beau soon too," says Charlotte.

"Well it's not like I went looking for him, you know," says Lyza.

"Tom neither. I found them both," I say.

"Well you are just going to have to find me one too," says Charlotte.

"You didn't find Julian, he found us," says Lyza.

"Well I got us on the train and if I hadn't . . ."

"Raine would still be with us," finished Charlotte.

"I told you, she's not dead," I say, acutely irritated.

"I know, I just miss her sometimes," says Charlotte.

"Well it's her own fault if she don't wanna' come back with us," says Lyza.

"Right, I know," says Charlotte.

We get to the camp and I can see that Julian, Tom, Kent, and

Freckles are in a heated debate. This does not look good. I see Julian has a newspaper in his hand, I hope it's not bad news.

"What's going on?" I ask.

"Besides the fact that you are the second most wanted person by the System?" asks Julian.

"Yeah, I already knew that," I say.

"Well I think you just upped your status and the reward on your head," says Tom.

"Really? What are they blaming on me now?" I ask.

Lyza takes the newspaper from Julian and we all sit down and listen while she reads aloud.

"The System Regulatory Unit has determined the cause of last week's explosion in Downtown St. Louis. The explosion demolished an entire block and caused an overwhelming loss of financial prospects. It is no surprise that the responsible parties of this explosion are none other than the notorious Abigail Steel and her band of pirates."

"What? I've never even been to St. Louis," I say.

Lyza reads on. "The loss of workers is uncountable as the explosion demolished entire buildings and caused numerous fires. However, it is noted that several persons are not accounted for and therefore are listed as suspects of piracy and therefore affiliated with the Steel Gang.

"The Steel Gang. Wow, I'm a whole gang of pirates," I say.

"I guess we're your gang," says Charlotte.

"Who are these other people they say are suspect?" I ask.

"There's a long list of names but none of them look familiar," says Lyza. She hands the paper back to Julian.

"I'll just bet these are the workers from the workinhouse that supposedly died in the explosion. Only they didn't die, they escaped and either they blew the building up on purpose or it blew up on its own. These poor toads were lucky they got out," says Julian.

"Like us poor toads when we escaped?" asked Freckles, taking the paper from Julian to read it.

"Yeah, sorry, but yes," says Julian.

"Does it say anything else?" I ask.

"Yeah, wanna hear it?" asks Freckles.

"Read on," I say.

"Abigail Steel is known to be in league with her father Bishop Steel who is now on the Black List by order of the System Regulatory Unit. As for Abigail Steel, she is wanted for questioning regarding numerous acts of rule breaking against the System. She is considered armed and dangerous and should not be approached but informed upon at once. Credits are being offered to those who come forward with any information about any of the Steel Gang. Full pardons offered for credible truths.

"What do they mean by credible truths?" asks Freckles.

"Good information that leads to capture," says Kent.

"What do they mean by offering credits and pardons?" I ask.

"The System offers those instead of money so that let's say a hobo has some information but might be afraid to tell it to anyone. Credits and pardons will get the hobo back into the System with good standing. If it's someone already in the System they can cash those credits in for money or use them and the pardon for a family member or a friend," says Kent.

"Oh, that makes me furious. They are trying to turn everyone against me, aren't they?" I ask.

"Yes, they are. They must want your papa real bad to go this far," says Julian.

"What's the Black List?" asks Charlotte.

"A death sentence," says Tom.

CHAPTER 22

"What?" I scream.

"Quiet, keep your voice down, and stay calm. It's probably just a threat to get their hands on him. He's got the System all wound up and you're not helping," says Julian.

"Of course not. Why would I?" I ask.

"It's just a form of speech. I wasn't askin' you," says Julian.

"We have to get out of here and now," I say. I turn and start packing.

"Abby's right, she had a look'in last night, we're not safe here. We have to get out of here as fast as possible, and we need to put the word out that Crushers are coming," says Lyza.

"Are you a seer?" asks Julian.

"I never have been before, but last night something did happen," I say.

"Right, then let's go," he says.

We pack up our stuff and head down the hill to leave the camp. As we go, I notice Kent and Julian stop and whisper to a few people here and there. I turn around as we are leaving the camp and see that the hobo jungle is in a mad business of packing

153

up. I guess Julian and Kent must have told the right people to get the folks moving.

"You know we could have just made an announcement," I say to Julian.

"Nope, you're wanted and maybe some of them know it now. We ain't the only ones who snuck into town this morning," says Julian.

"Yeah and we ain't the only ones who can read neither," says Kent.

"Where are we going anyhow?" asks Charlotte.

"We have to catch the train on the north side of town. We'll take the train to Fort Worth where it hooks up with the northbound train which goes all the way to Denver," says Tom.

It sounds like a lot of traveling, but it's the only way to get there and quick. I feel something hit my ankle and look down to see Boots running alongside me. Funny thing that cat following me all this way. Well I guess I kind of took him part way, but he didn't seem to mind. I wonder what he thinks of all this. I wonder what it would be like to be a cat and not have to worry about the System or any of this nonsense.

We walk a good bit the rest of the morning, none of us saying much but small talk. We keep to the outskirts of town not daring to go in at all. I know someone will recognize me for sure even if I am wearing boy clothes. The others though, they shouldn't worry too much about it; there's no pictures of them all over town. I guess they want to stay with me.

"Hey Abby, have you thought about dying your hair?" asks Freckles.

"And cutting it maybe too," adds Lyza.

"I already had it cut once, it's just now starting to grow back,"

I say.

"If you want to survive this trip you might consider the dye maybe," says Tom.

"How and where are we going to get hair dye?" asks Charlotte.

"One of us would have to go to a store and buy it, I guess," says Lyza.

"Okay, richies are the ones that buy that kind of stuff and none of us have the clothes to look like we are one of those, at least not anymore," says Charlotte.

"So were you a richie, Charlotte?" asks Julian.

"I was, but that was a long time ago," she says.

Silence falls thick like a fog around us as we all walk deep in our own thoughts. Poor Charlotte, she didn't know she belonged to a group of people that were despised by more than half the population. We weren't poor, but we weren't richies either. I never despised them though. I never wanted to be one either; I had been happy on the farm. I want it all back now. I wonder if that is what Charlotte wants or would she wish for something different if she could?

We come out of the woods around a bend where the train tracks incline before they go through a tunnel. This looks like it might be a good spot to catch the train but it will be tricky, I think. There is a drop off on one side and a tight cliff on the other and then the tunnel.

"How are we going to do this?" I ask.

"We're going to up above and jump down on the roof," says Julian pointing above the tunnel.

"Are you kidding me?" asks Charlotte.

"Oh Charlotte dear, don't worry I'll help you. You'll be fine," says Julian.

"Okay, what about the rest of us?" I ask.

"You will all be fine. It's not a far jump. You just have to remember to lie down as soon as you jump because we will be going through the tunnel and you could get knocked off and . . ."

"And what?" asks Lyza.

"Die," says Julian.

"Maybe we better find another place," I say.

"No, this is the best place, I promise, if you just remember to lie down after you jump," says Julian.

"What about all our stuff?" asks Freckles.

"Tie your bedding to your pack and put the strap over your shoulders. Then tie it around you with whatever you have so it won't move when you jump," says Julian.

"What about Boots?" I ask.

"Put him in the bag, I'll carry him," says Julian.

"No, I will, you need to help Charlotte," says Kent.

I don't like this idea but it doesn't look like we are going to be able to do anything else. We walk up the hill through the trees which is grueling and painful. The backs of my thighs ache and protest at every step until we get to the top. I wonder if we have enough time to rest before we have to get into this jumping business.

"So now we have to hide down until I give okay. The engine needs to go through the tunnel first, and we don't want the engineer seeing us. When I give the okay we stand up and go to the edge. Jump in the middle, land with your knees bent, and squat then lie down flat. Make sure you jump before the caboose comes around the bend or the brakeman will see you. Got it?" asks Julian.

I got it, but I'm not so sure I'm going to get it. I give Boots some love and then put him in the bag and lose it handing it to Kent. He takes the bag and gives me a reassuring smile.

"Don't worry, he will be safe with me. I've done this before," says Kent.

Well good, now I won't have to worry about Boots when I die from falling off a train. This is crazy and I don't want do this. I look at Freckles and she is looking down at the drop from the top, I'm certain I don't want to see that. Julian is talking to Charlotte, giving her pointers on what to do while Lyza listens. Tom is tying his bag around his waist tight. I guess I should do that too and make sure Papa's spyglass is secure as well. I'm not looking forward to doing this and I think I might have a panic attack.

We hunker down near the edge of the cliff above the tunnel behind some bushes. I'm nervous about this jump but I guess if Julian says it can be done then he must be right. The others are not complaining about jumping so I guess shouldn't either. Maybe I'm just still spooked about the dream last night.

It's not long before we hear the train whistle and the chugging sound of the wheels as the train pulls the cars up the steep grade. I peer out through the brush and can just see the train coming around the bend. Julian is right, the train engine is not moving very fast as it comes up and around then the tunnel.

"Come on," says Julian.

We all stand up and get to the edge. My heart is beating so hard and my legs feel wobbly. Kent jumps first with the bag and Boots inside. As soon as he jumps he lays flat and disappears through the tunnel. I watch as Tom and then Freckles jump and they seem to land pretty easy and then lie down flat. So maybe this is not so hard after all.

Lyza goes next, then Julian jumps with Charlotte and I watch them lay flat and disappear below me. Now it's my turn. I look down at the moving train below me. It's not that far a jump, I guess. Maybe it's about four or five feet, but it seems to me the train is picking up speed.

I look up and see the train cars are still winding around the bend. Julian said to jump before the caboose or the brakeman will see me. I can't believe I'm doing this but I take a deep breath to steady my nerves as best I can and then I jump.

I feel myself land on the roof of the boxcar and I remember now I have to lie down quick or I'll lose my head or get knocked off. I lay myself down flat and then the sunlight is gone and I guess I'm in the tunnel. Air is blowing against me and I'm glad I'm not wearing a skirt right now or the air might blow up my skirt and carry me away.

Though I lie flat the vibration from the train is making me slide a little. I reach in front of me and to my sides but there is nothing to grab onto. The roof is round on top and I feel myself slipping more and more as the wind keeps blowing me. I feel a sudden shock of pain as something hard hits me in the head and I see some rocks drop in front of me. At the same time the force of whatever hit me has pushed me sideways and I'm sliding off the train.

I reach out in desperation, grabbing with my hands at the roof, but all I get are splinters as I begin to slide sideways off the train. At the last second I manage to grab onto the edge of the roof and hang on the side of the train. I'm dangling on the side of the boxcar and I struggle to find a foothold or something, but my feet find nothing but air.

I don't hear my own scream over the passing air in the tunnel but I feel it vibrate through my chest. I'm not going to be able to hold onto the edge like this for very much longer; I can feel my hands slipping. I think this is it for me, but I don't want to die. I haven't even found Papa yet. I can't die now, I just can't.

Sunlight fills my eyes as the train exits the tunnel and is now gaining speed. I try and look around now that I can see but the boxcar is flat on the side and there's nothing for me to grab or step onto. I look down; maybe I can throw myself from the train and just roll away. I can always catch up with everyone later, maybe the next train. But I look down and see nothing but air below me, and now I know I'm going to die.

Just as the realization sets in that this is the end for me, I feel hands on top of mine. I look up and see old Jim there with his hands over mine. He smiles down at me like this is nothing. What the heck is he smiling at? He needs to just pull me up, then he can smile at me.

"I gotcha, girly. No worries," he says.

Funny thing but he doesn't yell or anything. It's like I can hear him clear as day over the wind but it's like we're sitting somewhere quiet. Then I remember last night when I saw Jim too, but last night he wasn't really there. I look up again and Jim is gone but I see Julian and Tom running along the top of the next car toward me. I don't see Jim anywhere but yet I swear I still feel his hands on mine, holding them.

This is confusing. The next thing I know Julian and Tom are leaning over and pulling me up on top of the car. I lie there trying to catch my breath for a moment. Before long I see Julian motioning me to get up and follow him. Now he wants me to walk on top of a moving train? Is he crazy?

I stand up with Tom's help. I keep my knees bent like Julian said to do, and we walk to the edge of the train but then Julian jumps to the other car. I look at him when he motions me to follow and I just shake my head. No more jumping for me. I see the ladder and I climb down it but I still have to jump over to the other car. To me it's less scary down here between the cars.

I make my jump without a problem, but my heart is still lodged in my throat. I climb back up to the next roof and am greeted by Tom who has already jumped over. We run across this roof to the next but this time we all climb down. We find everyone huddled on one side or the other of the brake step. It's quieter here and I can sit down and gather my wits about me. I look around.

"Where's Jim?" I ask.

"Jim? What do you mean?" asks Julian.

"Geeze, Abby are you okay?" asks Lyza.

"I thought we were going to lose you," says Freckles.

"Oh my goodness, Abby," says Charlotte, hugging me.

"I'm okay now, but that wasn't fun at all," I say, rubbing the back of my head.

"What's wrong with your head?" asks Lyza.

I bring my hand away from my head and see blood on it. I stare at the blood a moment partly in shock and disbelief that a moment ago I almost died. This is may be the second, third, maybe fourth, time I've come close to death. I can't keep track anymore.

"Something hit me and knocked me off the train," I say.

"We saw some rocks on the roof, I think some fell in the tunnel and one must have hit you," says Tom.

"You are so lucky you're alive. There's this one feller that this happened to some time back when a sharp rock stabbed a hole in his head. Funny thing about it is that his suspenders done got caught up on some of the other rocks. He stayed with the rock while the train moved below him. He died, of course. The next train that come up through the tunnel found him hangin' there. The engineer had to stop and let him down a'for he could move on," says Kent.

"Now you tell us how dangerous that is," says Freckles.

"Yeah, you could have warned us," says Charlotte.

"That wouldn't have helped, then you wouldn't have done it," says Julian.

"That's the point, Julian. We don't want to die before we even find Abby's papa, you know," says Lyza.

"Abby, why did you ask about old Jim?" asks Julian.

"Oh, nothing I just thought I saw him. I guess I'm in shock and my mind just started playing tricks on me," I say, dismissing it.

"Abby, didn't you say you saw him last night too?" asks Freckles.

"That was a dream," I say.

"No, you said it was a look'in," says Lyza.

"I don't know. What does it matter anyway?" I say.

"Well, it's just that I found out last night in the camp that old Jim got caught some time back. He passed away in the jailhouse," says Julian.

"What? When?" I ask.

"Gosh, Abby don't make me say this," says Julian.

"Say what?" I ask.

"Jim died before we even went to that hobo jungle that first time," says Julian.

"That's not possible," I say.

"Yeah that can't be right. You were with him when you found us and saved us from those horrible men," says Charlotte.

"Well, the thing is, I thought I was alone on the train that day, until I saw those boys running along the top of the train. Then when I heard someone screamin' I figure I better help out so I ran across the top to the car, that's when I saw old Jim. I figured he'd been just ridin' in another car or somethin', so we busted in together," says Julian.

"I just don't believe that," says Freckles.

"Yeah, so what you're saying is that Jim is a ghost?" asks Lyza.

"I don't know what I'm sayin', I'm just tellin' you what I know and what I heard," says Julian.

"But Jim is the one that gave me the map to find Papa," I say.

"And mayhap he did, but he died not long after that," says Julian.

"But he came to the workinhouse. I saw him in the courtyard. He brought Boots with him," I say.

"I don't know, Abby," Julian says.

I don't know either; I can't believe he is telling me that every time I saw old Jim after that night, he was a ghost. How is that even possible? I thought ghosts floated around in the air like a white pale thing in a sheet and moaned all the time. I've never seen a ghost. How is that even possible? It's just not. I won't believe it.

CHAPTER 23

The trip to Fort Worth is cold. Though there isn't as much wind down here on the end steps compared to up on the roof, we still catch a cold breeze between the cars. We keep huddled close together for warmth though there is not much room for all of us here. Julian, Lyza, Tom and Freckles are riding across from us on the front car. Kent, Charlotte and I, with Boots in the bag on my lap, are riding on the back car.

I'm sitting on the end, so afraid I'm going to fall off, but I have my arm wrapped tight around the rungs of the ladder that leads up to the roof. I'm sure Boots is snug and warm inside the bag with no idea the danger he's in. I feel myself dosing off from time to time and I think this might be dangerous considering where we're sitting. We've been on this train for several hours though, and I'm stiff, cold, and achy, and I have to go to the bathroom. I'm sure this is the most uncomfortable ride I've ever been on.

"Julian! How much longer?" I yell.

"I don't rightly know, I've never been this far west," he says.

"Why didn't we get into a boxcar?" I ask.

"Cows, the cars are full of cows," he says.

"Oh, is that what that smell is?" says Charlotte.

"I've ridden with cows before. It's no big deal," I say.

"It can be if they get spooked by something and there are a lot of us. Not much room," says Julian.

"There's not much room here either," says Lyza.

"You're complaining? I can move," says Julian.

"You stay right there, you're keeping me warm," says Lyza.

Finally I feel the train slowing down. I'm wondering if we are at Fort Worth or if it's a water stop. Either way, as soon as this train is going slow enough I'm off it and to the woods. I have noticed that the land around us is thinning out. When we started from Fort Smith there were mountains and trees galore and everything is so green. Now it seems to be thinning out and becoming flat.

The whistle blows indicating that we are coming to some sort of junction or stop. As the trains slows, though, our ride gets more precarious and jerky as the cars jolt and bump each other. This part scares me a lot because any one of us could get knocked off the train and dragged under the wheels. Suddenly an odd shadow passes overhead so fast I have no idea what it is.

"What was that?" I ask.

"It's the brakeman, he's running the plank to turn brakes on the cars," says Julian.

"He'll see us for sure," says Freckles.

"If he didn't already," says Lyza.

"No, not just yet because he's focused on the brakes and not fallin' off, but if he heads back to the engine he might get a look," says Kent.

"We should get ready to scram," says Julian.

We all very carefully and stiffly stand up, though it's difficult when the cars are bumping each other so much. The train is finally slowing enough to where it might be safe enough to jump off. I watch Julian peek his head around the side, then he climbs the ladder and peeks up top to see where the brakeman is. This part is tricky because if we're seen then we won't be able to get back on the train.

"There's a clump of bush comin' up, we have to jump and head for them and hide till the train passes," says Julian.

"Remember to jump away from the train and roll when you land," says Kent.

"I can't roll, I have a cat," I say.

"Yeah and our bags too," says Freckles.

"Ahh, just do whatever you need to do to not break an ankle, okay," says Tom.

"I'll take Boots," says Julian, and takes the bag from me.

The train slows down even more thankfully. Julian gives us the nod and we take turns jumping from the train. I don't see what the others do, I just concentrate on what I'm doing and I jump away from the train. There's no rolling for me, I just hit the ground running and my feet don't stop until I get to the bushes and plop myself down. Then I take a breath and look around to see where everyone else went.

I look up and see I'm all alone. I hope I ran to the right bushes. I peek out and see the train going by and the station it's heading for is not far off. There's a small building with a platform and a water tower where the train comes to a complete stop. I see a man walking across the top of the train who I guess must be the brakeman Julian talked about. He's not looking out my way so maybe he didn't see any of us. I don't see anyone in the open either.

"Abby," I hear Lyza's voice calling me in a loud whisper.

"Here," I answer back.

"Come over here," she says.

I look around for a minute until I see her over by the tree line further back from the bushes. I make my way over to her keeping low to the ground and behind the bushes as I do. When I get to the trees and in far enough where no one can see from the station, I see my companions huddled together.

"Everyone okay?" I ask.

"It appears so," says Tom.

"All here and accounted for," says Julian.

"So what do we do now?" asks Charlotte.

"I know what I'm going to do. You boys stay put while I find a bush," I say.

"Me too," says Freckles.

After we have taken care of our business we go back to where we left everyone. We find them talking about how they're going to get back on the train. I look out across the space between us and the train and wonder how it's even going to be possible without anyone seeing us. The caboose is right there and I'm sure someone must be there.

"They won't be here long, so we will have to move quickly," says Kent.

"We need some kind of distraction," says Freckles.

"Why? Everyone is at the front of the train getting water," says Charlotte.

"The caboose, Charlotte dear. There might be someone in there," says Freckles.

"Oh, but how do we know?" asks Charlotte.

"We don't, that's the problem," says Lyza.

"I'll just go check. If there is someone there, they will stop me.

If there isn't, then I wave you on," says Kent.

"But you might get caught," I say.

"Sometimes we gotta do this so the others can get aboard. I usually get away. Don't fret none," says Kent.

I watch in disbelief as Kent marches out of the bushes and straight to the caboose. He's right out in the open so if there's someone in there watching, they are sure to see him. He trots right up to the caboose and then up the platform and to the door. I'm in shock that he's just going right in. I hold my breath and wait. I look over at the others who apparently appear to be doing the same.

I release my breath when Kent comes back out of the caboose and shakes his head waving at us to come on. I look around to make sure there's no one on the back side of the building or walking around on the roof of the train that can see us. So far the coast is clear. We all make our way warily to the caboose, trying not to look like a band of hobos about to jump on a train.

Kent jumps down off the caboose platform and walks slowly up the line till he gets to a boxcar just two cars up from the caboose. This one is not a stock car but a freight car of some kind. As we get closer he pulls the door open a little and hops up. We all get to the car and one by one Kent helps us up in to the car and then he and Julian pull the door shut.

I'm about to say something when Julian puts his finger to his lips and shakes his head. I guess maybe if I speak they will be able to hear us. I turn to see that the car is dark but not so much that I can't see that it's full of grain bags and almost no room for us unless we climb up on top of them. We climb up on top and do our best to make ourselves comfortable and hidden should someone open the door.

After what seems like a long while we hear the whistle blow and commands shouted out. With a jolt the trains starts to move. Overhead footsteps run across the top and I guess it's the brakeman again releasing the brakes. As the train slowly picks up speed, I feel confident that we're safe, at least for now.

I open my bag to let Boots out, and he stretches and purrs and rubs against me while I pet him and love on him for a while. When he has enough he goes to explore and receive attention from someone else. It's kind of hard to see in this car since there aren't too many grooves between the boards. I also figure that it's almost evening too. My stomach rumbles a bit and I hear a little giggle from somewhere close by.

"It's okay to make noise now, but please keep the stomach rumbling down to a minimum," says Julian.

"I can't help it. I'm hungry," I say.

"Me too," says Freckles.

"That goes for me as well," says Tom.

"I'm hungry too. Who has the food?" asks Charlotte.

"You do, silly," says Lyza.

"I could eat," says Julian.

"I won't say no to a morsel," says Kent.

"I too could do with a meal," says a strange but familiar voice.

CHAPTER 24

Someone lights a match and then a candle, which gives the car an amber glow. My eyes adjust allowing me to see Lyza holding the candle. She sits atop the large grain sacks which are so high her head nearly touches the ceiling. I glance around and see Julian sitting beside her and then back behind them is Kent.

I turn my head and look to my left and see Charlotte about three feet from me sitting up on top of the sacks and back in the corner sit Freckles and Tom. No one else is sitting up on top of the sacks but us. I looked down to the floor and toward the door. There's about four feet of floor between the wall and the stack of sacks. In the far right corner of this stretch of floor, sits a man.

It isn't just any man though, but a very large black man. He turns his face up toward the light, and I realize why his voice sounds familiar. The man is the same man I met on the train some months ago who came from Africa seeking his fortune here in America. I search my memory for his name and I know it is a big long strange name but all I can recall is Mr. Bo.

"Mr. Bo, is that you?" I ask.

He turns his gaze in my direction and studies me a moment.

I'm a little afraid because I remember thinking he had turned me in to the conductor while we were on the train. I had found the newspaper in his bag that had the article about Papa and me.

"Little redheaded girl, I remember your face and your hair. You ran away from me after I fed you a very nice meal. That was very rude of you," he says.

"I didn't mean to be rude sir, but you were turning me in to the conductor and I couldn't let myself get caught," I say.

"Turning you in to the conductor? Oh, now I see where you might have thought that, I suppose. But that had not been the case. I was procuring you a ticket you see, to accompany me," he says.

"So you say," I say, not believing him.

"Well, you don't believe me, not a very trusting girl, and I can understand why," he says.

"Why are you here in the boxcar?" I ask.

"I believe this is what happens to your people when they get caught telling lies," he says.

"Don't you work for the System?" I ask.

"No, I have never worked for the System, and now I am apparently on the run from the System as well," he says.

"What's wrong with your face?" asks Charlotte, coming up beside me.

I look closer at him and see his face appears purple on the left side, and his left eye is almost swollen shut. His lip is bleeding as he dabs it with a wadded up cloth. It looks like he's been in a fight. It reminds me of the time Joey got into a fight with his brother Carl at school one time. Carl is several years older than Joey and much bigger so Joey lost the fight and ended up with a black eye and a busted lip.

"Did you get into fight?" I ask Mr. Bo.

"It's a funny thing, but I wonder is it a fight if you do not hit back?" he asks.

"Abby, aren't you going to introduce us?" asks Freckles.

I look about and see that everyone has come closer now to peer at the man down on the floor. I'll have to introduce this man to them though I hardly know him myself, and, I don't trust him, beat up or not.

"Everyone, this is Mr. Bo. We met on a train and he had been nice enough to buy me a nice meal, which I do appreciate. However, I had been under the impression he would turn me in so I left in a hurry. Mr. Bo, this is my family: Julian, Lyza, Kent, Charlotte, Freckles, Tom, and Boots is somewhere around here too," I say. They murmur greetings to Mr. Bo while trying not to look like they are staring at him.

"Well let's eat. I'm sure we have enough to spare for one more mouth," says Freckles.

"Yes, and I for one am sure we would all be interested in hearing Mr. Bo's story," says Tom.

"I agree, how come you're riding in a freight car to Fort Worth Texas," I ask.

"Come on up, Mr. Bo. No sense in staying down there. The party is up here," says Kent.

I help Lyza and Freckles get the food out while Kent and Julian help Mr. Bo up to the top of the grain sacks. Tom digs out some medical supplies he has in his bag and he and Charlotte help Mr. Bo clean up his face.

"I can't put a bandage anywhere on your face. I could wrap one around your head if you like," says Charlotte.

"No. Thank you Miss Charlotte, I think this will be fine," says

Mr. Bo.

"I'm sorry we don't have many supplies," says Tom.

"This is good. Thank you for your kindness, Mr. Tom," says Mr. Bo.

Everyone is being very nice to Mr. Bo and it makes me feel like I'm some kind of heel or something. I don't trust him. I haven't known him long enough to be nice to him. Why is everyone being so nice to him? It makes me just want to scream.

Does it make me a bad person for not being trusting enough? After all the things I've been through, I can't just jump at trusting. I don't even trust Kent; I'm not even sure why I included him as my family as I introduced everyone. I have no idea what is going on here but I intend to find out soon.

Our meal consists of some hard bread, soft cheese, some olives from a small jar, and apples. Kind of a strange combination but when you're on the road you eat what you can get and get what you can to eat.

We sit and eat in silence for a moment, sharing a water skin that Tom has to wash it all down. We will have to get more water at some point I'm sure, but I guess we will be in Fort Worth before long. Right now I just want to know how Mr. Bo got on this train and why he is riding in a freight car and not in the passenger section like before.

"I thank you kindly for the meal. I'm feeling more myself now, at least in my stomach," says Mr. Bo.

"You're welcome. Now please, tell us your story," says Charlotte.

"Well, it is true that I met Miss Abby on a train a few months ago. Anyway, the truth is that half of what I told you then was true, but not all. I told you that I came to America with a hunter and that he sent me to college and that I decided to stay to mine gold," says Mr. Bo.

"Yes, I remember," I say.

"I met with the business men and worked out all the paperwork. But something about the paperwork appeared odd to me. They put me down as a foreign company even though I live here in America. I thought perhaps it is just a formality since I am not born here. That of course should have been my first clue that something is amiss. But I dismiss it and move forward," he says.

"What did that mean?" asks Julian.

"I will get back to that in a moment. The other part of my misfortune has to do with a woman. You see the man who brought me here has two daughters, Summer and Josephine," he says.

"Wow, what interesting names?" says Lyza.

"We have a friend named Raine," says Charlotte.

"Shh, let him finish his story," says Freckles.

"Josephine, the oldest girl has brilliant red hair, like yours Abby, but she ran off with someone her father did not approve of. I remember seeing her once when she came to the house. She had a baby in her arms and wanted her father to accept the child as his grandchild. She cried and begged her father for forgiveness but he refused her and so she left. I thought it very sad that he would not accept his own grandchild," says Mr. Bo.

"Oh, that is sad," says Freckles.

"Did you ever see the father?" asks Tom.

"No, he sat in the carriage, or at least I saw a man who sat in the carriage waiting that I assumed must be her husband. He never left the carriage, he just sat there. Anyway the youngest daughter, Summer, she is the girl I fell in love with.

"Oh, now it's getting interesting," says Charlotte.

"Summer has hair like golden sunshine, and a smile that warms you like the rays of the sun," says Mr. Bo.

"What a poet," says Freckles.

"She and I were great friends at an early age and then it became more than friendship and I wanted to marry her and be with her forever. She loves me too and told me so but when we approached her father with the idea he became a monster. I have never seen him like that before. It was ugly and he said very hurtful things to me that I had never heard from any human being before," says Mr. Bo.

"Like what, Mr. Bo?" asks Lyza.

"I do not think I should repeat them in front of children," says Mr. Bo.

"We're not children," says Julian.

"If you've had to live the life we've had to live then you would know that any children in this country grow up fast," says Tom.

"Well then the ladies, it would not be proper," says Mr. Bo.

"Ladies? Ha ha. Where?" asks Freckles.

"I think what Mr. Bo is trying to say is that you've never been subject to the things some people call other people from different countries," says Kent.

"How come?" I ask.

"How come what?" asks Kent.

"How come we don't hear these things about other countries and what other people call them?" I ask.

"Because America is run by the System and the System keeps you blind to the truths beyond. They don't want you know about everything," says Kent.

"So, I'm confused, some people in our country know about

your country but they call you names? But the System of our country doesn't want the majority of the people to know about your country or the names that some of the people in our country call you?" asks Charlotte.

"Oh, Charlotte you just got me confused," I say.

"Look, let me put it this way," says Mr. Bo, "Only the privileged few of your country ever leave your country let alone know anything about me and my country. The System has kept you and your people within a wall of sorts. You don't know what is going on, not even people like you who live outside the System," says Mr. Bo.

CHAPTER 25

"$\mathcal{I}$ went to the mine in Georgia to make sure everything is in order and that the workers had arrived. When I arrived there were people there already running the mine and they promptly arrested me and chained me in my own mine to work. I believe that for some reason they needed my name, a foreign name, to put on the paperwork to continue. Though I do not know what the purpose is. I found a way to escape and decided to go look for Summer, but when I got to her home I found out from the servants her father sent away her," says Mr. Bo.

"Do you know where she is?" asks Freckles.

"I believe she may be in Fort Worth at a boarding school for young ladies," says Mr. Bo

"And you're planning to spring her?" asks Julian.

"Yes, that is the plan," says Mr. Bo.

"By yourself?" asks Tom.

"I have no one else," says Mr. Bo.

"Oh, that's so romantic," says Charlotte.

"What do you plan to do once you find her?" I ask.

"We will get married. I don't know, maybe we will find a way out of the country," says Mr. Bo.

"How would you get out of the country?" asks Charlotte.

"Oh a cargo ship or something the like," says Mr. Bo.

"A cargo ship?" asks Charlotte.

"Water or air?" asks Lyza.

"Water," says Mr. Bo laughing. "Imagine me trying to hide in an airship? That would be quite impossible since they account for every ounce of weight."

"They do?" asks Charlotte.

"A better question would be why there are cargo ships? Are they bringing goods or taking?" asks Kent.

"Both, I believe," says Mr. Bo.

"I thought America is a self-sufficient country? They taught us in school that the System created a way that our country didn't need to trade with other countries. That we produced our own goods," I say.

"They would have you think that, but it is not true. I have seen with my own eyes the goods coming in and going out on air, and water ships from a port in Long Island," says Mr. Bo.

"No that can't be. Long Island is a desolate useless island where waste is dumped," says Julian.

"Again, your System would have you think that, but it's not true. The barges that appear to be carrying waste actually carry goods that are shipped out from the port," says Mr. Bo.

"I don't believe you," I say.

"You do not have to believe me, child. You can believe what you want to believe. I'm only telling you what I saw with my own eyes. Whether you choose to believe it or not is up to you," says Mr. Bo.

With that he leans back, shut his eyes, and falls silent for a while. I just don't know what to think of all of this. I guess I never thought much about any of this stuff when I lived on the farm. It's bad enough thinking about the workinhouses and the way the poor folk are treated, now to think the entire System is lying to its own people about what it's doing. It's just like getting my brain scrubbed with a pine cone.

Papa said the System wasn't right and that things needed changing. I didn't understand what he meant. For people like us living on a farm in the middle of nowhere, it just didn't seem like there was much we can do. It also didn't ever seem like it would affect us, until it did. I wonder if Papa knew about the trading goods going in and out of an island that's supposed to be a waste area. If that ain't where the waste goes than I wonder where all that goes?

Mr. Bo sure has some story anyways, and maybe I'm too quick to judge him. It all seems so elaborate and detailed. How could it not be true? On the other hand, I remember Papa telling me that if someone puts so much detail in the telling of their story, there's a chance the story isn't true. On the other hand, he told us things that if they are true, I'm sure the System wouldn't want us to know about. Like the island and the goods shipped to and from other countries. I wonder what stuff comes from other countries.

I think about the things we learned in school and there wasn't much stuff about other countries. Nothing except maybe where on the map a country is and what languages they speak in that country. We learned nothing about their government or what their resources are. I know at the time I didn't care about all that stuff anyway. We mostly did math and reading, just the basics, I guess. There seemed to be a lot about farming and taking care of animals things like that. Looking back on my education, I think maybe I learned more from Papa and Granny than I learned at school.

I must have fallen asleep because I wake up and everyone is snoring. It's much darker in here which means that it must me night outside. We should be near Fort Worth by now, that or the train needs to stop for water soon because we have been traveling for an awful long time. Just as I'm thinking this the train starts to slow down.

I feel my way through the dark and slide down off the grain sacks to the floor. A familiar furry tickle rubs across my legs and I reach down and pet Boots. I wonder if he found himself any mice lurking around here with all this grain.

I reach for the door to see if I can peek through a crack but it's shut tight. I try and pull on it a bit but it's pretty heavy and I'm gonna need some help getting it open. I don't want to wake everyone up but since the train is slowing I think maybe I better anyway.

"Tom? Julian?" I say out loud in a question.

"Yeah," answers a sleepy sounding Tom

"I'm here, what yaw want?" says Julian.

"I think the train is slowing, I want to open the door a crack and peek out but I can't do it myself," I say.

"I can help I think I'm closest," I hear Lyza say. I hear a commotion and then someone sliding down off the grain sacks with a thump to the floor.

"Oops, sorry, didn't mean to be that loud," says Lyza.

"Where are you?" I say reaching out until I feel her arm.

"Yaw got me. Come on, I'll help. We don't need them boys. We're just as strong as they are," says Lyza.

Together Lyza and I pull on the door until it inches open and cool air flows in through the crack in the door. The crack is about half a foot wide, not too big so we would fall out but not too small that we can't see out. I look out with Lyza standing beside me and I see a moonlit land dotted here and there with shrubs and trees. A far cry from the abundant tree and shrub covered land we went through before, here it's near desert.

"Wow, what a change," says Lyza.

"You're telling me," I say.

The train makes a drastic reduction in its speed and Lyza and I pull the door open a bit more so she can stick her head out. I hold onto her just in case. She pulls back in, her hair windswept across her face.

"I see lights of a city coming up ahead of us," she says.

"That means it's time to pack up," says Freckles.

Everyone scrambles to grab their stuff and slides down the grain bags to the doors. Now it's just a matter of waiting until we are slow enough to jump off the train. It would be better to wait until the train stops but there are just too many of us to try and sneak off in the train yard.

I grab Boots and put him in the bag again. Then we wait while the train slows as it comes into town. In my experience this can sometimes be an excruciatingly long wait if you're in a hurry to get somewhere. On the other hand if you're just along for the ride I suppose it can be enjoyable and give you time to get a good look at the land around.

I'm thinking about all this when suddenly I realize there's no more land but buildings. I look down and see there's tracks running alongside our train as well which means we've come in to the train yard. No sooner do I think that when another train goes by us the opposite way pulling out of the yard. We all pull back away from the door in surprise.

"It just kinda snuck up on us didn't it?" asks Julian.

"Well now we ain't got but a choice to sneak outa here afore someone sees us all," says Kent.

"Any idea where we're going?" asks Lyza.

"Yep, we gotta go to the other side where the passenger station is and catch a northbound train," says Julian.

"Yeah, Julian and I worked it all out," says Tom.

"Okay then when the train stops we gotta get out quick and duck down under that train yonder," says Kent pointing to a stationary train across the yard.

The train comes to a slow stop with the brakes screaming as it does. Tom and Julian pull the door open further and we all jump out, keeping as low to the ground as we can. Single file, we make our way quickly to the other train across two sets of tracks hoping that the cover of night will hide us. We duck down under the train and wait in the shadows to check if anyone has seen us. My heart is thumping hard in my chest.

"You know as soon as someone sees that door open they're gonna start looking for hobos," Freckles whispers.

"Dang, shoulda closed the door," whispers Kent.

"No time," whispers Julian.

"Come on this way," whispers Mr. Bo.

He starts moving under the train to the other side where there's a wood shed. Julian looks over at me and though I can't see his eyes in the dark I know he wondering what I'm thinking. I see his shoulders shrug as if to say "why not?" and he follows Mr. Bo.

Lyza hesitates, looks around, and goes after Julian. Soon everyone follows one by one until it's just me holding my bag with Boots. There's nothing else to do but go after them. I find everyone huddled in the back of a wood shed. Now I think this is a very bad idea because it's even darker over here and someone could be lurking around for all we know.

CHAPTER 26

We're fortunate the wood isn't' fully stocked and there's room to hide behind it. We're also fortunate that this shed isn't the kind that is enclosed but rather an open building with a roof and a back wall. If we need to get away quickly we can exit through either left or right.

"Why are we here?" I whisper to Mr. Bo.

"We needed another place to go to buy us some time. I believe the first place they will start to look for anyone is under and around the other trains," he says.

"Yes, good point," I say.

"We have to get out of the train yard," says Freckles.

"No, we need to get across it," whispers Julian.

"Say what?" asks Freckles.

"Julian, are you crazy?" whispers Tom.

"Nope, across there in the middle is the depot where the passenger train going north stops," he says.

"Yeah but there's a lot of trains and cows if you haven't noticed," whispers Tom.

"I did, you can smell them," says Charlotte.

"Well then I guess we just walk on over there as dignified as we can and if anyone asks us why we are here, we will just tell them we're lost," says Mr. Bo.

"Good idea except where are you gonna tell them we came from?" asks Lyza whispering.

"Ahh, you kids think too much. Listen I must go into the town and find Summer. You go on with what you're doing and get out of here," says Mr. Bo.

"No, Tom and I are coming with you to help you," says Julian.

"I guess that means I am too," says Kent.

"You girls get to the train; it's just on the other side across the tracks. We'll meet you back here if we can," says Julian.

"What if you can't?" asks Lyza.

"Then we'll meet up with you later," he says.

"Where? When?" asks Freckles.

I can hear the panic in her voice. Lyza is better at hiding it than Freckles but I know they don't want to be separated from the guys. I admit it's handy to have them around; I do feel safer. Though I think I have proven I can take care of myself on many occasions, so I'm okay with them going. I just hope they don't get caught or anything.

I turn around and Freckles and Tom are kissing right in front of us all. It's kinda cute but then it kinda makes me want to barf. I guess because they are being so cute and lovey dovey it's sickening. Just as I'm getting used to that I turn the other way and there's Lyza and Julian kissing too. Ah, really?

I look over at Kent and he's kinda smiling at me. Oh no. He is out of his mind if he thinks I'm kissing him goodbye. I walk way over to the opposite side of the wood pile and lean down to make sure my shoe is laced. Then I realize I'm not wearing girl's shoes right now I'm wearing the boy's boots. I decide to say goodbye to Mr. Bo then to avoid Kent's ogling me.

"Mr. Bo, I hope you find Summer," I say.

"Thank you my dear. I appreciate your kindness and the meal you offered me," he says bowing.

"Well, I'm sure it's the least after I ran out on you last time. I didn't mean to . . ." I say, trailing off, not knowing what to say or how to apologize for trying to save my own skin when I thought I was in danger.

"Do not worry, I understand your motives and I believe you were in complete right to be afraid at the time. Perhaps the future will find us both in better circumstance," he says.

"I hope so," I say.

"Goodbye Mr. Bo. It was nice meeting you. I wish you luck," says Charlotte.

"Thank you," says Mr. Bo, bowing to Charlotte.

Lyza and Freckles say goodbye and then we watch as they leave the opposite direction as we're going. They'll go into town or the outskirts I suppose, wherever the boarding school is. I never did ask Mr. Bo if he knew where it is. I think about maybe going with them too but I need to get to Papa.

"Come on," I say.

Single file, we weave our way through the train yard. We hide behind train cars, buildings and wagons until we find ourselves out on a dirt path. We walk past stockades full of cows, steers and horses; the smell is overwhelming and endless. We keep walking at normal pace as if we are just on a stroll to the depot, hoping no one will notice what a strange and ragged group we are.

We're all dressed as boys right now, me in my brown breeches and oversized coat. I have a cotton shirt and vest on underneath. I have my satchel thrown over my shoulder so with my hat on I could pass for a messenger boy.

Charlotte's wearing dark brown baggy breeches with a dark turtleneck and a brown wool overcoat. Freckles and Lyza have on similar black breeches with light brown button down shirts. Over the shirts are dark vests, Lyza's is black and Freckles is dark blue. Then both have black wool over coats. We all wear the black leather boots and flat caps with our hair tucked up.

From a distance we look like messenger boys, but I guess if you were up close you could see we're girls. Well, maybe with our coats off and if you got a good look at our faces. We try and keep a little dirt rubbed on our faces so we don't look so much like girls. It's hard to disguise ourselves, but we do our best. It's much safer traveling as a boy than as a girl, that's for sure. Our dark clothes also help us blend into the night more easily.

At last we make it to the station. It's a large building with several trains pulled up and passengers getting on and off. There are gas lamps everywhere to light the way along the roofed walkway. We bypass the walkway and run along the back of the building.

"Which train is it?" I ask.

"I don't know," whispers Freckles.

"I don't know either," says Charlotte.

"Julian said we were going north, which way is that?" asks Lyza.

"Wait! I got an idea," I say. I start rummaging through my satchel because I remember I have a compass. An old lady with a funny accent at the first hobo jungle we went to, gave it to me. I feel my fingers touch it in the bag and wrap my hand around it. I take it out and look at it.

"I need some light. It's too dark," I whisper.

We all move back around the building toward the gas lamps until I have enough light to read the compass. The girls keep a lookout while I try and read it. I can't seem to hold my hand steady because it seems to be jiggling the little needle all over the place. Once I get it steady I watch as the needle swings around north to the direction we are facing.

"We have to take the train going that way," I say, pointing.

"Right then, these all look like passenger cars," says Lyza.

"I know. We can't ride in them, we don't have enough money," says Charlotte.

"Don't worry, there's other cars at the end. Come on," I say.

We walk down the train on the back side of where the passengers are getting on board and the trainmen are busy loading their luggage. I motion the girls to follow me underneath the train. We hug the ground as we go the length to the baggage cars.

We can see the feet of the men loading the people's trunks into the car which is pretty much the same as a boxcar, but probably cleaner. We have to sit and wait now until they're done loading. I had no idea this is such a busy place, so many people getting on board.

As we're waiting, I notice that the air seems warmer than before. In fact it seems a lot warmer. I thought it had been kinda cold when we first got here. I look up at the sky and all I can see is dark, I can't tell if it's all clouds or what, but I do know I can't see any stars.

We have to wait at least twenty minutes or so until they stop coming to the car to load it. I don't see anyone walking around near us so I take a chance and crawl under the mechanics of the car and to the other side to take a peek out. I look both ways and don't see anyone. I look up and see that the car is still open.

I wave to the girls to follow me and I crawl out from under the train. I keep looking around, making sure no one can see me. The people in the passenger cars can't see down this way unless they are sticking their heads out, and no one seems to be doing that right now. I climb up into the baggage car and see that there is a lot of luggage but plenty of room for us to hide. I make a check and don't see anyone so I whisper, "Come one now."

Lyza, Charlotte and Freckles come out from under the train. Charlotte has the bag with Boots in it and hands him up to me. I set him inside and then reach down and grab Charlotte's hand and help her up while Freckles and Lyza climb up themselves. One more quick look to assure we're alone and then we duck down behind the trunks to hide.

"How will the boys know where we are?" asks Freckles.

"Just keep a watch out for them. They're sure to check the cars, and we'll see them," I say.

We sit and watch in silence, but no one comes to the doors. A strong wind blows across the door and the scent of rain drifts in. In the distance there is a loud crack and then a rumble. A storm is coming; I hope the boys will be alright. I hear men's voices approaching but I know they don't belong to anyone we know.

"She's brew`n out yonder, mayheps we geter bad," says a man.

"Yep," says another.

"Y'all close em up, they're aleavn'," says a third man.

Suddenly the doors slams shut and that's it. No boys, they didn't make it. I look over at Freckles but it's dark and I can't see her face. I know she's probably crying though. I'm sure Lyza wants to cry but she'll wait for a time when no one is looking.

"They didn't make it," whispers Charlotte, stating the obvious.

"It's okay, they'll catch up. They know where we're going. We'll be fine," I say. "They'll be fine," I add.

The words sound empty here in the dark as the train starts to roll away from the station. The horn lets out a whoop, whoop, and we're moving. I feel the train motion slowly pick up speed as it leaves the town. I think it's safe to get up now so I get up and walk over to the doorway.

I pull hard on it trying to get it open. Charlotte comes over by me and tries to help me but it's not enough. Then Lyza comes over and joins in and I feel Freckles behind. We all pull and pull until at last the door gives way opening a crack. Enough for me to get a better hand hold and pull it open a little more, just enough for us to look out at the landscape.

In the distance we can see the storm as it's rolling to us. It looks like it's a big long line of thunder and lightning and we are inevitably going to be going through it. I'm glad we're not riding outside; that would be miserable in that sort of weather. We all sit down, and without speaking we watch the storm for a while as the train picks up speed and the landscape zooms by us.

CHAPTER 27

$\mathcal{I}$t's almost as if the trainman is trying to outrun the storm. But you can't beat a storm; it's coming and there is nothing we can do about it. I take a deep breath and reach over and unlatch my bag so Boots can get out and stretch his legs. He won't come too close to me when I'm near the door but he watches from a safe distance. He soon becomes bored though and goes off exploring the luggage.

"Do we have any food left?" I ask.

"Yeah, we have some. Oh my goodness, I didn't give them any food," says Freckles.

"It's okay, those boys will find food. They're resourceful," I say.

"Yeah, Julian and Kent know what they're doing. It'll be alright," says Lyza. I wonder, is she reassuring us or herself.

We close the door after a while but not all the way. We leave it open a crack so we can peer outside from time to time to keep an eye on the storm. I light a candle while Freckles gets the food out and we solemnly eat the last of the bread and cheese. Since Tom still has the water skin none of us have anything to drink. We open a can of peaches and share that, drinking the juice to quench our thirst.

After we eat, we divide what's left of the food among our bags so no one has to carry a heavier load. There's not much left anyway, only a couple of cans of preserves, some dried meat and a few apples. I give Boots a bit of the dried meat, which he eats, but when I offer him some peach juice to wash it down he snubs his nose at it. Too sweet for him, I guess.

"You think there's any food in any of the luggage?" asks Lyza.

"Lyza, that's stealing," says Charlotte.

"You didn't have a problem with it when we got the clothes," says Lyza, her tone defensive.

"Oh Lyza, that was different, those clothes belonged to the System not people," says Freckles.

"I bet there's probably a trunk or two with System markings. Let's look around," I say.

We get up and light a few more candles, one for each of us and go in search of anything marked by the System. There are a lot of steam trunks, but so far the ones I've seen have name tags on them.

"Hey, I think I found one," says Charlotte. We all meet her over in the corner of the luggage compartment and there is a crate marked 'System R U.'

"Here's another one," says Freckles, pointing to the crate next to it. I hold my candle up so we can see that there is a whole stack of System crates here in the back.

"What does R U stand for?" I ask.

"Regulatory Unit," says Lyza.

"Well, should we pop one open and see what the System has for us?" I ask.

"Indeed," says Lyza. She smiles and pulls a small hatchet out of her bag.

"What are you going to do, hack it open?" asks Charlotte.

"No, just to pry it open with this, silly," says Lyza.

After a bit of work prying all along the edges of the box, the lid finally pops open. Inside there's lots of packing material that looks like straw. After digging around we pull out some long metal pipes. They actually look like gun barrels to me but they're not attached to anything.

A sudden wind blows the train car and it almost feels like it will blow us right off the tracks it's so strong. We all look at each other in shock for a moment. I wonder if maybe we should look outside but I'm kind of afraid to. Then there is the sound of rain hitting the roof. The rain starts out soft at first but then it starts to get harder and harder until it sounds like someone is dropping rocks on the rooftop.

"What is that?" asks Charlotte.

"I'm afraid to tell you what I think it is," I say.

"It sounds like hail," says Lyza.

"Hail! Are you serious?" asks Freckles.

"Why, what does that mean?" asks Charlotte.

"It could mean nothing," I say.

I go over to the door and peek out, and my heart nearly stops in mid-beat. The sky is dark but it has a green tint to it. Everyone in Missouri knows that a green sky means tornadoes. The train feels like it's going faster now which is not good when a strong wind hits it making it rock all the more.

"I think the engineer is trying to outrun the storm," I say.

"That's crazy," says Lyza.

"I got a bad feeling about this," I say. I grab Boots and put him back in the bag. "Sorry buddy, but things are about to get bumpy

195

around here."

"What do you mean Abby, what's going on?" asks Charlotte.

"Abby thinks there's a tornado coming," says Freckles.

"Oh my gosh!" says Charlotte.

Everyone grabs their things together in a panic and we get ourselves ready as if we're getting off the train. It just seems like the smart thing to do in this case. Back home we had a root cellar where Granny, Papa, and I would have to go when a bad storm came up. We never had a tornado hit our house, but one time we saw one from afar. Papa said it wasn't on a path to our house, but it would be safer in the root cellar anyways because of the flying debris. There's always the chance that another tornado could pop up too on account of how the one tornado blew the air around.

I didn't understand how it all works, though Papa tried to explain it to me. I remember him saying it had something to do with cold air meeting hot air and mixing up. All I know is that these storms are powerful scary when the wind blows. Sometimes the trees will bend so far down it looks as if they might snap in two. I'm looking outside now and I see that same kinda wind and the eerie sky, and I just feel something is wrong.

"Do you think we're safe on the train?" asks Charlotte.

"I don't know," I say.

"I doubt it," says Lyza.

"Why would you say that?" asks Charlotte.

"Yeah Lyza, why would you say that? Can't you see she scared?" says Freckles.

"Yeah! Well we all are and we should be. I've seen those thing take brick building and break them apart like sandcastles, so a train is nothing to that," she says.

"Okay, let's all stay calm about this, the train is going too fast for us to jump off anyway so we just have to wait to see what the engineer is going to do," I say.

We peek out the door and the wind is just blowing like crazy, lightning cracks and the sky lights up. Ahead of the train I see a dark ominous cloud and my stomach feels sick. Another crack of lightning and I can see the cloud is funnel shaped and we are going right into it.

"Oh my gosh, Abby do you see that?" asks Freckles.

"Yes, I see it," I say.

"Doesn't the engineer see it?" asks Freckles

"Well, he must," I say.

"See what?" asks Lyza

"It's a tornado just like we thought," I say.

"What do we do?" asks Charlotte.

I can see the look of fear in my friends' eyes as they all look to me for the answer. I don't have an answer. I have no idea what to do. There is no root cellar on a train. Suddenly the train screeches to a halt.

The luggage and crates slide forward with the momentum as do we, falling against each other. There's a violent jolt as our car slams into the front passenger cars while the freight and boxcars behind us slam into the luggage car. I'm confused and feel lost for a moment, dizzy and sick to my stomach. I hear sounds but they seem so far away. Someone is talking to me but their voice is so distant I can hardly make out what they are saying.

Then it all comes rushing back to me along with the pain in my head. I feel like something hit me in my head and I'm lying on the floor of the luggage car. I hear frantic voices and it takes me a moment to realize it's Freckles.

"Abby get up!" she yells.

"We stopped, why have we stopped?" asks Charlotte.

"Maybe the engineer finally came to his senses," says Lyza.

"Abby are you alright? You have to get up," says Freckles.

"Something hit my head," I say.

"Yeah, I pushed a crate off you. How do you feel? Anything broken?" she asks.

"I don't think so," I say.

Slowly I get up with Freckles' help. My legs feel weak, but they're okay. Nothing feels broken but my head. I feel all over until I find the sore spot and wince at the pain.

"What?" asks Freckles.

"Sore spot," I say.

Lyza pulls the door open and a gush of air blows in. I suddenly remember Boots and frantically look around for his bag. I know I had it in my hand when I fell but I don't see it anywhere.

"Where's boots?" I ask. I try to keep the panic out of my voice.

"I have him. I checked him. He's fine. He's not very happy right now, but he's fine," says Charlotte.

I turn and see she's holding the bag he's in. I'm relieved. Boots is part of the family after all and I can't imagine being without him. I think it would break my heart if something happened to him.

"People are running off the train," yells Lyza.

Freckles, Charlotte and I go to the door and look out. The passengers are getting off the train and running away from the train. What I find to be strange is that there is no place to run to. Off in the distance, I can see a tree line but all the land that lies before it is flat and desert for the most part. There are a few rocks and shrubs here and there, but that's all I see.

I turn my head and look toward the front of the train and

see the monster in the distance: a huge black funnel cloud. The thing is so large, I reckon it has to be miles wide. I've never seen anything like it. It looks like a mountain growing up from the ground and touching the clouds. All around us it's dark, and dust and debris is flying through the air, but this thing is much darker in contrast.

"Look!" I say, pointing. I didn't have to even say that though because I see the girls are all looking at it as well.

"Jeepers!" says Charlotte.

"Oh, mama!" says Freckles

"Tarnation!" says Lyza

"Lyza!" says Charlotte and Freckles at the same time in surprise.

"What? It just came out," she says.

"I don't blame her. I feel the same," I say.

"Should we go with those other people?" asks Charlotte.

I have to figure out what to do. Running off into the open doesn't seem right to me. I scan the horizon, and there doesn't seem to be any kind of shelter close enough.

"There is no way anyone can outrun that thing," says Freckles.

"Papa," I say.

"What?" asks Charlotte.

"I remember something Papa once said about trains. He said the engine is the strongest and heaviest part of the train. He said it's well built and the sturdiest link in the train, but next to the engine is the caboose," I say.

"What is that supposed to mean?" asks Lyza.

"No time to explain, come on," I say, and jump down off the train running toward the back where the caboose is.

CHAPTER 28

$\mathcal{I}$ look behind me as I run and see the girls are following me. All around me the wind is whipping about. My hat is gone and the wind is blowing my hair around my face making it hard to see. I grab my hair and pull it around and hold it as I run. The train somehow seems longer than I remember it being, did they add some cars after we got on, I wonder?

There are six cars we have to pass before the caboose at the end. Then I hear a sound like the train engine and I think it's the tornado. Papa said a tornado sounds like a big train coming for you, getting louder and louder. I turn and see that funnel coming at us but at the same time I see the train is starting to move backwards.

I get to the caboose and grab the rail and jump on. I realize that the train is moving. The engineer is trying to back the train away from the tornado. I reach my hand down and grab Lyza, helping her up. Then we both help Freckles and then Charlotte up. I take the bag Boots is in and we all go inside the caboose.

"Okay, now what," says Lyza slamming the door behind her.

I look around the room to assess the situation. We're the only ones in the room, if anyone had been in here they must have ran out with the passengers. There are two doors on either side of the door here, from past experience I know one is a closet, and one is a washroom. Then there are two bunks, one on each side of the room. Then there is the wood stove set in the middle and above the cupola, and some chairs and a desk after that.

"Grab the mattress from that bunk and bring it over to the other one," I say, pointing to the bunk on the west side wall.

"Why?" asks Charlotte.

"Charlotte, we don't have time. Look, tornadoes travel west to east, which means debris is more likely to hit the west side of the train than the east. We will barricade ourselves in the bunk with mattresses and bedding on the east side of the train and hope for the best," I say.

"Got it," says Lyza, and she and Freckles start pulling the mattress and bedding off the other bunk.

"Charlotte, come help me," I say.

Charlotte and I pull the bedding off the mattress and lift it up against the wall. Then we tuck all the bedding from both beds around the ends. Freckles runs and grabs the cushions off the chairs and brings them back, then she and Charlotte climb inside. I hand Charlotte the bag with Boots inside.

Lyza and I position the mattress within the bunk. It takes a little work because the bunks are framed in. We have to get the mattress inside the frame, and then we have to crawl inside ourselves before pulling the other end of the mattress in with us.

Freckles and Charlotte have put down the cushions and taken their own bed rolls and wedged them in the top of the mattresses to cushion above us. We are now enclosed within all this and it's a little stuffy and hard to breathe, but by now I can hear the roar of the tornado. The motion of the train rolling backwards has halted, and we remain stationary for a moment. We can hear a loud screeching sound above the train. It's as if the tornado is pulling the train while the engine fights against it trying to move backwards. We are held within a tug of war battle.

We all hold hands and wait for whatever it is to happen because there is nothing else we can do. The train lurches back and forth and the sound is so loud I want to scream. I feel my ears pop, which makes my head hurt even worse and I think it might even explode from the pressure.

There is a moment when it feels like the train is free from the grip of the storm and the caboose is rolling. The loud thunderous train sound starts to move away and the screeching of the wheels on metal stops. I let out a breath I had been holding. Maybe we will be alright, and maybe it's over.

Then abruptly the screeching begins again and there is a hard bump as something large hits the caboose. I can hear the sound of cracking and wood breaking, metal sliding on metal mixes with the pounding of what sounds like rocks hitting the roof. The caboose shudders and then leans over and we feel ourselves falling over toward the east. I'm thankful that we have the mattress between us and the wall but the jolt is still a shock.

I lie still a long while; I don't feel anyone around me move at all. I'm scarred to know if anyone is dead, so I just lie still listening as the wind fades away. Eventually the sound of rocks hitting the side of the caboose stops and turns to light pelts of rain. I can hear breathing so I know I'm not the only one alive.

"Is everyone okay?" I ask.

"Are we alive?" asks Charlotte,

"Is it over?" asks Lyza.

"I can't tell if I'm okay or not, my heart is beating so hard," says Freckles.

"Well, at least you can all talk," I say, breathing a sigh of relief.

"Should we try and get out now? Do you think it's over?" asks Freckles.

"I think it's over," I say.

Together we push out on the mattress until it gives way. Carefully we stand up helping each other to our feet and looking around at what has happened. The caboose is lying on its side or at least the half we are in is. The other half the caboose is gone, smashed in by one of the boxcars which is lying on its side as well, stopped short by the wood stove. I can't tell if it's where it just stopped or if the wood stove stopped it. Whatever the case may be, it didn't reach us or it would have crushed us too.

"I have to go to the bathroom," says Freckles.

"I think I already did," says Charlotte.

I look over at Charlotte and see that she is about to cry. I feel like crying myself and I'm shaking all over. Of all the things I have ever experienced in my life, this is one of the scariest. I put my arm around Charlotte.

"It's okay Charlotte, we're alive," I say.

"Suck it up Charlotte, we're not out of this yet," says Lyza.

"Geez Lyza, grow a heart," says Freckles.

"No she's right, I'll be okay," says Charlotte wiping away her tears.

"What do we do now?" I ask looking around.

Freckles steps out of our little hiding place and walks to the washroom and lifts the door open. She looks down and makes a face and drops the door.

"That's not going to work," she says.

"Look there's a bucket over in the corner," says Lyza.

We all busy ourselves getting out of the bunk while Freckles makes use of the bucket. Then in turn we all use it as well. I realize I hadn't checked on Boots. I open the bag and gently take Boots out. He's shaking a little and I cuddle him and pet him, talking to him in a soothing tone telling him it will be alright.

"Ah, poor Boots. Is he okay?" asks Charlotte.

"I think so. There doesn't seem to be anything hurting him, he is just shaking," I say.

"Can I hold him?" asks Charlotte.

"Yes of course, in fact, can you see if he'll drink any water and try and calm him down a bit?" I ask.

"Sure," she says, taking him from me and sitting back down in the bunk.

This will keep her calm as well as Boots I figure. Charlotte's a strong girl but there are some things I have learned that are just too much for her to deal with. Charlotte grew up in a completely different environment and isn't used to having to deal with so much strife and stress. Sometimes I think this annoys me and maybe even Lyza and Freckles, but it also makes us more protective of Charlotte too. After all, she is part of the family. She is, in essence, our sister and we have to look out for her.

I turn my thoughts to what we should do next. It's dark outside still and raining. I'm sure the passengers will be coming back to the train now that the tornado is gone. Maybe another train will come or some wagons after a while. Of course, how would anyone know what had happened.

"We should to get out of here before the authorities come," I say.

"It's dark outside and it's still raining," says Freckles.

"There might be more tornadoes too," says Charlotte.

"She's right, those things can pop up anywhere," says Lyza.

"I know, I'm just afraid that someone will find us and we'll get caught, that's all," I say.

"I see your point," says Freckles.

"You know, because it is dark, it will be easier for us to leave without anyone seeing us. I mean, considering we seem to be out in the open here," says Lyza.

"Where are we gonna go?" asks Freckles.

"I guess we could follow the tracks," I say.

"How is anyone gonna know what happened here?" asks Charlotte.

"I'm sure they'll send someone back along the tracks the way we came to fetch help, if they haven't already.

"How do we know anyone is still alive?" I ask.

"Good question, I suppose we should find out," says Lyza.

Lyza slips out the door to see if she can find out what is going on outside with the crew and passengers. Freckles and I scavenge around the caboose for anything useful. We find some food and medical supplies which we distribute between our bags. We don't take all the food though, just a few cans of preserves and pickles, a loaf of bread and some cheese we cut out of a wheel.

There is still a box of canned goods and three other loaves of bread and the rest of the wheel of cheese. We decide to leave this in case it's a while before the passengers are rescued. We find a wine skin which is half full and decide to take that as well.

"We can use the skin for water," says Freckles.

"Yeah, it's just like Tom's isn't it?" says Charlotte.

"What should we do with the wine that's in it?" I ask.

"We could dump it out," says Freckles.

"What if someone out there needs it like for medicine if their injured?" I ask.

"I'll find something to put it in," she says.

We gather up the blankets that are not ours and the medical supplies we don't need and put those in a box as well. We haven't decided if we will just leave all this stuff here or take it out to anyone who needs it. I guess that will depend on what Lyza finds out. We just finish when we hear a sound at the door and instinctively, Freckles and I jump into the bunk with Charlotte to hide.

"It's me," says Lyza.

"Oh thank goodness," says Charlotte.

"What took so long?" asks Freckles.

"Sorry, it's just crazy out there. The train is all over the place, and there are dead bodies too," she says.

"Oh geeze," says Charlotte.

"Is there anyone alive?" I ask.

"Yeah, I saw some people huddled in and around one of the boxcars, they were trying to start a fire. I had to sneak up and behind the car so they wouldn't see me and listen to what they were saying," she says.

"And?" I ask.

"They talked about the engineer being dead and the engine on fire. Someone said they needed to send someone down the tracks to get help. It seemed like only one guy is telling everyone what to do. He also sent out two or three other people to scout out for passengers and bring them back," says Lyza.

"It won't be long before they decide to come over here then, we need to get out," I say.

Charlotte puts Boots backs in his bag and I put the bag up on my shoulder and then strap it around me so it's close to my body. Partly so I know it's sturdy, and partly so he can feel me through the bag and know he is okay, at least this is my logic.

"Your hair," says Charlotte

"What about my hair?" I ask, pushing back some of the wet strand from my face.

"You lost your hat, someone will see your red hair," says Charlotte.

"Here take mine, I'll just pull mine back and tuck it under my collar. I don't mine is as noticeable as yours," says Charlotte, handing me her hat.

"Thanks," I say. I take the hat and tuck my hair up inside the hat.

"That's better," says Charlotte.

"If we take the supplies we gathered with us, we can say we were gathering supplies if anyone questions us," I say.

"Good idea, and even if no one sees us we can leave the stuff near the boxcar where they are all at," says Freckles.

"Y'all are just too nice, you know that don't you?" asks Lyza.

We ignore that statement as we leave the caboose. Lyza's telling of the train being everywhere falls short of what my eyes behold. It's dark out and there's a light rain. The fire from the engine gives off enough light to see a good bit of the wreck and I am astonished that we are alive.

It looks like the tornado threw the engine, the tender, and the first two passenger cars off the tracks about five hundred feet away.

The other train cars are lying on their side and with the momentum of the train in reverse, slid back and slammed in to the caboose where we are. There is wreckage of wood, metal, luggage, and cargo all over the area as far as I can see. A couple

208

of people are dragging what looks like dead bodies to one of the passenger cars lying on its side.

Groups of people are walking around in the rain picking up items from the ground. Some people are pulling on trunks or boxes and dragging them to another car lying on its side. I can't even imagine where those crates might have gone that contained those gun barrels. I can guess they are out there with the rest of the stuff lying about the wreckage.

My knees feel weak and I can hardly make myself walk as I see the carnage before me. We could have died in this. We could all be dead lying on the ground in the rain and there would be no one to save Papa. I feel the tears threaten to fall and I will them away. I'm not dead. We didn't die. We are alive and we are walking away from this, there is no reason for me to cry about this.

"What have you boys got there?" says a voice suddenly out of nowhere.

"We found supplies, we're taking them over to the main area," says Lyza, using a deep voice.

"What supplies? Where did you get them?" asks the man. He comes up to us from the left; I hadn't seen him in the shadows.

"We found them in the caboose; it's food and blankets," says Freckles. She too tries to deepen her voice to sound more boyish.

"And medical supplies," adds Charlotte. She tries to talk deeper too but she still sounds like a girl.

The man looks through the boxes and looks at Lyza. I can tell he's suspicious. I can't think of what to do or say. We have to do something quick I think because I notice that the man is wearing a gun belt.

"Where did you come from? I don't recall seeing any of you before," he says.

CHAPTER 29

"Well we ran outta the passenger car, the last one before that tornado come, Oh my, you shoulda seen it. Oh, but I think you did, didn't you?" asks Lyza.

"Oh my goodness it was so scary. We didn't know what to do and we couldn't find my sister we just ran looking for her," I say.

I shove the box I'm holding into the man's hands, and throw my arms around Charlotte.

"We thought the conductor said to go into the caboose when the train stopped so I did, thinking my sisters were right behind me," says Charlotte. She sets her box right on top of mine and the man struggles a bit with the weight for a moment but recovers.

"Well, you're alright then, all of you?" he asks. His tone too has changed from suspicion to concern.

"Oh, yes we're all just fine now, and we thought we'd help out," says Freckles.

"What's goin' on here Nevil?" asks another man coming up alongside the man holding the two boxes.

"Oh, thank goodness," says Freckles. She hands her box to the other man who takes it looking bewildered.

"These kids were just tellin' me of their horrific experience," says the man called Nevil.

"And how since we survived thought we ought to do our part and help out," says Lyza, piling her box on top of the other man's box.

"Now let's see that's some food and blankets and medicine, and did anyone get the jug of whiskey we found?" asks Lyza.

"No, I couldn't carry it, my arms were full," says Charlotte.

"I think it got left by the wood stove in the caboose. Do you want us to go get it," I ask, looking at the men.

"Oh no, you just go on back to the fire and we'll take care of all this," says the other man.

"Okay," says Freckles.

"That's just where we were headin'," says Lyza.

We walk with a quick pace toward the fire. After several paces and we are almost within the vision of the other people at the fire pit, Lyza casually looks over her shoulder.

"They're gone, well, I mean they are walking to the caboose," she says.

"There is nowhere to hide out here," whispers Charlotte.

"There, behind that other boxcar to the left," says Freckles.

Quick as we can, we dodge behind the boxcar and wait a moment. Lyza peers out from behind and watches the men and their progress to the caboose. I peer out the other side to see if anyone is looking our way but it appears that no one has noticed us.

"Okay, they've gone in, now what?" asks Lyza.

"The tracks are right behind us. We can just run up the tracks until they can't see us anymore," I say.

"Everybody up for a run?" asks Lyza.

"I'm good," says Charlotte.

"Me too," says Freckles.

"Let's go," I say.

We run to the tracks and then along them, keeping low at first so no one will notice us. Then when we think we are far enough away, we put some speed into our run. I watch where I'm going, but I keep glancing to my right to make sure no one sees us either. After a while my side aches and I can't run anymore so I slow down. The others follow suit, but I keep watching the encampment for any signs that we've been spotted.

"Do you think anyone has seen us?" asks Charlotte.

"No, but we have to keep going because eventually they're going to realize we're not there and start looking for us," says Lyza.

"Do you honestly think they will, though? Do you think they actually care after what has happened?" asks Freckles.

"You know, I have no idea," I say.

We keep walking into the dark with the steel rails as our path. The rain gradually stops and the wind slows down. I'm hoping that means the storm is dissipating. However, this could also mean we are in the mix of another tornado getting ready to hit. Gosh I hope not.

"How long do you think we have to walk before we are far enough away?" asks Charlotte.

I think we've been walking for near an hour now in silence and we can still see the camp but it looks very far way. Ahead of us is a shadowy area that could be line of trees or a building or rocks but it's so dark there is no telling what it is until we get there.

"Whatever that is up there, I think we should at least try and make it to that," I say.

"What do you think it is?" asks Charlotte.

"Hard to tell," says Freckles.

"I hope it's some kind of shelter," says Lyza.

We come up on the dark mass and find that it's a clump of trees and rocks. I'm relieved because now we can find some shelter from being in the open. Also because I'm so tired and I know everybody is tired.

"Let's make camp inside these trees," I suggest.

"Good idea, I'm spent," says Lyza.

"Oh, thank goodness. I'm so tired," says Charlotte.

"Yeah, I'm ready to stop," says Freckles.

We walk into the trees where it's even darker, but the rain has started up again so I think it will be better up under the trees. We won't get as wet anyway. As my eyes adjust, I think I see a sort of overhang of rocks but we are going to have to climb up to the rock to get to the area.

"That looks like it might be a dry shelter if we can get up there," I say pointing to the overhang.

"Let's try. I'm so tired of being wet," says Charlotte.

We walk through the trees and up a hill until we get to the rocks and I start to climb. The rocks are slippery from the rain and muddy so I go slow and careful until I get to a cliff. I can't see any way to get up the cliff to the overhang. The cliff comes to the top of my shoulders but it's sheer with no foot holds.

"I can't see any way up," I say.

"I'll boost you up, and then Freckles can boost me up, and then we can help her and Charlotte up," says Lyza.

I undo the bag with Boots and hand it off to Charlotte to hold. Then Lyza braces herself and locks her hands together. I step into her hand and she pushes me up while I jump. This gets me up to my belly where I squirm and wiggle until I'm over the ledge and can stand up. I turn and help Lyza as Freckles boosts her up. Then Freckles hands up all the bags and packs and then we pull her up and then Charlotte.

It is a nice overhang; it's almost a cave but does not go back in too far. It's wide enough for us to lay our bed rolls down and the overhang covers us enough to where we don't get wet. I think about maybe making a fire but then we are all just too tired and besides it's not cold. In fact it's quite warm and muggy. I think a fire might attract attention to us anyway so I don't suggest it.

"Do you think it's safe here?" asks Charlotte.

"I think so, not much can get up here to us," says Lyza.

"Do you think we should take turns keeping watch?" asks Freckles.

"Maybe we should, just to be safe. I'll go first and when I get too tired I'll wake one of you," says Lyza.

"You can wake me next," I say.

Before I lay my head down I open the bag to let Boots out and give him a little food and water. He doesn't seem to be hungry, but he drinks a little rain water out of my hand. I think he is still pretty shook up as we all are. I don't want to think about it though. I don't want to think about all the people that died. With my luck the System will more than likely blame that on me too, though I'm not sure how they are going to pin a tornado on me.

Someone is shaking me and calling my name but the sound is so far away, it's like a dream. I'm in the train and the train is flying through the air, we're inside the tornado and the train just keeps going around and around in circles. I hear my name again but louder this time. I can't see who it is but it sounds like Lyza. Then I hear the sound of wolves howling and I'm awake.

"Abby, I've been trying wake you up," whispers Lyza.

"I heard wolves," I say. I sit up looking around wide awake.

"You're not far off, coyotes actually. They are a ways off but I'm worried they might come closer," says Lyza.

I look over and Charlotte and Freckles are still asleep. Boots is awake and sniffing the air and pacing. This worries me because I've never seen him do that before. Of course we have never heard coyotes before, and we have never been in a tornado before. A whole bunch of new experiences for us that's for sure.

"Do you think it's almost morning?" I ask.

"Maybe, but it seems like it's only been a couple of hours. I'm real tired I need to sleep," says Lyza.

"That's fine, Lyza, you lay down, I'll keep watch," I say.

"I found some dry wood and weeds in the rocks here and put it all together there," she says.

"Okay," I say not sure what she wants me to do.

"In case the coyotes come near us, then you need to light it to scare them away," she says.

"Oh, right, got it," I say.

I go to my pack and get my matches out and put them near the fire ring she built to have them ready. Lyza must have been bored or sleepy trying to stay awake because she built this fire ring three rocks high. She built it all the way around under the eave near us and has it filled with wood and kindling set to light. She has another pile of sticks close by for fuel. I hope I don't have to light it.

No sooner do I think this than I hear the coyotes howl again. I watch as Boots goes over to Lyza's bedroll and crawls under the covers with her. I don't blame him. I'm sure he'd make a nice meal for a coyote.

I choose a big stick as a weapon and then I remember the derringer in my bag and the snake venom gun. I dig those out of my bag and put the derringer in one side of my pants waist, and the other gun I set on the rock nearby. I don't want to risk getting snake venom on me. Then I have the stick in my hand and I patrol the area on the ledge.

CHAPTER 30

$\mathcal{I}$ stand watch for a long while it seems. I have no way of keeping track of time, but when I start feeling sleepy or nodding off, I hear the coyotes and I wake right up. They never seem to come near though, thank goodness. After a while I notice the sky turning gray and getting lighter. Soon enough I stop hearing the coyotes anymore, I guess they must have gone to sleep. I think maybe it's time I wake someone else up for a while. It's too hard to wake Charlotte up so I decide to wake up Freckles for the next watch.

"Hey Freckles, wake up," I say, gently shaking her.

"What's wrong?" she asks.

"I'm tired, I need some sleep," I say.

"Okay," she says. She sits up, stretching and looking around. "It's almost morning," she says.

"I know, just let me sleep for at least an hour okay?" I ask.

"No problem," she says.

I lie down on my blanket, feeling the drowsiness setting in along with the relief that my watch is over. I'm trying not to think about anything because if I start to think about anything then my mind will just start working and I won't be able to sleep. I try to imagine myself back home lying under the tree by the pond and it's a warm summer day.

Did I sleep? I hear soft voices talking and I think I smell coffee. I must be asleep if I smell coffee, we don't have coffee and I'm pretty sure of that. I roll over and open my eyes. The day is still gray but it's much brighter now. I swear I smell coffee. I sit up and see Charlotte, Freckles and Lyza sitting on the edge of the ledge with feet their dangling down.

"Hey, how come I smell coffee?" I ask.

"Oh you're awake," says Freckles getting up from her seat.

"You smell coffee because of Freckles," says Lyza.

"When we were rummaging through the caboose I grabbed the coffee pot and found a bag of coffee and put it in my bag," says Freckles smiling.

"We didn't have a grinder so we ground it up like the natives do with the corn," says Charlotte.

"What do you mean?" I ask

Freckles pours some coffee into a cup and brings it to me.

"She means with rocks, we ground it up on the rocks. You know we need to get you your own cup next time we go into a town," says Freckles.

I take a sip of the coffee; it's hot and bitter but it's the best thing I have tasted in such a long time because it tastes like home. The smell is calming and after a few drinks I don't mind the taste so much. I know it's going give me a little energy too, something we are all going to need for the long walk ahead of us.

"Here's breakfast," says Charlotte. She hands me some warm bread with melted cheese in the middle.

I take the bread and nibble on it while I drink the coffee and enjoy the morning. Even though it's a gray sky the birds are singing in the trees and bugs are humming in the grasses. The wind blows across my face, smelling fresh and clean, though there is the threat of more rain hanging in the air.

"It's pretty out here. I wish we could just build a house right here and live in it," says Charlotte.

"If you had heard those coyotes last night you wouldn't be thinking that," says Lyza.

"Coyotes! Really?" asks Charlotte.

"Really," I say.

"Yeah, looks like you were loaded for bear," says Freckles, holding up the snake venom gun.

"Hey be careful with that. It's a deadly weapon," I say.

"I'm sure it is. How come you didn't tell us you had weapons?" asks Lyza.

"I dunno, I just didn't think of it I guess," I say.

"What else you got?" asks Freckles.

"This," I say, pulling the derringer out of my belt. I can't believe I forgot I had it on me and slept with it like this.

"Geeze," says Charlotte.

"Give me the snake venom gun back; I'm the only one who knows how to use it. Besides, I borrowed it and I don't want anything happening to it before I have time to give it back. Someone else can take the derringer if they want," I say.

"I've never shot a gun," says Charlotte.

"Me neither," says Freckles. She hands me the snake venom gun.

"I have. I'll take the derringer," says Lyza.

"Figures you would know how to use one," says Freckles.

"Julian taught me," she says.

I hand her the derringer. It's better that there are at least two of us armed in case something happens along the way. There may be outlaws or more coyotes out here in the wild.

"Why do any of us need to be armed?" asks Charlotte.

"Really Charlotte, don't be so naive, we're heading into the west. haven't you ever heard of the Wild West and its dangers?" asks Lyza.

"I've read stories, but I didn't think they were real," she says.

"Oh they're real all right, those coyotes prove the wild animal theory anyway," says Lyza.

"I wish the boys were with us," says Freckles.

"Yeah, I know. In a way, I'm kinda miffed at them for leaving us on our own. On the other hand, they are doing a good thing," I say.

"What else is out here?" asks Charlotte.

"Charlotte dear, there are dangers everywhere. We just need to be careful," says Freckles.

"Hey that's some pretty quick thinking last night by the way, Lyza. I meant to tell you good job," I say.

"Oh you mean with those men? I am just glad y'all caught on," says Lyza laughing.

"When you start acting all helpless and scared I know something is up," says Charlotte.

"Why thank you, Charlotte. I'll take that as a compliment," says Lyza.

"I think we should get moving. I'm betting there won't be a train coming along for a while until they get all that mess cleaned up," I say.

"Which means we can follow the tracks for a while so we won't get lost, right?" asks Freckles.

"My thoughts exactly," says Lyza.

"Where's Boots?" I ask. looking around.

"Oh, he's around somewhere. He didn't leave the camp until daylight so I'm sure no coyotes got him. He's probably hunting," says Lyza.

We pack up our stuff and clean up the camp. Lyza puts out the little fire they made for the coffee and breakfast. I'm all packed up and looking around for Boots. I always worry that he won't come back. Maybe he will think it's my fault he got bumped around in the bag during the tornado.

"Boots! Here kitty," I call.

"There he is," says Charlotte. pointing at the bottom of our ledge.

I look down and see Boots sitting there looking up at me as if to say he is ready to go. We help each other down and hand down the bags. I'm the last down and I'm kinda afraid to jump which is what it looks like I'm going to have to do.

"Just get on your belly and slide down as far as you can go and then jump down. We'll catch you," says Freckles.

So I lie down on my belly and scoot down opposite of the way I came up and jump back. For a moment there is a funny feeling in my stomach, as there is nothing under my feet but air. It's a matter of trust, I think. To know that those girls are behind me to catch me and not let me fall backwards and break my neck. Of course they catch me and of course I knew they would.

We grab our packs and head down the way we came until we see the railroad tracks. We check both ways to make sure there is no one around. We far enough from the accident that we can't see it, but we can still see the smoke rising from the engine fire. I have an idea. I get Papa's spy glass and look through it toward the area where the train derailed.

"Can you see anything?" asks Freckles.

"Yeah, there are people sitting around the fire they made. Some people are walking around picking stuff up off the ground. I guess they are just waiting," I say.

"Well we're not. Come on, let's go while we can," says Lyza.

We head up, following the tracks to an unknown destination. Eventually I'm sure the tracks will lead us to a town. I hope there is another train that can take us up to Colorado. If not, we will have to figure out some other way to get there. For now we just walk along the steel rails.

We let our feet carry us along the rail. The land around us is a mixture of flat grass lands and tufts of trees and bushes. Every now and then I see some hills and rocks in the distance. But where we are now is flat for the most part. It's not hot, so that's good, and it hasn't rained on us yet, though the sky seems like it wants to. I just keep thinking that we are a long way from nowhere.

"What if I'm wrong about all this?" I ask out loud, breaking the silence.

"What do you mean?" asks Freckles.

"Well what if what I'm doing is wrong?" I ask.

"What do you mean, what if it's wrong? Abby, you've seen how it is out here; you've seen what the System does to people. They took everything from you, including your papa maybe," says Lyza.

"Well, what if my papa did something to deserve it? I mean what if he is actually doing something wrong?" I ask.

"Do you really believe that?" asks Freckles.

"I guess not," I say.

"Look at poor Charlotte; she had everything you ever dreamed of having. Did she deserve to have her family and everything she owned taken from her?" asks Lyza.

"No, of course not," I say.

"Well, then stop being so silly. You know what we're doing is right," says Lyza.

"But what exactly are we doing?" I ask.

"We're finding your papa," says Lyza.

"But what about all that other stuff Julian and Tom were talking about? You know the revolution stuff?" I ask.

"Well, we will just have to figure that out when we find your papa," says Lyza.

"Yes, that makes sense," I say.

"Stop worrying, geeze. We just survived a terrible ordeal, enjoy the day," says Freckles.

"I for one am glad to be alive, but tired of walking," says Charlotte.

"You want to take a break?" I ask.

"No, that won't help. we'll just have to walk again after that," says Charlotte.

We walk for a time in silence, I guess just each of us in our own thoughts. I'm wondering what Papa is doing and if he's okay. I hope he's in the same place at least. After we get to Colorado Springs I have no idea where else to go. Once I find him we'll still be on the run so I guess Lyza is right. We'll figure that out when we get there.

CHAPTER 31

$\mathcal{I}$ guess we've been walking for a couple of hours, or at least it seems like it, but I see something ahead that might be a town. It could be a mirage. I've read stories about people stranded in the desert and they thought they saw water. When they get to the spot there's nothing there, and it turns out to be their eyes and mind playing tricks on them. Of course it's just a story, who knows if that sort of thing is real unless you experience it? I stop and take out Papa's spy glass to look through it and see what's ahead of us.

"What, Abby, you see something?" asks Freckles.

"Maybe," I say. I adjust the scope and sure enough, I see buildings and people and horses.

"Oh please tell me there's a town or something," says Charlotte.

"There's a town, Charlotte," I say.

"Really? Truly? You're not making that up, are you?" asks Charlotte.

"Nope, see for yourself," I say, handing her the spyglass. She takes it from me and looks through it in the direction I point to.

"Oh my goodness, she's right," says Charlotte.

"But how far away is that?" asks Lyza.

"I dunno," I say.

"It's still pretty far, I wager," says Freckles.

"Yeah, but it's there," I say.

"Let's stop for a few and have some water," suggests Lyza.

"Good idea," says Freckles.

We sit down by the tracks and pass around the water skin that Freckles found in the caboose. The water has a hint of wine taste to it, making it bitter. It's not a horrible taste but it makes me wonder if she poured out the wine first.

"Freckles you did pour the wine out of this, didn't you?" I ask.

"Yeah, I wondered about that too," says Lyza.

"She did. I watched her," says Charlotte.

"Of course, sillies. I poured it in a jar and put it in one of those boxes we gave those men," says Freckles.

"How come it still tastes like wine?" I ask.

"Dunno, I guess cause I didn't rinse it out," she says.

"Why didn't you rinse it out?" asks Lyza.

"Because, Lyza, there is precious little water as it is, okay?" says Freckles.

"Alright, no need to get upset, just askin'," says Lyza.

"I think we're all just tired and hot and should get moving again and get to that town as soon as we can," I say.

"You're right, let's go," says Freckles.

"Okay, I'm ready," says Charlotte.

We all get up and start walking again. Just knowing the town is there puts a little pep in our step and I think it makes us all feel a little better. It would be great if we could make it to the town before it gets dark. I don't relish the idea of spending the night in the open with the coyotes again.

It is near dark by the time we get to the outskirts of town, and

I know the girls are just as beat as I am. I'm surprised that Boots kept up the walk with us, but as we get into town I think maybe I better put him back in the bag. I'm sure his little legs must be tired anyway.

"Stop for just a second I have to put Boots in the bag," I say.

"Oh poor Boots, he walked as far as we did," says Charlotte.

"Where are we gonna go? Do we have any money left?" asks Freckles.

"A couple of dollars I think, not much," I say.

"I say we just follow the tracks to the train station, maybe we'll get lucky and there'll be a train there," says Lyza.

"Maybe," says Freckles.

"Well if nothing else we can at least sit on the benches there like we're waiting for one and no one should bother us," I say.

"At least for a little while," says Charlotte.

"We better slip our skirts on over these breeches, don't you think?" asks Freckles.

"Why?" asks Lyza.

"I just think maybe it would look better if people see girls walking into town instead of boys. Four boys walking into town looks like trouble," says Freckles.

"She might be right," says Charlotte.

"I suppose we can always play off the lost passenger scenario," says Lyza.

"Oh, like we could pretend we were on a train that got hit by a tornado?" I ask.

"Ha ha, very funny, but something like that, yeah," says Lyza.

"The breeches are hot anyway," says Charlotte as she pulls on her skirt and drops the breeches underneath, tucking them back in her bag.

"Okay then, Charlotte has spoken," I say. We all do the same, donning our female attire and smoothing our hair down to try and look as proper as we can. Personally, I don't think we're fooling anyone but ourselves.

"Abby, take that scarf off your waist and put it on your hair," says Freckles.

"Oh, yeah, right I forgot," I say, and I put the scarf over my red hair.

It looks like the train tracks go behind the main part of town, which is good; we don't want to draw attention to ourselves. It must be supper time because I smell food in the air. We never even thought about eating while we walked here, we just wanted to get here. Now that we're here I'm feeling powerful hungry and thirsty. It occurs to me that it never did rain; it just stayed gray and muggy all day.

We pass by some houses, they look like nice little farm homes. Not as big as the one I lived in, but they look cozy. It makes me kind of homesick and makes me wonder if Granny is doing okay at the oldies home. As soon as I find Papa we can set out to get Granny.

"Oh my stars, my stars," says a woman running out of a house toward us.

The woman is tall and thin, about middle age, though her hair is already almost all gray. She has it pulled back in a bun but loose strands of hairs blow about her face as she runs toward us. She holds up her skirt as she runs, revealing her stockings and laced boots.

I hesitate, wondering if we should run or stand our ground. It's hard to tell if she's coming at us or if she's just upset in general and running. I look over at Lyza, and she looks as confused as

I do. Charlotte grabs my arm and Freckles stops walking and is staring at the woman.

"You girls look awful, what on earth has happened to you? Are you okay?" asks the woman.

"Yes ma'am," I say.

"We were traveling on a train when it got hit by a tornado," I say.

"We just started walking and got lost. We don't know what happened to the other passengers," says Lyza.

"Oh my poor, poor dears, you must be exhausted. Come inside and we'll fix you right up," says the woman. She ushers us to the house she ran out of.

When the woman goes up the steps in front of us to get the door I look over at Lyza. She just shrugs her shoulders and goes on up the steps. Well it's not as if we're telling a lie. We were on that train when it wrecked, and we did sort of get lost from the other passengers, and we did in fact just keep going.

"Oh, don't be shy girls, come on in, after what you have been through, my stars," says the woman.

"Thank you ma'am. We appreciate it," say Freckles.

"What town is this?" asks Charlotte.

"This is Wichita Falls. Oh my stars, let me get you some lemonade, I bet you're parched," says the woman.

She brings us into the kitchen and she sits us down while she goes and gets the lemonade. I'm a little concerned because my face is on posters now and some are placed in the train stations. I look over at Charlotte, who looks a little frightened over the situation, but Lyza and Freckles look at ease. I guess we will just play along for now and hope this doesn't lead to trouble.

"Now here you are girls, this is a start," says the woman. She brings over a pitcher of lemonade and some glasses with a plate of cookies and sets them down in front of us.

"Excuse me, but I don't suppose you might have a small saucer of milk do you?" I ask very timidly.

"A saucer of milk, why whatever . . ." the woman stops in mid-sentence and then smiles at me. "Do you have a kitten in your bag by chance?" she asks.

"Umm yes ma'am, only he's not a kitten. He's full grown, but he's pretty hungry if you don't mind. I'll be happy to pay for it," I say.

"Nonsense, of course he can have some milk, let the poor dear out," she says, and turns to get some milk.

I take Boots out of the bag and set him on the floor. It's obvious he has been asleep because he's groggy. I'm a bit worried about him because he hasn't eaten much in the past few days or, at least I haven't seen him eat. Last night really spooked him.

The lady puts the saucer of milk on the floor and Boots runs to it and starts lapping it up. The woman reaches down and pets Boots and he starts to purr. That satisfies me a bit because food or no food, Boots is a good judge of character. If she wasn't a good person he would instinctively know it, and he wouldn't be purring.

"Thank you ma'am," I say.

"You're certainly welcome, and so is your cat," she says.

"Did you say this is Wichita Falls, ma'am?" asks Freckles.

"Why, yes. Have you heard of it?" she asks.

"Oh yes ma'am, I heard about the falls and how beautiful they are," says Freckles.

"Were, dear. Alas, they are no more. A flood destroyed the falls several years ago. People keep coming to see the falls but they're not here anymore. It's sad, truly sad. But my stars, where are my manners? My name is Ms. Meredith," she says.

"A pleasure to meet you Ms. Meredith, my name's Elizabeth, this is Franny, Charmaine and Bonnie," says Lyza.

"My goodness. You're not all sisters are you?" asks Ms. Meredith.

"Oh no ma'am, we're cousins. We were visiting Charmaine's family and now we're off to visit another cousin in Denver," says Lyza.

"Oh my, but isn't school starting for you girls?" she asks.

"We go to Merriweather's School for girls in Boston, it's a year round school so the off times are different," says Charlotte.

"Our cousin in Denver doesn't go there, So we have to go see her," I say.

"Oh, I see," says Ms. Meredith.

"That is until last night and that terrible storm hit us. It was so awful," says Lyza.

"Oh, my stars you poor dears. Well you just sit tight and enjoy that lemonade and I'll be back in a jiffy," says Ms. Meredith.

"Yes, ma'am," we all say.

Ms. Meredith leaves the room and I give Lyza a glare. I don't dare say anything though in case that woman is listening in on us. What a mess this is. I remember Papa telling me it's always best to tell the truth because lies will only lead to more lies until a person gets caught in their own web of deceit. I admit I've told a little fib now and then just to survive, but this takes the cake by far. Boy we are in it for sure.

CHAPTER 32

$\mathcal{S}$uddenly I hear the screen door slam. I get up and look out the window and see Ms. Meredith walking swiftly over to the next house. Oh, this can't be good.

"She's going over to the other house," I say.

"Oh no," says Charlotte.

"Suppose she's going to tell them to get the Crushers," says Freckles.

"You gooses worry too much, she's going to tell her neighbor that she has survivors from the train wreck in her house. That's bragging rights," says Lyza.

"How do you know?" asks Charlotte.

"I've seen her type before," says Lyza.

"Yes but how does she know about the train wreck already other than what we told her?" asks Charlotte.

"She's coming back," I say, and sit back down. I take a long drink of the lemonade and grab a cookie. I might as well enjoy what I can while I can.

"You girls do look a fright, you'll want baths and some food and rest," says Ms. Meredith.

"Oh yes ma'am, but we just realized that we don't have much money on us," says Freckles.

"We managed to find some of our things but, well Papa told us not to carry all our money on us, so most of the money we had is in the trunk," says Lyza.

"I lost the rest with my purse," says Charlotte.

"Maybe in the morning we could send a messenger to our families to let them know were okay. They can send us some money," says Freckles.

"Oh, you poor dears, don't you fret about any of that. We'll take good care of you, don't you worry about a thing," says Ms. Meredith.

"Where are they, Meredith? I brought some lemon cake," says a woman from another room.

"In here, dear, but I hardly think lemon cake is appropriate, these girls need some real food," says Ms. Meredith.

A plump woman in a gingham dress with blonde hair pulled tight into a bun comes into the kitchen from the other room. She's holding a plate with half a yellow cake with white frosting on it. She swoops into the kitchen, plops the plate down on the table and instantly begins to assess each of us.

"Are any of you hurt?" she asks.

"No, ma'am, just shook up a bit and tired from walking," I say.

"Girls, I would like you to meet Mrs. Gubbels. She's the chairperson of our ladies auxiliary, and she runs the train station here in town," says Ms. Meredith.

"Oh, Meredith don't tell them that, you know Buber runs the train station. I just sort of help," says Mrs. Gubbels.

"It's nice to meet you ma'am," says Lyza.

"Yes it's nice to meet you," says Charlotte.

"Pleased to meet you," says Freckles.

"Nice to meet you," I say. I'm trying to keep my face down a bit because if she and her husband run the train station, then I know she's seen the poster with my papa and me for sure.

"Well I am just ecstatic to meet you. I know we had a bad storm last night but a tornado hitting the train! My word what a thing! I suppose there will be more survivors coming to town," says Mrs. Gubbels.

"Melanie, why did you bring half a cake may I ask?" asks Ms. Meredith.

"Well it's all I had at such short notice. When Stephanie arrived at my place, I hurried over as fast as I could. But not to worry, I sent Stephanie out to alert the rest of the Auxiliary and they will be right along," says Mrs. Gubbels.

"Oh good, Melanie then we'll want to get the girls freshened up before they meet the ladies," says Ms. Meredith.

"Oh yes, we would love to freshen up," says Charlotte.

"Well, I'm afraid I there's just one bathtub so you'll have to take turns. But I have a small water tank so there is enough hot water for everyone if you conserve it," says Ms. Meredith.

"Well Meredith dear, what are we waiting for let's get these girls cleaned up and comfortable," says Mrs. Gubbels.

"Yes of course, come with me," says Ms. Meredith.

We follow her out of the kitchen and through a parlor and then a hallway where there are three rooms; one room on the left, one on the right, and another room in the back. The one on the right turns out to be the bathroom where Ms. Meredith goes in and starts the water in the bathtub. She then leads us to the room in the back.

"This is my room; you can change your clothes in here and

wait for your turn to bathe or whatever. There are towels in a basket in the bathroom. We'll let you know when it's all clear to come out," she says, and leaves the room.

"What does she mean when it's clear to come out?" asks Charlotte in a whisper.

"I don't know but I'm not passing up a bath," says Lyza.

"I think we should all stick together," I say.

"Fine with me but I'm getting in the bath first," says Lyza.

"Oh, whatever just don't take up all the hot water," says Freckles.

"The bathroom is kinda small. Maybe we should go in pairs," says Charlotte.

"That's fine, I guess, just no one alone. These woman are being kinda weird," I say.

"I'll go with Lyza," says Charlotte.

Freckles and I wait in the bedroom as Charlotte and Lyza go into the bathroom. Freckles sits down on the bed, lets out a sigh and then lays back. I think if I lay down on that bed right now I'm sure to fall asleep so I sit in a chair that's situated under the window. There's a table next to it and a little oil lamp that I light with the matches next to it.

"Don't you think they are being a little too friendly?" I ask Freckles in a whisper.

"Yeah," she says, "a little over the top but then maybe they have nothing better to do around here."

"Maybe, but if that other woman Mrs. Gubbels runs the rail station she is sure to have seen a poster with my face on it. Don't you think she would have recognized me?" I ask.

"Good point. But I sure want a bath," says Freckles.

"I know, me too," I say.

It's been a while since I've had a chance to relax so I lie back on the bed and let myself doze a little. I'm not sure, but I think it's been only a few minutes, when I hear a soft knock on the door. I don't answer right away or fast enough because the person who knocked opens the door and comes in.

It's a little girl about ten or so with brown pigtails. She's dressed in a little pink dress with eyelet lace at the bottom. She just looks at me and smiles for a moment and then, as if she has forgotten that her hands are full, remembers the packages in her hands. "These are for you," she says in an adorable little voice. Then, without another word she puts the packages on the blanket trunk at the foot of the bed and goes back out the door. This place is getting odder by the moment.

I get up from the chair and see there are four wrapped packages. I unwrap one and find a pretty turquoise blue gingham dress with the same type of eyelet lace around the bottom, sleeves, and neckline. The dress is floor length and has a large ribbon that can tie in the back. There are also some undergarments including a petticoat and bloomers in the package as well.

I check each package and find that each package has the same clothes but with variations in color. There is a lavender one, a yellow one, and a dark maroon one. They are all a little different in style but for the most part the same pattern. They are pretty and feminine, but now I'm even more suspicious.

"What's that?" asks Freckles sitting up.

"Clothes, I am guessing for us," I say.

"They brought us clothes?" she asks. She gets off the bed and comes around to look at the clothes.

"Weird huh?" I ask.

"Well, maybe they are just being nice because we were in that train wreck," says Freckles.

"I guess," I say. Just then the door opens and Charlotte and Lyza come in wrapped in towels and nothing but.

"We left our bags in here with our clothes," Charlotte giggles.

"Well, how about some new ones?" I say.

"What?" asks Charlotte.

"They brought us clothes," says Freckles.

"Oh, my they are pretty," says Charlotte.

"That's a little over the top," says Lyza.

"You're telling me," I say.

"Oh can I have the purple one?" asks Charlotte.

"I want the yellow one," says Freckles.

"I don't care. I want to take my bath. Did you leave us any hot water?" I ask.

"Yes, and we even started the water for you so you better hurry up," says Lyza.

I start for the bathroom with Freckles behind me. I don't care which dress I get. What I'm concerned about is what they are going to want for those dresses. Are they going to turn us in to the Crushers? Do they need servants of their own? Do they think they are going to adopt us? I mean what could be going through these ladies' minds?

As I walk to the bathroom I stop to listen in the hallway. All I can hear are muffled voices. They are too far away to hear what they are talking about. Seems like there are more people than before but they're still in the kitchen. Freckles nearly runs into me while I'm standing there. She gives me a questioning look but I shake my head directing her into the bathroom and close the door.

"I'm trying to hear what they were talking about," I say.

"Oh, well I could hardly hear them," she says.

"I know me neither. Do you want to go first?" I ask motion to the bath.

"No, it's fine. You can go," she says.

I undress and climb into a nice warm tub of water. It feels so good. I immerse myself underneath and get my head wet, pulling my hair down. I can't believe how fast my hair has grown since they cut it at the workinhouse. It's already past my shoulders; of course it's always been thick.

I realize that Freckles will be waiting to get clean too, so I try and hurry and scrub myself and wash my hair. While I do that Freckles busies herself going through all the soaps and things Ms. Meredith has in the bathroom. She finds a jar of face cream and takes out a glob and smears it on her face. I can't help but laugh at her as she turns to me all covered in white goop.

"Do you ever wonder why grown woman have so much of this stuff?" she asks.

"Maybe to help keep themselves young, I guess," I say.

"My ma didn't have any of this stuff that I can remember," says Freckles.

"When they took you from your ma, did you ever see her again?" I ask.

"No, but there were other girls, older girls who treated me like their own. It's sad, but when they move you out of one workinhouse, you never see them again. You are all the family I have now. I probably wouldn't even know my mother if I ever saw her again," she says.

"I'm sorry," I say.

"It's okay, at least I knew her for a little while, you never even knew yours," says Freckles.

"No, and maybe that's easier than knowing your mother for a little while because you can miss her. I don't miss mine because I don't remember her," I say.

I climb out of the bath so that Freckles can have hers. While she is bathing I dry off and pick up the package that she brought in for me. I see Freckles brought the maroon dress and the yellow dress in. I know she wanted the yellow one so I figure the maroon one is for me. I'm pleasantly surprised that the undergarments fit and the petticoat is a tie up so it can be adjusted.

By the time I'm ready to put the dress on, Freckles is out of the bath and getting into her undergarments. I decide to do my hair first so I won't mess up the dress. I find a brush on the sink and painstakingly brush through the tangles of curls. When I'm done I look at the brush filled with red hair. Now I have to pull all the hair out of this brush so I'm not discovered and then I realize that there is no way I can hide my red hair.

"Freckles what am I going to do about my hair? I can't put the scarf back on. It will look funny, don't you think?" I ask.

"We'll pull it back and braid it, maybe it won't be so noticeable then," she says.

Freckles braids my hair and I braid hers. Then we help each other into our dresses and straighten up the bathroom before we go back to the bedroom with the Charlotte and Lyza. When we get to the room Charlotte is wearing the lavender dress and I notice that the color makes her eyes stand out. Lyza is wearing the turquoise dress which makes her look so lovely. She has her hair pulled back on the sides with her dark curls hanging down in the back.

"Well, aren't we all pretty?" says Lyza.

"Oh, you two look so beautiful!" says Charlotte. "Watch me

spin," she says.

Charlotte does a little spin and her dress twirls around her. She giggles a little. I can just imagine her when she lived with her parents. I bet she had clothes like these, maybe even finer dresses than these.

"Yeah, maybe you like it, but I feel like a dressed up pony," says Freckles.

"Oh don't be silly, you look nice! We all do but the question is, why are we all dressed up?" I ask.

We all jump when we hear a knock at the door. "I guess we're about to find out," says Lyza.

"Come in," I say.

Ms. Meredith comes in holding an oil lamp in her hand. "Oh girls, you all look so beautiful," she says.

"Thank you for the clothes, ma'am, but we can't pay you anything for them right now," says Lyza.

"You're not to worry about that. Now everyone is here ready to meet you if you're ready to meet them," she says.

"Umm, who exactly are we meeting?" asks Freckles.

Ms. Meredith just smiles and says, "Come with me."

CHAPTER 33

We follow Ms. Meredith out of the bedroom but with hesitation. We have no idea what to expect or what we have gotten ourselves into. She leads us to the parlor where all the drapes are pulled shut and the lights are low. There seated around the parlor are several women including Mrs. Gubbels and the little girl who brought the dresses.

There are a couple of young girls about our age too and one man who is standing near the door looking very nervous. Every now and again he peers through the curtains as if watching for someone. He's tall but medium build with a long thick mustache, and he twirls a bowler hat in his hands.

As we enter the room the voices become hushed and then there are a few gasps as the ladies see us for the first time. I feel like a show pony for real. I feel like I and my friends are on display for these people and I just want to run right out that door as fast as I can. But I can't. Whatever this is, I need to see this through, we all do.

"Ladies, girls, Mr. Gubbels, these are the girls," says Ms. Meredith.

"You look so much better now that you've freshened up," says Mrs. Gubbels.

"Girls, these are the Ladies of the Auxiliary plus a few other trustworthy people," says Ms. Meredith.

"Whom you can trust?" I ask.

"Please, sit down, we'll explain while you eat," says Ms. Meredith. She shows us to some chairs brought out from the kitchen.

"Buber, stop that fussing at the drapes, no one is coming here, no one knows and no one can see," says Ms. Meredith.

"Oh, I don't think I can eat in front of people," I whisper to Ms. Meredith.

"Right you are Miss Abby, we'll just get you all some tea and cake for now, then you can eat later," says Ms. Meredith. She walks away to get the tea but my heart has just stopped.

Did she just call me Miss Abby? She knows my real name. We told all those lies for nothing; these ladies know who we are. I turn to look at Lyza but she's not looking my way. No one else heard her call me by my name. I'm confused and unsure of what to do. Should I just run? Should I make an excuse to talk to the girls? Should I just grab them by the hands and run out the door?

All our things are still in the bedroom; even Papa's spyglass is in there. I don't even have Boots; I have no idea where he is. I start looking around for him while in the back of my mind I hear small talk going on between Lyza and some other lady. Charlotte is talking to someone else. I think Freckles is too but I can't seem to concentrate on anything right now because I'm in a panic.

"Here's some tea, ladies," says Ms. Meredith as she brings out a tray of tea and cups and cream and sugar. She sets it down on the little table in front of us.

"How do you like your tea?" asks a woman next to me. I can't seem to answer her because my throat has gone dry.

I'm finally able to speak, "sugar please," I say.

She fixes the tea and hands it to me. I take the cup and saucer but my hands are shaking so bad. I can hear the rattle of the dishes in my hands. Everyone stops talking and looks at me. I take a long drink of tea and then set the cup and saucer down. I look up at Ms. Meredith in expectation. She turns and looks at Mrs. Gubbels.

"Well, we should go on then, shouldn't we?" ask Mrs. Gubbels.

"Yes please, I think Abby is about to have a nervous breakdown," says Ms. Meredith.

Lyza, Freckles and Charlotte look at me with frozen terror on their faces. Well, at least now they know, but what comes next I haven't a clue.

"Are you girls familiar with a lady by the name of Mama Sampson?" asks Mrs. Gubbels.

"I'm not sure. Why do you ask?" asks Lyza. I'm so glad Lyza is thinking clearly.

"She's my sister, and we are very close," says Mrs. Gubbels.

"How do we know that's the truth?" asks Freckles.

"You don't. But I'm telling you anyway," says Mrs. Gubbels.

"We also know who you are, especially Miss AB'Gale Steel. We did appreciate the lovely story you told us earlier about the tornado and the train. Oh and the school and traveling to meet your cousins," says Ms. Meredith.

"But the tornado really happened," says Charlotte.

"If you knew we were lying, why did you let us go on with it?" asks Freckles.

"We wanted you to feel at ease and relax a bit. It's hard to know who to trust and when it's okay to be yourself," says Ms. Meredith.

"We were on that train and we really were in that tornado. That part wasn't a lie," insists Charlotte.

"It's alright dear, we understand. Sometimes you have to fib a little to hide your identities or the System will find you," says Mrs. Gubbels.

"That is where we come in," says the lady who served me my tea.

"I don't understand," I say.

"We're on your side dear; we're here to help you. We will divert the enemy away from your direction," says another woman.

"But why? I don't know you, why would you do this?" I ask.

"We are not who or what you think we are, dear," says another lady.

"We may look like we are upstanding System citizens but we are actually part of a vast organization," says Ms. Meredith.

"An organization that does what, exactly?" asks Lyza.

"We help people out of the System," says Mrs. Gubbels.

"How long have you been doing this?" asks Freckles.

"Help them go where?" I ask.

"We've been do this for just a couple of years," says a lady to my left.

"Wait, this doesn't make any sense. You live here in a town that's run by the System; I mean the railroad goes right through here. Mrs. Gubbels, you say you work at the station. How is it even possible that you can do this right under the nose of the System?" I ask.

"Well that's just it dear, we are right under their noses aren't we?" says the lady next to me.

"It's all about the paperwork," says another woman.

"Basically, we make new papers for everyone. Mrs. Howard

and her husband run the local newspaper so we have access to a printing press. It's quite easy to make new papers," says Mrs. Gubbels.

"My name's Mrs. Kemp. My husband runs the general store. I'm the one who brought you the clothes. I'm so sorry I didn't have shoes for you," says the lady next to me.

"Thank you very much for the clothes. We do appreciate them," I say.

"Is the whole town in on it?" asks Charlotte.

"Oh no, to be sure that would be a miracle. No, we have to do these things in secret," says Ms. Meredith.

"Okay, though I'm not quite sure how all that works with the paperwork, I mean don't the Crushers check?" I ask.

"Well, how can they? When you show them credentials and they look real, how are they to know they are not?" says Mrs. Howard. She is a stout older woman sitting in front of me.

"I guess they don't actually have a way of checking," says Lyza.

"So why don't you just give the hobos papers too and help them out?" I ask.

"Oh dear no. That sort can't be reckoned with. They are very hostile. Besides they don't want our help. They are happy traveling the way they do," says Ms. Meredith.

"Not all of them? Maybe some of them are not nice, but most of them are just trying to survive and live without the System grabbing them and throwing them back into the workinhouses," I say.

"Do you have any workinhouses here?" asks Charlotte.

"No, we don't have any workinhouses, but we do have some cotton farms out yonder," says Mrs. Gubbels.

"They have some kids out there working them but we don't

know how to go about shutting them down without attracting attention to ourselves. Besides, I don't believe they are doing much harm to those young'uns there anyway," says Ms. Meredith.

"How would you know unless you go out and see for yourself," I say.

"Well, we just can't get that involved. That would put our lives at risk," she says.

"Maybe it wouldn't hurt just to check and see that they are not abusing the children and if they are, maybe you could just ask them not to," says Lyza.

"Well, I suppose that couldn't hurt," says Mrs. Gubbels.

"So where do you send people once they get these papers?" I ask, again.

"They go wherever they want. Once we give them the papers to legitimize their citizenship, it's up to them to figure out how to survive," says Ms. Meredith.

"I see," says Freckles.

"We do what we can for them, and that is to give them papers and send them on their way. It's their responsibility to figure out where to go and what to do from here. We can't do everything for them," says Mrs. Gubbels.

"Of course you can't," says Lyza.

I sense a sudden change in the tone of Lyza's and Freckles' voices. It's the sort of tone that is almost patronizing but not to the point of detection. It means to me that they are pretty much done with this conversation and are just ready to move on. I don't think they're being fair, after all these people are at least trying to help.

"I think it's very noble what you are doing, but what has it got to do with us?" I ask.

"You're well known, Miss Abby, and your father has quite

the reputation. We are going to help you get to him," says Mrs. Howard.

"Yes, we're going to help. You don't have to worry about a thing," says Mrs. Gubbels.

"We're working on your papers right now, except there is a problem with Miss Abby," says Mrs. Howard.

"Oh, I see," I say.

"It's just that your face is all over the train stations and post offices. Anywhere they can put them, with your father's too," says Ms. Meredith.

"So we won't be able to make you any papers," says Mrs. Howard.

"But we will get you a ticket on the train to Denver. You will just have to try and keep your face hidden," says Ms. Meredith.

"You three ladies have not been sighted yet, so you should be okay, just keep Abby hidden until you get out of public view," says the lady to my right.

"Why Denver?" I ask. I'm curious if they know something about where Papa is or if Denver is just a random city they picked.

"The Denver train station has a lot of trains going in and out to different places. You will have a better opportunity of getting where you need to be from there than from here of course," says Mrs. Gubbels.

"When does the train leave?" asks Charlotte.

"It leaves tomorrow morning so you will spend the night with Mrs. Gubbels and her husband. They will get you to the train station in the morning," says Ms. Meredith.

"We thank you all for your hospitality, it's so kind of you to help us," I say.

"It is the least we can do for a celebrity. And one day when this is all over, you can say the folks in Wichita Falls helped you out," says Mrs. Howard.

"Yes, we can, and we will," says Lyza, smiling.

"Hush now," says Mr. Gubbels, "There's a rider coming."

"Here?" asks Ms. Meredith.

"Looks like it," says Mr. Gubbels.

"Well, everyone is here who's in the group. Who on earth could it be?" asks Ms. Meredith.

"Don't know but they're ridging that horse awful fast. Quick, get them girls hid," says Mr. Gubbels.

"This way," says Ms. Meredith. We get up and follow her through the first door on the left instead of going to her bedroom like we did before.

"Stay in here and keep quiet," she says. She leaves and closes the door behind her.

"What about our bags and things, and where's Boots?" I ask in a whisper to the other girls.

"I think Boots went outside. I'll sneak out and get our stuff out of the bedroom. Better for just one of us to go," says Lyza.

"No, better not, someone might see you. Just wait and see who comes to the door," I say.

I'm wondering who is at the door and why these people are so worried. There are so many questions going on in my mind when I distinctly hear someone put a key in the door and lock it. I can't believe I just heard that so I go to the door and try the knob. Sure enough, the door is locked. I put my ear to the door and listen but I can't hear anything but muffled voices. How are we going to get out? Perhaps the bigger question might be why did we just get locked in?

CHAPTER 34

"Oh geeze, Abby what'll we do?" asks Charlotte.

I turn and look at Freckles and Lyza maybe to see what's on their mind. Freckles is standing over by the window looking out. Lyza is giving me the "I told you so" look. I ignore Lyza and go to the window.

"Can you see anyone?" I ask.

"No, we're on the wrong side of the house," she says.

"Maybe we should crawl out the window," says Charlotte.

"No way! Are you two kidding? They're giving us free tickets to ride the train the rest of the way," says Freckles.

"We can just keep walking down the tracks until a train comes along," says Lyza.

"How will we know if it's the right one?" asks Charlotte.

"Does it matter? As long as it's going west and away from here, it's better than standing around wondering if it's safe or not to trust these people," I say.

"Oh, all right, come on," says Freckles.

"What about our stuff?" asks Charlotte.

"Maybe we can get into the other room through the window,"

says Lyza.

"I guess it's worth a try," I say.

Just as we are about to go out the window we hear the key turn in the door. I turn around and the door opens. The little girl steps in holding a light in her hands.

"No need to worry, it's just the messenger boy coming to tell us about the train wreck. You can come out now," she says.

We follow her out of the room and back into the parlor where everyone seems to be having a joyous time now. They're all talking excitedly amongst themselves until they see us, and the room goes quiets. Whatever is going on in here, I can see a few faces in the room look a little penitent.

"I'm sorry ladies, it looks as though we owe you an apology," says Mr. Gubbels. He is standing with his head hung and wringing his hands as if worried about something.

"For what?" I ask.

"Well dear, it's just that we didn't exactly believe you about the train wreck," says Mrs. Gubbels.

"We thought you just you concocted the story to hide your identity and why you're traveling alone. I admit it confused me that you went on with the story even after we told you we knew who you were. We are just so sorry we didn't believe you," says Ms. Meredith.

"My word, that must have been a horrible experience for you," says a lady with a hat that looks like she killed a bird and stuffed it in a ring of flowers.

"You are so lucky to be alive," says Mrs. Howard.

"How ever did you manage? What did you do?" asks Ms. Meredith.

"I'll tell you if you answer one question honestly for me," I say.

"Of course dear," says Ms. Meredith.

"Why did you lock the room when the rider came?" I ask.

"I locked the door so that if anyone from the System came in they would not be able to open the room. You would at least have a chance to hide or get away while I fumble with the keys to unlock it. I assure you, it's not to keep you locked up," says Ms. Meredith.

"That actually makes sense," says Freckles.

"You have to understand that we have all been through a lot with the System. Locked in a room is one of their fortes so when you locked the door, well, it made us all a bit nervous," I say.

"Oh, I am so sorry. I never meant to frighten you. Please forgive me and my over thinking," she says.

I look at her and I see a pained look in her eyes like she is worried that maybe I will be angry with her and not forgive her. I can see that she really didn't mean to do any harm. I realize now that maybe I have grown somewhat tainted by my life on the road. It's hard for me to trust people now. Just like Mr. Bo. Apparently he never meant any harm to me either and look how I treated him.

"You're forgiven," says Charlotte. To my surprise Charlotte throws her arms around Ms. Meredith and gives her a big hug.

I just look at her and nod my head in agreement. I'm still not ready, but I'm trying. I sit down in the chair and someone hands me a piece of cake. I'm famished so I eat and let Freckles and Charlotte tell the story of how we survived the tornado. I notice Lyza isn't doing much talking either. She too is busying herself with some cookies and tea.

When I have to talk to someone, I try to keep my conversation short and sweet, trying not to say too much about anything.

If these truly are good people trying to help, then the less they know, the better for them. Sooner or later someone will come around and start asking questions. I don't care how nice a person is or how good their intentions are, some people are not good at keeping secrets.

After a while I start to feel sleepy, and a yawn slips out. I don't mean to be rude but it has been a long few days and I didn't get much sleep last night. In fact, I can't remember the last time I had a good sleep.

"Oh dear, we've kept them up too long, Meredith," says Mrs. Gubbels.

"Yes, yes, everyone it's time to go home, this meeting is adjourned," says Ms. Meredith.

"Is this a real meeting?" asks Mrs. Kemp.

"Of course not dear, but if anyone asks, then it was," says Ms. Meredith.

"Oh, then what did we discuss?" asks Mrs. Kemp.

"Updating the train station," says Mrs. Gubbels.

"But we discussed that last week," says Mrs. Howard.

"And we continued to discuss it this week too. Everyone needs to leave the house all at once so we have a distraction while the girls get into the carriage," says Ms. Meredith.

"We're leaving?" asks Charlotte.

"Yes, I don't have room for you here and you will need to be at the train station early. It makes more sense for you to be at Mr. and Mrs. Gubbels house," says Ms. Meredith.

"We need to get our things," I say, getting up.

"Oh dear, I forgot about your bags. Well hold them low and don't look conspicuous. I have nosy neighbors," says Ms. Meredith.

"I've got Boots," says Charlotte.

"Good, put him in the bag, please," I say.

We make our way down the hall to the bedroom and grab our things. Charlotte puts Boots in the bag and closes it. I think it will be hard to hide our bags with bed rolls and all but we can do our best. We hold our bags in front of us instead of slinging them on our backs. We get out to the parlor and everyone is waiting for us at the door.

"Well I guess this is goodbye to some of you. We thank you all so much," I say.

"You are most welcome, dear," says Ms. Meredith, and she gives us all a big hug.

Someone opens the door and everyone goes out in a big crowd, while talking at once about nothing. It's kind of funny I think. It's as if they all rehearsed this part for this particular moment and have been waiting to put the play on. Everyone crowds around Mr. and Mrs. Gubbels' carriage, and Mr. Gubbels opens the door for his wife. She starts to get in then she stops and turns to someone else and starts talking. At the same time she motions with her hands waving us in.

We all duck into the enclosed carriage with the curtains drawn. We make sure to leave room for Mr. and Mrs. Gubbels who get in after us. It's a tight squeeze with them and all our stuff but we manage. Then Mr. Gubbels bangs on the roof with his cane and the driver takes off.

We are all silent as the carriage drives through town. I want to peek out the curtains but I don't dare for fear someone might see me. I wouldn't want to get these nice people in trouble.

The ride doesn't seem to take long and before I realize it the horses have slowed down. I thought this meant we were near our destination. But the horse goes on for a while longer at this slow pace and I can't stand the silence any longer.

"Do you have a steamcarriage?" I ask.

"Of course, dear, but we couldn't all fit in it. Besides, there's no privacy," says Mrs. Gubbels.

"No, I guess you're right, there wouldn't be," I say. "I'm only curious."

"Our town even has a mule-drawn trolley just like Fort Worth," says Mr. Gubbels.

"Really? That's pretty jiggy," says Charlotte.

"Jiggy?" asks Mr. Gubbels.

"She means that's fine," says Freckles.

"Yes, yes of course, the lingo of the youth today. It's very new to me," says Mr. Gubbels.

"Our children are all grown and gone, I'm afraid it's just us these days. Though sometimes they come for a visit," says Mrs. Gubbels.

"That must be nice," I say.

"For a moment, then the madness drives me insane," she says.

I smile to myself, most definitely Mama Sampson's sister, no doubt about that. I wonder how Mama Sampson is doing. I hope nothing has happened to her. I'm concerned that the System will find out that she helped us.

"Have you heard from your sister recently?" I ask.

"Not for a month or so, but that's not anything new," she says.

"But she told you about us. Isn't that a bit risky? I mean, anyone could have gotten a hold of that letter," says Freckles.

"I suppose you're right, she should be more careful about that," she says.

"Here we are. I've told the driver to pull around to the back of the house," says Mr. Gubbels.

"Won't the driver be suspicious?" asks Lyza.

"Oh probably, but he works for me, so if he wants to keep his job he won't say anything," says Mr. Gubbels.

"Just keep your head down, Abby dear, until we get inside," says Mrs. Gubbels.

The carriage stops and Mr. Gubbels opens the door and gets out. He helps us out one by one and we find ourselves in a small courtyard outside what looks like a grand house. A trellis with ivy and honeysuckle vines covering it surrounds the courtyard like a great green wall. They usher us inside through a small wooden door into a mud room.

"Follow me, dears," says Mrs. Gubbels.

We follow her up a narrow staircase which I think might be the servant's stairs. I wouldn't know for sure but I will remember to ask Charlotte later. When we get to the top she leads us to a room with a large bed in it. It's so large that I do believe the four of us can sleep in it together, which I think is the idea.

"This should be fine for you. There's a bathroom across the hall with running water. I'll have some food brought up for you and some milk for your cat, too," says Mrs. Gubbels.

"This is great, thank you," says Freckles.

"Just be sure to keep the drapes closed. You can light a candle but keep the drapes closed. The neighbors are not used to seeing a light in here and they would wonder," she says.

"We'll keep them closed," says Lyza.

"In the morning we will sneak you down to the station very early so it will look like you are travelers. Until then I hope you can get some rest," says Mrs. Gubbels.

"Good night," I say. I close the door behind her and turn and look at my friends.

"Wow," says Lyza.

"Oh my goodness, what a day," says Charlotte.

"I don't even know what to say. This place is just crazy," says Freckles.

"Yeah well, crazy or not, tomorrow morning we will all be on a train in style and on our way to Papa," I say.

CHAPTER 35

$\mathcal{W}$e take our dresses off but keep everything else on so it will be easy to dress in the morning. A knock at the door startles us. After a quick debate of who should answer the door, Freckles finally gets up and opens it. We are relieved to find a young girl about our age holding a tray of food.

The girl brings the tray of food in and without a word leaves it on a table by the window. She is wearing a nightgown with a nightcap on her head which tells me she had to get out of bed to serve us. I kind of feel bad about that. But she's gone before we can even thank her.

On the tray we find some various cold cuts, fruits, nuts, bread, butter, four cups and one bowl of warm milk. I set the bowl down on the floor and let Boots out of the bag so he can have a meal too. I also open the window for him. He likes to go out at night, but he better get back in time before we leave.

We all stuff ourselves with the food and milk and what we don't eat, Freckles tucks away in a bag for later. We've learned to save what food we don't eat. Exhausted, we all just lie across the bed every which way. I barely remember my head hitting the pillow.

A gentle shake rouses me from my slumber and dreams. It's still dark outside but Mrs. Gubbels is here in the room encouraging us to get up so we don't miss the train.

Sleepily, we all get up and put our dresses back on and freshen up. I call out the window for Boots and am pleasantly surprised to see him come right away. This time I coax him into the bag with a piece of meat I saved from last night.

Dressed and ready, we grab our bags and head down the back stairs as quietly as we can. We find Mr. Gubbels waiting for us below. As we did the night before, we leave through the back door and into the carriage. I notice Mrs. Gubbels isn't with us this morning, but Mr. Gubbels is and he tells us the plan.

"Now ladies, we are going around the back of the station where we will get out and go in through the back door. Once we are in there you sit down on the waiting benches until Mrs. Gubbels comes in to the ticket booth. When she turns the sign to open then you can go up to the ticket booth and she'll give you your ticket and papers," he says.

"How long until the train comes?" asks Charlotte.

"It will be along about twenty minutes after you get your ticket," he says.

"So we just have to wait," I say.

"Yes. And I must ask that you do not attempt to engage in any conversation with either myself or Mrs. Gubbels. We must remain as if we are strangers from here on," he says.

"We understand," says Freckles.

"Yeah, we know this is dangerous for you and we don't want you to get into any trouble," says Charlotte.

"You don't have to worry," says Lyza.

"We do appreciate everything you have done for us. I want you to know that," I say.

"You are most welcome. Just remember if for some reason you ever get caught, please leave our names out of it," he says.

"Yes sir, we will," I say.

No sooner do we finish our conversation than we have arrived at the station. Mr. Gubbels gets out first and unlocks the back door and goes in. We wait a minute or two and then we go in after him, closing the door behind us. I turn to look out the window in time to see the carriage leaving.

Inside it's cool and still a little dark. Mr. Gubbels is making the rounds, pulling the lights down from the ceilings to light them. As the room grows brighter the station comes to life. A red tile floor glimmers alongside polished wood benches. Framed maps of train routes become visible along the walls as well as painted art of the Texas landscape.

A lattice wall in the back of the room, sections off the office and work area while in the middle a small archway looms over a polished oak counter. A little sign centered in the archway reads 'Tickets Sold Here' while another sign next on the counter reads 'Closed.'

We sit down on the bench facing the ticket window and wait. Outside the sky is growing gray with the first light of dawn. Mr. Gubbels finishes lighting the station and disappears through a door in the lattice wall.

"Abby, your hair," says Lyza.

"What about my hair?" I ask and touch my head. My hair is still in a tight braid hanging to one side.

"Do you have a hat to put on?" she asks.

"I lost my hat in the tornado," I say.

"What about your scarf?" asks Freckles.

"Oh yes, I forgot," I say, digging in my bag for my scarf.

"That'll work, it matches your dress. Here, let me help you put it on," says Lyza.

"Won't it look funny if none of you are wearing a scarf or hat and I am?" I ask.

"Not much we can do about it," she says.

"I have a ribbon I can wear in my hair," says Charlotte.

"Come here, I'll tie it in for you says," Freckles.

"I can roll mine up in a bun, at least," says Lyza.

Lyza rolls my hair up and ties it in a knot so it won't fall out. Then she ties my scarf around my head and loosely around my neck and ties it off in a bow on the side. She holds up her hand mirror for me to see, and it looks fashionable. Then I help her roll up her hair into a bun. She has two hair pins exactly so I try to use them well and in the right place. We all assess each other and decide that we have done the best we can in disguise. So now all we can do is wait.

After a while I hear movement behind the ticket window and looked up. Mrs. Gubbels appears to be getting things ready for the day. I looked over to see Charlotte curled up on the far end of the bench asleep. Freckles and Lyza are leaning against each other with their eyes closed as well. A slight clearing of her throat causes me to look over at Mrs. Gubbels. She has taken the closed sign down and is now looking over at me in anticipation.

I nudge Lyza awake and get up and go over to the ticket booth. Lyza must have woken up the others because when I turn around they are all standing in line behind me. Mrs. Gubbels doesn't say a word but puts her finger to her lips and then smiles. She slides me a ticket with an envelope across the counter. I smile and nod at her and turn to walk away when she grabs my arm and stops me.

I turn back around and she slides a basket across the counter to me as well. I take the basket thanking her and return to the bench. While she is handing each girl a ticket and envelope I take a peek in the basket and find it's packed with food.

Lyza comes and sits next to me as we wait until Freckles and Charlotte join us. Then we watch as Mrs. Gubbels again busies herself behind the counter. We all look in our envelopes and as the girls find their official papers I have none. Instead of papers I find some money which I appreciate and show the girls before I tuck it into my bag.

Then I open the basket for the girls to see inside before they even ask me. I am about to tell them that maybe we should wait to go through it until we get on the train, when a small bell rings. I look over at the front door and someone has come in.

Quickly I look down as if I am adjusting the contents in the basket. I sneak a peek when the person approaches the ticket booth and see the back of a man standing there. I'm thinking that maybe we're sitting too close to the ticket booth and if any other people come in before the train gets here they are sure to look over at us. I mean it's only natural to scope out who is in a building, especially this close to the door and ticket window.

Then I hear it, the sound of freedom, that ever loving whistle that has so often comforted me and saved me in so many ways. Getting up from the bench to move won't seem so awkward now. We all get up and walk to the window to watch as the train comes into the station. Funny but I don't remember seeing it from this vantage, except maybe once when I first went to look for Papa. That seems so long ago but it really hasn't been. I wait with anticipation to board the train that I hope will carry me to Papa.

We have to wait for the train to stop and the conductor to make sure no one is getting off the train before we can board. While he is standing by the door we watch men load and unload the baggage and boxcars. This is something I've never watched from this perspective, and it seems kind of tedious and long. At last the conductor opens the door and waves us through. He takes our tickets and punches them with a hole puncher as we pass by him.

"Do you have any luggage, miss?" he asks Lyza who is the first to board.

"No sir, none of us do, just our carry on things," she says, speaking for all of us.

"Very well then, make sure you keep it out of the aisle and mind your step up to the train," he says.

"Thank you," she says.

He gives her a hand up and then Charlotte, then Freckles, and then it's my turn. I keep my face turned down on the pretext that I am watching my step so I don't fall. Having the scarf over my head helps, but it doesn't hide my face. Given the fact that this man has been to many a rail station, I'm sure he has seen the poster and has even read the paper. I think my disguise as a boy must be better than this.

We make our way down the aisle and I'm feeling a bit queasy remembering the last time I tried to do this. At least this time I have a ticket. There are several seats available since there are no other passengers in this car except an elderly couple sitting in the middle. We move closer to the front to some seats that are four facing each other. As I turn to sit facing the back I notice another man we passed unnoticed sitting near the back. He is asleep with his head against the window and his hat pulled down over his face. I decide to sit facing the front of the train instead, I would rather not face a stranger, sleeping or not.

It isn't long before the train lurches forward and begins to move. I just now start to relax a bit and have the time to wonder how the boys are doing and if they are okay. I can't remember if we had told them where to meet us. They did say they would find us so I guess that means we should look for them in Colorado Springs. I don't dare ask Lyza or Freckles, I don't want them to fret, that is, if they aren't already.

I watch out the window as Wichita Falls passes by. I notice a great many buildings now that the sun is up, and I can see that the train yard is immense. There must be a lot of trains that go through here. Then I wonder where this train came from because I know it didn't come up from Fort Worth. I doubt anything can get through yet.

"Hey Lyza, ask the conductor where this train came from," I say.

"Why?" she asks.

"I'm just curious is all. I mean it couldn't come from where we came from, they wouldn't have had time to clear the tracks," I say.

"You're right, I didn't think of that," she says.

It's about ten minutes or so before the conductor comes through on his way to the engine. He stops and chats with the elderly couple behind us for a moment. I hear him take his leave of them and then walk toward us and stop.

"You ladies doing okay here?" he asks with a pleasant tone.

"Yes sir," says Charlotte.

"Yes thank you. I wonder can you tell me where this train hails from?" asks Lyza.

"Oh we come down from St. Louis. We just got word that

the southern train got hit by a tornado so we don't have as many passengers as we're supposed to. Don't know how bad the damage is or how many people are hurt or even dead. Those tornadoes are a scary thing, I tell you. Rest assured you ladies will be fine on your trip. We're supposed to have fair weather save for a bit of snow," says the conductor.

"Snow?" asks Freckles.

"Yes, snow, not bad though. Snow only gets bad when you get up in the mountains; we got a flat ride through here until we cross the border of New Mexico. Once we cross there we start hitting the high desert, but I don't expect the storm will be much to Pueblo. Now if you're going on up to Denver, well you might want to wait a day or two," he says. He pulls out his watch from his pocket and looks at it a moment.

"Thank you, we might just do that," says Freckles.

"Okay, well if you're good here I've got to mosey on up front now. Just sit back and enjoy the scenery. There's a head up front through that door if you need to use it. Mind you don't drop nothing down it though or it's gone for good," he says. He tips his hat and leaves us.

"Oh bother, another snow storm," says Charlotte.

"Don't worry, we're not going as far as Denver, silly," says Freckles.

"Oh, okay. Where are we going?" asks Charlotte.

"Colorado Springs, remember?" I ask in a whisper.

"No one is listening," says Freckles, looking around. "The old couple is playing cards and the creeper is sleeping still."

"I hope he's just a creeper and not a Crusher," I say.

"You know, he looks like one of them detective types," says Lyza, looking up.

"Oh yeah, like that one that used to come and see you at the workinhouse, Abby," says Charlotte in a hushed voice.

"Charlotte, turn around don't let him wake up and catch you looking at him," says Freckles.

"I remember that guy, Detective Walker. He had been looking for Papa and he asked me a lot of questions," I say.

"Yeah, that's the one," says Charlotte.

"It's not him is it?" I ask.

"I doubt it, Abby, besides we never got to see him. You're the only one of us who did," says Lyza.

"Charlotte look what you've done. You've got Abby all wound up now," says Freckles.

"Sorry, Abby," says Charlotte.

"It's alright, I'm sure it's not him," I say.

I accept her apology because I know she'll fret until I do. But the truth is my heart is pounding now that she has mentioned that guy. But I'm sure Lyza is right, it can't be him. We are far away from that place now where he can't find me. Of course, there is always the chance that there are others looking too. After all, I'm on the System's most wanted list.

CHAPTER 36

We watch the countryside morph into a flat desert through the window. As far as I can see, there is nothing to see. Sometimes we pass a field of crops and a farm house, but those are few and far between. We stop once for water for the engine at a lonely water tower. The conductor didn't allow anyone to get off, not even to stretch our legs for a moment.

"Hey, anyone hungry?" I ask.

"As a matter of fact we never ate breakfast, did we?" asks Freckles.

"Nope, I believe it's right here in this basket," I say picking it up.

"Look, there is a table that folds up from the wall," says Charlotte.

"Jiggy," says Lyza.

We fold out the table and inventory the items from the basket Mrs. Gubbels provided for us. Inside are biscuits, two apiece. A small jar of honey, four apples, some cheese slices and bacon wrapped in paper. There's also four ham and cheese sandwiches and some canned pickles. I'm guessing that is for lunch later. We also find a deck of cards and a newspaper.

We settle on the bacon and biscuits with honey and keep the rest for later. I must say there are times when I'm so hungry and I don't know where my next meal will come from. Yet when we do eat, we eat real well.

After we're done eating and clean our mess, I check on Boots and give him some bacon and a little water. I can't take him out of the bag because I don't want the train conductor to see him. I put the bag on my lap and open it and pet him for a while before setting the bag on the bench between Charlotte and me.

Lyza and Charlotte keep themselves occupied by playing cards across the table. Freckles and I share pieces of the newspaper to read. The paper is local out of Wichita Falls so most all of the news is about the goings-on in the town. At least it's something to pass the time.

Another stop comes up, and this time they let us get off the train to stretch our legs. I'm inclined to believe it's not a good idea for me to get off the train; if I get off the train with all these people I risk being recognized. I just keep my head bent and get off anyway. I've been sitting for so long I need to walk a bit. I have no idea what town we're in, but I do know the land is still flat and it's getting cold outside. I feel something wet hit my face. I look up and see little speckles of white falling from the sky.

We have twenty minutes before they blow the whistle and call us to board again. When we get back on there are more people in the passenger car now. In fact it's about half full. I hadn't even noticed anyone getting on. I don't see the creeper guy anymore; I guess maybe he's gone, so that's a relief.

We sit back down and analyze the new passengers. From where I'm sitting I see the passengers in front of me and beside us. I tell Lyza and Freckles who I see then Lyza and Freckles narrate to Charlotte and I who they see. That way we don't look odd staring around at everyone.

"The creeper is gone now but the old folks are still there. A new family is sitting across from them. Looks like a mom and two small children," says Lyza.

"Small children can be dangerous," I say jokingly.

"Yes of course. We will have to keep our eyes on them. There are two old business men, they look suspicious though," says Lyza.

"Yes, and two more men just got on in the back that are dressed like that creeper guy," says Freckles.

"Oh that's great," I say.

"By the way, I found these glasses someone left behind. You should put them on," says Freckles. She hands me a small pair of clear round glasses.

I put them on. "They are a little weird but not too bad. I think they are for reading, they make things a little bigger," I say.

"Well, maybe just wear them when we are close to people or if someone is approaching us, I guess," says Freckles.

"Thanks," I say.

"So what have you on your end of the train?" asks Lyza.

"We've got four old biddies in front of us yakking away," I say.

"Yep, I can hear them," says Lyza.

"A couple of cute young men across the way," says Charlotte.

"Really Charlotte, don't be so crude," says Lyza.

"It's true they are a bit cute," I say, "If you like them that young, Charlotte."

"I'm just kidding," says Charlotte.

"I know," I say laughing.

"What's the joke?" asks Freckles.

"They might be about five years old," I say.

"Wow Charlotte, you're getting desperate for a beau huh?" asks Lyza.

"Now who's being crude?" asks Charlotte.

We pass the time making jokes about the other passengers and the conductor. We make up stories about who they are and their lives. For a moment in time we feel normal having fun and laughing. It's as if nothing bad has happened in our lives and we are just taking a fun ride on the train. It feels good.

After a while we break out our lunch and enjoy the ham and cheese sandwiches with bread and butter pickles. We wash it all down with water from our water skin because that's all we have. The water still tastes a little like wine but I'm getting used to it. We decide to save the apples for later since we're not sure where we will be when dinner time comes around.

Outside the snow is falling thicker and heavier. It's growing colder and we have to break out our coats and blankets to stay warm. I remember there being a stove in the caboose to keep the crew warm. I wonder why they don't have one in the passenger car. I look around the room but I don't see one.

"What are you looking for?" asks Charlotte.

"Just looking to see if there's a stove to light to warm it up in here," I say.

"Only if you're first class, dear," says a woman across the way from us.

"Oh, you mean there is another passenger car?" asks Charlotte.

"Yes, but like I said it's for first class passengers who can afford to pay for it," she says.

"That's typical," I say to know one in particular.

We bundle up together under our coats and blankets to stay warm. It's not like we haven't done this before. In fact this isn't as cold as I have felt it either. After a while I must have fallen asleep because I open my eyes and see that it's nearly dark outside. Charlotte is asleep but Lyza and Freckles are gone. I guess they went to the bathroom.

I stand up and stretch my legs and arms and look around the coach and see everyone else is bundled up and sleeping too. Everyone except me and one other person. I see the creeper in the back of the car is back in his spot and is sitting up and looking right at me. The light is dim but not so dim that I don't recognize his face. I try to act like I don't notice and turn back around and sit down, nudging Charlotte to wake her.

"Charlotte, wake up. We're in trouble. Sit up slowly and don't look around, just listen," I whisper in her ear.

To her credit Charlotte hears me and does as I tell her. She sits up and stretches and leans into me as if to lay her head on my shoulder.

"What's going on?" she asks quietly.

"That creeper is back and it's him. It's the detective. I recognize him. He looked right at me," I say.

"What do we do?" she asks.

"We have to wait for Freckles and Lyza to get back. When they do we better get our stuff together in case we have to make a run for it," I say.

"Okay," she says.

We do our best to gather our things together and put it all away except for our coats and blankets. Boots has been lying asleep under the blanket so I have to coax him back into the bag. The best way to do this is with food since he has been content lying on the bench beside me. I saved some ham from my sandwich from our lunch so I put some pieces in the bag. He smells it immediately and crawls inside to investigate.

By the time we're done getting everything packed back up, Freckles and Lyza come in through the door. Freckles sits down but Lyza hesitates a moment and I see her looking around. I realize she must notice the guy too. She sits down and looks around at our area and then she looks at me expectantly. I lean down and I am just about to whisper to her and Freckles when I notice the shoes standing by our benches. I work my way up from the shoes to the pants. I look up and there he is standing there looking right at me.

"Well, Miss Steel, it is a pleasant surprise seeing you here on this train," says Detective Walker.

"Excuse me, but I think you're mistaken," I start to say.

"Let's not cause a scene shall we? You and I both know it's you. Now suppose you walk back here and talk to me for a bit," says Detective Walker, motioning to the back of the car.

"I don't think so, mister, she's staying right here," says Lyza.

"Well if you like, then I will just arrest all of you," says Detective Walker.

"Wherever she goes," Charlotte starts to say, but I stop her.

"No, this isn't your problem. I appreciate you girls riding with me on the train but there's no need for you to get involved in my problems. Especially since we just met," I say. I look right at Lyza hoping she understands that if we all get arrested then there is no one to help us out.

"That's very responsible of you, Miss Steel. Now come along quietly so we don't make a scene," says Detective Walker.

I walk with him to the back of the train as he holds my arm

tight, afraid I'm going to make a run for it I guess. All I have is my coat on. I've left all my things with the girls, including my bag and Papa's spyglass, and of course Boots. I know they will take care of everything. I trust them. Papa's spyglass is safer with them than with me now. I don't want the map falling into the wrong hands.

"Sit here," he says, motioning to the bench.

I sit down next to the window, within sight of my friends. There is nothing I can think of doing right now. No sooner do I sit down than he puts cuffs on me and attaches me to the metal part of bench.

I look around at the other passengers. Most of them are still asleep but some of them have woken up and are watching us with interest. I can't imagine what they must be thinking.

"Do you really think that's necessary?" I ask.

"Yes, I do. I have been chasing you all over the place. You do get around don't you? You have been pretty busy it seems," he says.

"It's all lies, everything they are saying about me is lies. I didn't blow up that workinhouse," I say.

"Well, I'm sure we will get to the bottom of it all in time. I'm not a foolish man either. I know those girls are your friends from the workinhouse. But they don't have a bounty on their heads so I'm willing to overlook the fact that they are escapees for the moment. But if you give me any trouble, I swear I will arrest the lot of you. Are we clear?" he asks.

"Yes sir," I say.

"Now I don't suppose you know where your papa is, do you?" he asks.

"You know I don't. Why do you think I've been traveling all

over the place? I've been looking for him," I say.

"And where are you headed now to look for him?" he asks.

I think a moment. I'm not going to tell him where I think Papa is, but I have to tell him something. We are heading west so where would it be believable for me to tell him we're headed? I stall as long as I can because if I answer him right away he'll know I'm lying.

"I would appreciate some cooperation. Again I could arrest them, as well," he says.

"No, please don't. We're headed to California. I don't know where, I just heard somewhere out there," I say.

The train starts slowing down and I realize we are pulling into a station. I'm wondering which town this is.

"Well now, that wasn't so hard, was it?" he asks.

"No sir," I say.

"Looks like we are pulling into Pueblo now. It's a shame you can't be truthful with me," he says.

"What do you mean?" I ask.

"The System has reliable information that your papa is not in California, and you know it. You are headed to somewhere here in Colorado," he says.

My heart is pounding because I have come so far to find Papa and now I may have led them right to him without even meaning to. I'm listening to him talk, but at the same time I watch the city of Pueblo come into vision. The snow is still falling, covering the hills and houses with a light dust. It's still twilight so the light hasn't faded yet and the train station comes into vision. Up ahead I can see Crusher carriages waiting at the station.

I yank on the cuffs trying to break free because I realize this is all a trap. He's not just going to arrest me, he's going to arrest everyone and he's going to find Papa and arrest him too. I have to get free and find Papa and warn him, but how?

"Stop doing that. You'll just hurt yourself," he says.

"You're not a nice man. I thought you were on my side when you came to see me at the workinhouse. I thought you understood things weren't right and what they did to me and my family wasn't right. Everything they've said about Papa and me is lies. The System made up stories to make us look like we're horrible people," I say.

"That may be true, Abby, but you're still a criminal, and so are your father and your friends. We all have to follow the rules of the System," he says.

"The System is wrong, don't you see? It's all wrong," I say. My voice has elevated and people are waking up and looking alarmed.

"No, you're wrong. The System has kept our country in a peaceful balance for years. Until you and your father started an uprising with the hobos, that is, now it seems we have pirates as well," he says.

The train is now at a pace that is slow enough for a person to jump off if they needed to. We are still far enough away from the station and the Crushers. If only I could get lose, but I know there is no way I can. I make a decision and take a deep breath.

"Get off the train. It's a trap!" I scream as loud as I can.

"That wasn't very smart," he says, standing up.

I grab his legs with my other hand and trip him so he falls. I look up to see the door shut behind Charlotte. They were ready, they knew it too. I watch to see that they make it as they jump off the train. The other passengers gasp and holler in the excitement. Once they pass the train jumpers they turn their attention to me and Detective Walker. He stands up and looks down at me; I can see the anger in his face. The only thing I can think of doing is to smile.

CHAPTER 37

"You think you're clever, helping your friends get away, don't you?" he asks.

He sits down across from me and fixes his hair that has been disheveled from his fall and readjusts his hat. I look at him and don't say anything. I remember the first time I met him and how afraid I felt because he represented the System. The next time I saw him again I had been abused by Ms. Marcs. That time he seemed almost kind to me. Now he's different, more by the rules and cynical than I remember him.

"Cat got your tongue?" he asks.

I shake my head. I have nothing to say to him. I will just wait and plan my escape. I look out the window and watch as we pull into the station. I ignore the stares from the other passengers as they get up to exit the train and we still sit here.

"They won't get far, you know? We'll catch up with them now that we know what they look like. Ms. Marcs wasn't clear on the particulars of your friends. She is certain about you though. She said you caused the explosion," he says.

"Ms. Marcs?" I ask, surprised.

"Oh yes she's alive. She believes you blew the workinhouse up on purpose before you escaped," he says.

"I told you that's a lie, and she knows it," I say.

"Mr. Grugen is not too pleased with you either, going around blowing up his mines and helping his workers escape," says Detective Walker.

"All lies," I say.

"And there are the train fires which are attributed to the airship pirates for the most part. The System is certain that you have a hand in them as well," he says.

"Are you serious? How can one little girl do all that stuff you're telling me I did?" I say.

Of course, I'm not going to admit that there were a couple of accidents. Well, one accident actually. I guess I did kind of tell those boys that it wouldn't hurt to make sure that mine didn't work again. Either way, if I even admitted a little bit they would take that as a confession I'm sure. I never meant for anyone to get hurt, but the workinhouse in Bryson City had been an accident.

"Still not speaking? Well it doesn't matter. They will make you talk eventually. Come on, let's go. They're waiting for us," he says.

He unlocks the manacles from my wrist and helps me up. He keeps a tight grip on my arm as we exit the train. Outside the wind is cold and the snow is falling harder and deeper. All around the building roof tops are covered in white and the ground is wet and muddy. There are more than a dozen Crushers standing around talking. One man sees us and comes over.

"I see you finally caught the lass, Detective Walker," says the man. He is round and stout with a gray mustache. His voice is pleasant but his look is stern.

"Yes, but her cohorts have gotten away. They jumped the train about a mile back heading west I think," says Detective Walker.

"I'll send my boys out right now. We should have them in no time," says the man. He bows slightly to Detective Walker and leaves.

I watch as he goes over to his men and starts shouting orders to them. Then he speaks to two other men who nod and walk toward us while the other Crushers leave. I'm guessing they're all going out to look for Lyza, Freckles and Charlotte. I hope those girls just hide somewhere safe rather than try and outrun these guys.

"You need a ride, sir?" says one of the two Crushers who have approached us.

"Yes, thank you. We do," says Detective Walker.

We follow the Crushers to the dreaded Crusher box and they open the back and usher me in. I remember the first time I road in one of these. Everything felt as hopeless then as it does now. I sit down on the bench, resigned for the moment.

"I will ride in the back with her," says Detective Walker.

"Suit yourself," says the man.

Detective Walker climbs in and sits across from me. They shut and lock the door. So there it is, I'm trapped again. I listen as the motor starts up and sputters a bit as they crank it. After a moment it gets going and we start to move.

"It's a long ride to Denver so you might as well get comfortable," says Detective Walker.

"Do you know anything about the System other than the rules you follow?" I ask.

"I'm not sure what you mean," he says.

"Do you have any idea what goes on in those workinhouses or the workinfarms?" I ask.

"Yes I do. People who would be starving to death are given shelter and food, and in return they work," he says.

"Wrong. People are taken from prominent lives they have been living and thrown into those places to be slaves. Children grow up to be about five years old and then taken from their mothers. Husbands and wives are separated. Families are torn apart. Old people are thrown in oldies homes to work the last bit of life out of them until they die," I say.

"I think you have been misinformed. Perhaps you think Ms. Marcs treated you a bit harsh, but I assure you not all the places are like that," says Detective Walker.

"Do you know that for a fact?" I ask.

"Well, I haven't been to every one of them but the System has standards," he says.

"Yes, yes, I'm sure they tell you all that, but until you have lived it and seen it you wouldn't truly know," I say.

"I'm sorry you feel that way," he says.

"This happened to me because of something my papa did. Is that fair to me?" I ask.

"Well, I'm certain the System has their reasons but that does not give you free reign to go around causing more problems," he says.

"I'm not trying to cause more problems; I'm trying to find out what happened to my papa. But people are keeping secrets, trying to kill me, steal from me, and my own government makes me the enemy," I say.

"You put yourself in this mess. You could have just stayed put and everything would be fine," he says.

"No it wouldn't!" I yell. "That workinhouse blew up. If we hadn't been trying to escape that night we would have died with everyone else in there," I say.

Then it occurred to me, maybe that's what the System wanted. Maybe those boilers blowing up wasn't an accident at all and they were trying to kill me. But that would be stupid. They could just take me out and kill me without having to waste an entire workinhouse and workers. Anyway, I'm not that important. Unless they were trying to get to Papa. No, it couldn't be possible. That would just be too much to believe.

"I think you need to calm down now, you're getting too excited over this. It's over now," says Detective Walker.

"That's what you think," I say.

"It will be over soon when we catch your friends. It won't be long before we have your father in custody too," he says.

"If you think you're going to get any information out of me you're crazy. I've told you what I know, which is nothing," I say.

"Well, we will see about that," he says.

"What are you going to do with me, put me in another workinhouse? I'll just escape that one too," I say.

"I have no idea what they are going to do with you to be honest, but it can't be good. I suggest you cooperate if you want to get through the interrogation alive," he says.

"What is that?" I ask.

"The System is going to ask you questions. Just tell them the truth," he says.

"Or what?" I ask.

"Or you won't like what they will do to you," he says.

Then comprehension comes to me; he's telling me that wherever I'm being taken, they plan on questioning me and torturing me. That's awful. How could they do such a thing? I'm only fifteen years old.

"What do you think you're going to find out from me?" I ask. I try to keep my voice calm but I'm shaking inside.

"I'm not going to do anything. I've done my job. I found you. It's someone else's job to find out what you know about your father and his friends," he says.

"What if I don't know anything?" I ask.

"For your sake, I hope you know something," he says.

"But I don't. How can you just turn me over like this if you know what they are going to do?" I ask.

"Like I said, I've done my job. I found you. Now I have to go continue looking for your father," he says.

"You are a cruel heartless man. Don't you have any children of your own? What if it were you? What if they took everything away from you and threw your family in a workinhouse and your kids. What if your kids were going to be tortured?" I ask.

"I don't have a family," he says quietly.

"So you don't care then, is that it? You just do your job like a windup toy. They wind you up and you go," I say.

"I think maybe you are just too young to understand how things work," he says.

"Exactly my point. I'm too young to be thrown in a workinhouse never to go to school again. I'm too young to torture for information about my papa that I know nothing about. Did it ever occur to you that maybe he left to protect Granny and me? That he didn't tell us anything so that the System wouldn't do this to us?" I ask.

"I'm sorry, but there is nothing I can do. It's out of my hands," he says.

I am so angry now I could hit him, but I know it would accomplish nothing, so I scoot down as far away from him as I can. I am done talking to this man. He has no clue and never will. All these people who work for and with the System, think that the System is right and the rules are good and work. That's why Papa and his friends are starting a revolution, because nobody listens and there is nothing else they can do.

The carriage hits a bump and we're jolted and thrown about the inside of the Crusher wagon. Then it hits another one causing the carriage to start swerving back and forth on the road in a violent manner. I can't keep in the seat. I see a strap attached to the wall and I grab it and hold on tight. I look over and Detective Walker is doing the same.

The next thing I know, the Crusher carriage is tipping, and it keeps tipping until it falls over onto its left side. I'm hanging onto the strap with my feet in the air. The carriage keeps sliding down the road on its side for a ways until it stops. I let go and jump down. Detective Walker isn't moving. I reach down to feel if he is breathing. I feel his breath but there is blood on his head.

It's dark and quiet. The two men in the front are quiet too, and the lights have all gone out. I'm trapped in here with no way out. The window is too small for me to climb out of, and the door's locked. I crawl over to it and try the door, but it doesn't budge. I bang on it, but it still won't open. Then someone outside bangs on the door from the outside. I bang again and wait. They bang back.

"Who's out there? I'm trapped. Can you help me?" I shout.

"Abby, is that you?" asks a voice.

"Yes it's me, please help," I ask.

I'm wondering who it is that's out there who knows me. The voice sounds familiar but I can't quite place it. I hear a noise and the door pops open a little. Gloved hands reach in and pull the door the rest of the way. I see a figure standing there and a hand reaches in for me. I grab the hand and I'm pulled out of the Crusher carriage.

It's snowing and it's dark outside but a faint moon gives off a hint of light. Yet even if it were the darkest night I would know who my savior is. I remember his voice now, I remember his smell, his touch, and I remember everything about him. I just can't believe he is here, the love of my life, my best friend, my Joey.

CHAPTER 38

"Joey, how did you find me? What are you doing here?" I ask.

"No time to explain, Abby, we gotta go before those men wake up," he says.

I turn and look at the wreck. The snow continues to fall and melts as it hits the twisted metal. Steam rises out of the engine compartment. The wagon part of the carriage is lying on its side dented and twisted, and I wonder how I even survived.

"You could have killed me," I say, turning back to Joey.

"Not me, the natives," he says pointing behind him.

I look past Joey and all I see is his horse standing there waiting. Then out of the snowfall, like ghosts, the natives on horseback emerge. A few at first, and then several until I've lost count. I look back at the Crusher wagon and see arrows sticking out of the flattened tires. I understand now what happened. The Crushers must have lost control of the wagon when the tires went flat from the arrows. It skidded on the wet road, hit something and flipped.

"Geez," I say.

"I'm sure they didn't mean for it flip like that. They were just trying to stop them," he says.

All I can do is nod my head. I think I'm in shock or something. I feel as if I'm in a daze. I'm seeing natives shooting arrows at a Crusher wagon and Joey here to rescue me. This must be a dream.

"Abby, come on, we gotta go now," he says.

He grabs my hand and pulls me to him and picks me up, putting me on the horse. Then he gets up behind me, shouts something to the natives and sets the horse to a gallop. The cold wind hits my face but doesn't seem to bother me right now. For some reason I feel warm all over. My heart is thumping hard in my chest and I'm aware of Joey's arms around me as he holds the reins.

We gallop through the snowy night for a long while until I see trees. I don't remember there being trees before, only flat land. Somewhere along the way the desert turns to a forest of pines and mountains. The snow is not so thick here; I guess the trees shelter the area. Something large looms in the trees, a wagon of some sort but it's so dark I can hardly make it out.

We're up on it in no time and it's a wagon and there are familiar voices echoing from it. The voices sound like Mr. Clark, Lyza, Freckles, and Charlotte. It can't be them because they jumped off the train. In my haze I hear them speaking to me but I can't seem to answer back.

"Is she alright?" asks Mr. Clark.

"I think she's in shock," says Joey.

"Get her inside and warm her up. We have to get going," says Mr. Clark.

"We got her," says Freckles.

I climb the steps to go inside the wagon and someone lays me down on a bed and covers me up. I watch them mill about me as if in a dream. Someone is pouring a warm liquid down my throat. It doesn't taste so good, but then they give me water. I lie back against a pillow and feel the wagon moving beneath me at a quick pace.

"I think she's falling asleep," I hear someone say in a tone far, far, away.

I'm home again, looking up at the tree across from the house. The big oak tree with the golden leaves looms above me. It looks so big, almost too big to climb, and I reach up to grab a branch but it moves away from me. Something touches my foot and I look down to see the roots of the tree moving and stretching. They appear to grow and stretch into a train rail leading into the mountains. High in the sky the sun is setting spreading peach and pink colors across the sky.

I open my eyes and I'm not home. I'm in a bunk, in a wagon that's moving. The wagon creaks and rumbles as it rolls. Baskets and bottles hanging from the ceiling sway to and fro with the movement. I sit up and look around and realize I'm in Oliver T. Clark's snake oil wagon.

"How on earth did I get here?" I ask aloud.

"Oh, Abby, you're awake!" exclaims Charlotte.

I look down and see Charlotte is sitting up from a pile of furs and blankets on the floor next to my bed. I looks as though she has been sleeping there. Her hair is tousled and her eyes sleepy but she has a smile on her face.

"Charlotte, how did I get here? How did you get here? Where are we going?" I ask.

"Whoa, slow down, we'll get to all that in a minute. How are you feeling?" asks Lyza, popping up behind me.

"Is everyone here?" I ask, looking around.

"Yep," says Freckles. She comes over and sits on the bunk and plops down a furry mass on my lap.

"Boots!" I exclaim. Boots comes up to me purring and nuzzling me. It seems he is just as happy to see me as I am him.

"So what happened? How did you meet up with Mr. Clark?" I ask.

"First things first. Let's take a look at you. You had an awful spill last night I hear," says Lyza.

"I'm fine, I think. It all seems like a dream though. I'm not sure if any of it is real," I say.

"If you're talking about that handsome redhead out there, he's definitely real," says Charlotte.

"Is Joey really here?" I ask.

"Yes, he's out riding with the other boys," says Freckles.

"Julian and Tom, and Kent?" I ask.

"And Mr. Bo and a few others. It's like we have an army now," says Charlotte.

"Oh Charlotte dear, were going to need a lot more people than that for an army, but it's a start," says Lyza.

"Did Mr. Bo find his girlfriend?" I ask.

"No, she had already left. Apparently she has gone back home. But he's still hopeful he will be able to find her," says Freckles.

"Ah, love is so grand," says Charlotte.

"Really Charlotte, what do you know about love?" asks Lyza.

"That's not nice. Especially since you all have beaus, including Abby now," says Charlotte.

"The natives? Are they here too?" I ask, changing the subject.

"Some are. The others went back to gather their warriors together," says Freckles.

"They're going to meet us at our destination," says Lyza.

"Which is where?" I ask.

"Well, that's what we need you for. So you need to get up,

refresh, have something to eat, and get it together, girl," says Lyza.

I get up and realize that I'm stiff and ache all over. I must have hurt myself in that tumble after all. I don't have time to think about it right now. I hastily drink the tea Lyza offers me and eat the sandwich Charlotte has made me. By the time I'm done eating the wagon has stopped.

"Why didn't you just look at the map yourselves, you have it," I say.

"Well, Abby, it's your map and we didn't want to mess with it," says Charlotte.

I appreciate this gesture in part, but there is another part of me that wishes that they could have just looked for themselves. I just want to go out and see Joey right now. But I open Papa's spyglass and take the map out, spreading it over the table. Just as I do, the door of the wagon opens and Mr. Clark comes in followed by Julian, Tom, and Joey.

"Hello there Miss Abby, how you feeling this fine day?" asks Mr. Clark.

"I feel okay, thank you. I'm awful sorry I didn't meet you when we were supposed to meet. Things sort of happened that were out of my control," I say.

"Yes, yes, I know. Your friends have recounted me with your tail and adventure thus far. I am simply glad we have managed to meet up with you in time," he says.

"Oh yes sir, so am I," I say.

"And I reckon I have brought you a gift in the meeting," he says.

"Yes sir you have," I say. I look at Joey and smile. I would love to give him a big hug right now but the wagon is very crowded and there is no way I can get to him. Instead I will have to make do with the smile he returns me. I look back down at the map and study Colorado in depth.

"I'm hoping Papa is in Colorado Springs," I say

"Why do you think he is?" asks Julian.

"Because of this right here," I say, pointing to the word Ormes.

"Ormes, what is that?" asks Freckles.

"Or who?" I ask.

"You think it's a person?" asks Tom.

"I haven't a clue," I say.

"That, my dear, is your clue," says Mr. Clark, stroking his beard in thought.

"Maybe it's a place in Colorado Springs," suggests Joey.

"Yeah, maybe it's an inn or something," says Charlotte.

"I think you're close, hang onto that thought," says Mr. Clark.

He starts rummaging around in boxes. This is difficult since there are so many of us in here he has to move us around to get to the boxes he wants to look through. I would never imagine so many people could fit in here, but then I never imagined any of this anyway.

I look over wistfully at Joey who catches my eye and smiles at me again. I'm getting that warm feeling all over again. There are so many things I want to say to Joey and ask him about, but there hasn't been a moment where we can talk yet.

"Here it is," announces Mr. Clark. He holds up a rolled up paper about as long as my arm.

Mr. Clark takes the rolled up paper and spreads it across the table so we can all see. It's a map like mine but twice the size and labeled with cities and towns and lakes and roads. It appears to be a larger version of my map and maybe more updated and just more intricate.

"This map has more of the names of places here. Look, there's your Ormes," he says, pointing to a spot on the map.

I look close and there opposite and a little northwest of Colorado Springs is Ormes Peak. There are several other names south and west of this one with the word peak and mountain as well. However, this is the only Ormes noted on the map.

"So you think it's a mountain peak?" asks Julian.

"Well, if the shoe fits," says Mr. Clark.

"It's the only Ormes I see and the one clue we have," I say.

"Is it far do, you think?" asks Freckles.

"Oh, perhaps half a day at best. We can be there just after supper if we leave now," says Mr. Clark.

"I say we go for it. We can't stay here. We have to go somewhere," I say.

"If nothing else, we can at least hide out there if we have to," says Tom.

"The snow has stopped for the moment, so if we are heading into some mountain we had better do it now," says Julian.

"Don't you think maybe we ought to send a scout on ahead?" asks Lyza.

"Good idea, we'll send the boys on up ahead to check things out," says Mr. Clark.

Well there goes my time with Joey. Oh well, at least I got to see him again. I suppose the most important thing right now is to find Papa. It's just that Joey being here now is such a distraction, and I need to know why he's here and how he got here. His mother is the one who turned me over to the Crushers in the first place. Now suddenly Joey appears out of nowhere? I hate to be suspicious, especially about Joey, but I wonder why he's here and how he even found me.

The wagon rolls on and so do we, up and through the forest into the mountains. Funny how a little while ago we were in the desert and now we are climbing higher into the mountainous pines. It's too cold to ride outside, so the girls and I ride inside the wagon and try not to get too bored.

I keep thinking that we are almost there and soon I will see Papa, but the hours seem to drag on and on. I wonder what if we get to this Ormes Peak and Papa isn't even there. What if we are going the wrong way? Or what if Papa has left already and I have missed him again like I have been doing this whole time.

Then there is the ultimate question, what if Papa didn't want me to find him? What if this is all for nothing and he sends me back? That thought keeps straying into my mind even though I try and tell myself that is ridiculous. My papa loves me and will be happy to see me.

"So how did you girls end up with Mr. Clark and the boys?" I ask.

"When that detective took you we knew we had to get away. I knew he'd try and get us too and then there would be no one to help any of us out," says Lyza.

"I was hoping you'd puzzle that out," I say.

"Yeah well, we were halfway out the door when you yelled for us to run," says Freckles.

"I didn't want to leave you Abby, but Lyza said it would be for the best," says Charlotte.

"And she was right, Charlotte. I'm glad you ran," I say.

"We hid in the woods but figured they'd come after us sooner or later so we lit out to the town," says Lyza.

"That's when I saw the wagon with the snake on it," says Charlotte.

CHAPTER 39

"We remembered you telling us about Mr. Clark and how he helped you. We caught up with him and asked him if he knew you," says Freckles.

"He didn't want to say much at first but then Boots here started fussing in the bag," says Lyza.

"What do you mean fussing?" I ask.

"He acted kind of weird, moving around and meowing in the bag which is not normal for him," says Lyza.

"Mr. Clark asked us if we had a cat in the bag and I said yes his name is Boots. Then he asked if he could see him and I opened the bag and Boots jumped right out and into Mr. Clark's wagon," says Charlotte.

"Mr. Clark said he knew that cat and it belonged to Miss Abby," says Freckles.

"I told him that's what we are trying to tell him and that you needed help. For that matter so did we cause the Crushers came around about then," says Lyza.

"Mr. Clark told us to get in his wagon, so we did," says Charlotte.

"Okay but then how did you meet up with Joey and the rest of the gang?" I ask.

"Joey was inside the wagon sleeping when we hid inside. We got to talking and figured out from conversation he'd been looking for you," says Freckles.

"Yeah Abby, he left his ma and town and has been traveling all over trying to find you. He happened to run into Mr. Clark on the road and had that poster of you. Mr. Clark recognized it and said he knew you," says Charlotte.

"While we talked to Joey, Mr. Clark drove the wagon out to the other side of town. He started setting up his camp. That's when Julian, Tom, Kent and Mr. Bo saw him. Julian and Tom remembered him from your telling and thought to ask if he'd seen you," says Lyza.

"We saw the boys from the window and came out. Mr. Clark liked to have a fit when he realized we were all together," says Charlotte.

"So that's when we made the plan to get you. Mr. Clark knew the local natives so he got them to help," says Freckles.

"Wow, it's amazing you all found each other," I say.

"I know, it's like it's fate or something," says Charlotte.

"It's something, that's for sure," says Lyza.

The wagon stops abruptly and I jump up quick. My stomach is all a flutter and I'm giddy with anticipation. I can't believe we're finally here and I'll get to see Papa. Without a word I throw the door open and I'm about to jump out of the wagon.

"Abby wait," says Lyza.

"What?" I ask, impatient.

"Take this, just in case," says Lyza.

I look down as she presses the derringer into my hand.

Without thinking, I stick it in my boot, nodding to her in understanding, and rush out the door. Behind the wagon I see nothing but natives mounted on horses. There are so many of them among the trees I can't even count them. I turn and head to the front of the wagon where Joey is talking with Mr. Clark. Joey turns and comes toward me.

"We found the hide out, or at least we found someone's hide out. Julian figures you better be up front and center. If it's where your papa is, they need to know we ain't the System, Abby," he says.

"Okay," I say. I'm a little disappointed we aren't there already.

Joey reaches his hand down to help me up behind him. He takes his foot out of the stirrup so I can put mine in and pulls me up with ease. I sit behind him wrapping my arms about his waist.

"Just follow on up, Mr. Clark, but take your time," says Joey.

Mr. Clark nods and Joey nudges his horse up the hill. I have so many things going on in my head right now that I'm unsure where to begin. I should concentrate on seeing Papa but if Joey is a spy I need to know before we get any closer to Papa.

"Joey, why did you come looking for me?" I ask.

"Mama told me what she done. How she turned you in to the Crushers. She made me so mad, Abby girl. She shouldn't have done that. She got no right tellin' me who I can and can't be with. I came lookin' for you cause you're my girl, Abby, aren't you?"

"Well that depends on what your reasons is for finding me, and how you found me, Joey," I say as calm as I can. My heart is just pounding. Dare I hope that he came looking for me because he loves me?

"I followed the trail. I asked people questions, if anyone seen you, found out the Crushers took you to a workinhouse. By the time I got to the place they took you, it had blown up. I thought for sure you died in that workinhouse. I felt so bad, and thought I would just die myself, Abby. I couldn't stand the thought of you being gone forever," he says.

I can hear his voice crack a little and I can feel his emotions coming through, but I can't see his eyes. If I could see his eyes I'd know if he's telling me the truth.

"I didn't know where to go from there so I just sort of wandered around for a while. Then one day I saw the wanted poster with the likeness of you and your name. They spelled it wrong but I knew it was you and I realized you were still alive. I found my hope and will to live. Right then I knew I had to find you. Not long after, I happened on the road where Mr. Clark traveled and he picked me up. It turns out he had just dropped you off near a mountain pass. When he heard I'd been lookin' for you he turned right around to take me to you, only you wasn't there anymore. I got scared somethin' bad mighta happened in the ravine," he says.

"A man named Bisket tried to kill me. I think I would be dead if it hadn't been for the Sky Riders. They picked me up in their dirigible. Didn't you see that man's body?" I ask.

"No, there weren't no body Abby, but I could see blood all over the rocks," he says.

Joey stops the horse and jumps down. He reaches up and pulls me down off the horse. We stand looking at each other. I look into his eyes and I feel like I'm about to melt.

"Abby, I think I know what you're afraid of. You think I might be a spy, but I ain't, I swear to you. You're my girl and I came lookin' for you cuz I knew you were in trouble. Maybe you don't wanna be my girl and that's okay, but I'm gonna see you through this first and make sure your gonna be okay," he says.

"Oh Joey, of course I'm your girl. I'm so glad you did come for me. I never thought that I would ever see you again and it hurt my heart to think about it but I had no choice. I had to leave," I say.

Joey smiles, and it's the most wonderful smile I've seen in a long time. He leans down and he kisses me gently on the lips. A rush of warmth flows all over me and I feel a tingling feeling like thousands of butterflies lighting on my skin. My heart beats fast like a drum but this time not out of fear but out of joy.

"Let's go find your papa, Abby. I got something I wanna ask him," he says smiling.

Joey puts me back on the horse and leads it up the hill. As he walks the horse I wonder what it is he wants to ask Papa, but I dare not even try and guess.

As we reach the top of the hill, I see Julian and Tom on their horses, waiting. Across from them is an entrance to a cave with five sentries standing guard with guns at the ready. The whole scene looks volatile. The last thing I want is for anyone to get shot.

"That's far enough, red," yells a sentry as we near the entrance.

He and the other men are wearing matching clothes. I take it for a uniform of a sort. They have on light tan button-down shirts and dark green breeches tucked into dark brown boots. The one variation to their attire is their coats. Two are wearing fur coats that look like they took the fur from several different animals and sewed them together. The other three are wearing dark green dyed wool coats. Overall the effect helps them blend in with the woods around them.

"Like I told yer friends, this here's private property so you can jist turn around," says another man.

"I'm here to see my papa, Bishop Steel," I say. I pull the scarf off my head and let my red hair fall across my shoulders.

"How do we know you is his daughter," asks one man.

"Shush, you pumquat, they didn't know he was here till you said somethin'," says a man on the far end.

"Well, now cause of you they know for sure, pumquats all yaw," says the big man in the middle. He comes forward a little and studies me.

"Is my papa here or not?" I ask.

"Could be a trick of the System," says another man.

"Okay you're all not too bright are you? It's obvious he's here from the way you're talking. Why don't you go and find out if there is someone who can verify this is AB'Gale Steel," say Julian.

"Better yet, just go get Mr. Steel, and have him come up like I asked before," says Tom.

"Geeze, we ain't stupid, just not expecting this," says a scrawny man on the other end.

"Go get Roger," says the big man.

Two men run into the cave. Joey helps me down while we're waiting. Tom and Julian dismount as well and we stand and wait for whoever this Roger guy is. I notice that the air is getting colder by the minute and wonder if another storm is coming. There's already about an inch or two of snow on the ground, though most of it has melted or turned into mud in some places.

Finally I see someone coming out of the cave but I'm again disappointed because it's not my papa. I've never seen this man before but he looks like he holds some authority here. He's wearing brown breeches with suspenders and a tan cotton shirt with the sleeves rolled up. Over that he wears a vest. He doesn't have a coat on and he's not wearing boots but scuffed dress shoes, the kind you'd wear out to dinner or the opera maybe. On his head he wears a top hat with a feather stuck in the band on the left side.

His face is weathered, but his long mustache is well manicured, ending in a curl on both sides. He wears round spectacles that have a blue hue to them. He carries himself with importance walking upright with long strides.

"Miss Steel, I presume," he says, bowing to me, "I am Roger Willow."

"Hello, I'm AB'Gale Steel, and I'm pleased to meet you. Now if you would be kind enough to take me to my papa I would appreciate it," I say.

"You must understand, we are a bit surprised you found us. As you may see, we are a bit suspicious," he says, eyeing the boys.

"I used the map with clues that Papa left for me," I say.

"Do you have this map? May I see it?" he asks.

Now I'm suspicious. If we are wrong and these people are the System then we have just played into their hands and given them the map. Even if they are not the System, they could be some other people who want to find Papa. I hesitate, unsure of what to do, and Mr. Willow notices and smiles at me.

"A stalemate I see neither one of us willing to trust the other. This is what the System has done to us. Very well, I will let the four of you pass, but if it turns out that you are spies, you will be eliminated immediately. Is this acceptable?" he asks.

"Yes, since we aren't spies and have nothing to hide. I just want to see Papa," I say.

"Then come with me and we shall see," he says.

We follow the man through the cave entrance and into darkness except for the lantern that he carries. Why must it always be a cave or a mineshaft? I am so sick of having to go underground. Suddenly he stops and turns to us.

"I almost forgot, we'll need you to leave your weapons here," he says.

"We haven't got any weapons on us," says Joey.

"You don't, but she does," he says, pointing to me.

"No I don't," I say. I wonder how he knows. Am I walking funny or something?

"Are you certain?" he asks.

"Very!" I say. I'm starting to get irritated.

"Search them," he says, motioning to the guards that accompanied us.

After the men searched the boys, finding nothing, they started to come toward me to search me but I back away. There is no way these men are putting their hands on me. I feel the derringer in my boot but there is no way I'm letting them have it. I have been through way too much and have come too far.

"You keep back, or my papa will hear about this. I swear to you I have no weapons," I say.

"Okay then, come on," says Mr. Willow.

We continue on through the cave until the darkness starts to get lighter. Mr. Willow turns the lantern off and I can see sunlight shining through a large opening in the wall. It looks as though this is not a real cave but a natural tunnel of some sort. As we come out of the tunnel we are standing atop a small canyon.

Below us are shacks and houses and tents scattered all over. People are walking around doing things. Some are loading carts, others are filling boxes. Above us are scores of dirigibles tethered to makeshift moorings. In the distance are men and woman practicing shooting and archery.

It's almost as if we have stumbled upon an army preparing for battle. In the center of it all is a large square building with an extremely tall pole in the center of it. It's so tall that it towers above the trees and dirigibles. I can hardly believe something like this has gone unnoticed by anyone.

We take a pathway that leads from the tunnel down into the canyon. It's a bit of a walk and I'm feeling sorry that they made us leave our horses behind now. My legs ache from going downhill for so long. We reach the bottom and head toward the main building. I notice people stop their work and watch us as we walk past them. I wonder why and what they're thinking.

Finally we get to the building and Mr. Willow opens the door for us. Inside there is a familiar smell of burning chemicals just like Papa's workshop in the barn at home. The building is a large open room with all sorts of strange equipment with men working on them. We walk past these toward a table against the wall.

Two men have their heads bent over something in deep discussion. Our footsteps echo off the walls bringing attention to our presence. The men lift their heads to see who is approaching. They stop their discussion for a moment and look at us in puzzlement. One of the men, the oldest of the two, sees first the boys, and then me. Our eyes meet and I see recognition and surprise in Papa's eyes.

CHAPTER 40

"Ab'Gale," says Papa.

I rush into his waiting arms and he folds them into a loving embrace. So long have I waited for this moment that I can hardly believe it's real and not a dream. He holds me tight and I breathe deep the smell of his aftershave and hair gel. I close my eyes and I'm home again and all that has passed has been a dream and nothing more. But I open my eyes, and we're not at home.

"Papa, I never thought I would find you," I say, pulling back from his embrace to look at him.

He's much older than I remember him, but it hasn't been that long has it? His hair is much whiter and his beard is thick with speckles of red among the white. His eyes are tired and wrinkled around their edges but they still sparkle that deep blue I remember.

"Abby, I never meant for this to happen," he says.

"I know, Papa, but I found you and now we have to go get Granny, they put her in an oldies home," I say.

"Granny is fine. I had her rescued and taken home to her kin where she will be safe, for a time at least," he says.

"Oh, I'm so relieved, I didn't know what to do or where to find her but I had the map that old Jim gave me to find you," I say.

"I'm glad you have the map because it proved to be much harder for me to find you. I had intended on getting you and Granny out of the house before anything happened. I apparently moved too late and then I had to go into hiding or they would have found me as well. I had people searching for you but other than the rumors and then the posters the System put out, you could not be traced," he says.

"I kept moving and never stopping in one place for long," I say.

"I'm so proud of you. But now we can discuss all this later," says Papa.

"Mr. Steel," says Roger, gaining Papa's attention.

"Oh, yes Roger it's all right they are with me. This is my daughter," he says.

"What about the rest of them?" asks Roger.

"The rest of them?" Papa asks.

He looks at me curiously, and then suddenly realizes that there are three other people with me.

"Yes Papa, you remember Joey from home?" I ask.

I grab Joey by the hand and pull him up closer to Papa.

"Joey? My goodness, did you come all this way with Abby?" asks Papa, shaking Joey's hand.

"No, sir, well it's a long story," says Joey.

"And this is Julian and Tom. They have helped me and the girls along the way," I say.

"Boys, thank you for bringing my daughter to me safely," says Papa.

"The girls are coming in Mr. Clark's wagon," I say.

"The girls?" asks Papa.

"It's a very long story but I have more friends who have traveled with me to find you," I say.

"That's my little Abby. When she was just a tot she smiled at me and warmed my heart right from the start. Now that's my little boxcar baby, making friends everywhere she goes," says Papa. He caresses my face and smiles.

"Actually sir, she has done more than that," says Julian.

"Oh, how so?" asks Papa.

"Abby has become somewhat of a hero I guess. I think it's partly because of you and partly because of the System and their propaganda," says Julian.

"The more the System accused her of doing things like blowing up a workinhouse and causing a train wrecks, the more people loved her. They see her as an example," says Tom.

"Really? Abby blowing up a workinhouse?" asks Papa. He looks at me with alarm.

"No, not really. Well not on purpose. The thing is, Papa, things happened around me while on my way to see you. The System sort of blamed all of it on me whether I had even been to the place or not," I say.

"In an effort to get people to turn Abby in, they made up stories about her. What the System didn't figure on is that it made people want to rebel even more. Because Abby broke free from the System and told others about the people out there trying to survive. Pretty soon Bishop Steel's Boxcar Baby had a following," says Tom.

"What we mean to say, sir, is we have somewhat of an army to join with yours in revolting against the System," says Julian.

"My word, we really do need to sit down and discuss this,

don't we?" asks Papa.

"Roger, we will need to meet with the head of the army to discuss matters before we let everyone in, do you agree?" asks Papa.

"Yes sir," says Roger.

"That would be heads of armies," says Julian.

"What?" I ask, "I saw the natives but who else is here?" I ask.

"The airship pirates and the hobos will be joining us," says Julian.

"AB'Gale, you have been busy," says Papa.

"I had no idea. They just told me to say a few words to the hobos. I didn't know anyone else would even bother," I say.

"Right then, I guess I should show you what I've been working on," says Papa.

"Oh yes, please," I say.

"Come with me," he says.

We follow Papa through the building which I now see is a giant lab for Papa's work. There are a lot of other people in here working on various projects. I can't tell what all these gadgets are but everyone appears busy. I hear a loud zapping noise and look to my left to see something like the contraption I saw in the mine where I found Tom. Only this one is much bigger.

Papa leads us through a door which that goes right into the hillside. Here we are again inside some sort of cave or mine shaft. Doesn't anyone keep anything above ground? We walk down a path a ways until he stops us and then reaches over and turns a switch on the wall. The room lights up as if by magic. I'm so amazed by the bright light that I almost miss the real surprise standing right in front of me.

Rows upon rows of metal men stand in front of us. They

stand at attention and don't even move but look forward through large goggled eyes. Other than their eyes, there are no other facial features except long wide slits where the mouths would be. On top of their heads, which are octagon in shape, there are an upside down funnel like contraptions and some wires on either side. The bodies are smooth metal with arms and legs and rivets here and there holding everything in place. For the most part the bodies are large and square in shape and adorned with nothing.

"What are they?" I ask.

"This is our army of automatons," says Papa.

"Autonomatons?" I ask.

"Automatons," he corrects me.

"What do they do?" asks Tom.

"They're soldiers. We radio commands and they follow the commands. Remember the little squirrel we made back home, Abby?" asks Papa.

"Yes Papa, I remember. It worked on clock parts," I say.

"Well these men are clockwork inside as well, with a little added wireless electricity," says Papa.

"Wireless electricity?" I ask.

"Yes, an invention of a colleague of mine. It's the radio system to send commands," says Papa.

"Do they have weapons?" asks Julian.

"Oh yes, several. They shoot electricity out of the fingers of their right hand to stun. There are real bullets and gunpowder in their left arm which they shoot out of the index finger. They also spit fire, so to speak," says Papa laughing.

"These are amazing. How are they powered?" asks Tom.

"Natural energy my boy, they harness energy from the sun. They also grasp electrical energy from the air around us so we don't have to wind them up," says Papa.

"Electrical energy in the air?" asks Joey.

"Yes my boy, it's all around us you just don't always know it. But with the right
substance you can harness it. The bodies of the automatons are made with a special mixture of metals to help them harness this energy as well as the solar energy from the sun. It's also bulletproof so whatever our enemy shoots at them will bounce off," says Papa.

"Do they talk?" I ask.

"No, they don't speak, though I'm sure we could work that in. We didn't feel it necessary. They are actually war machines," says Papa.

"They are so amazing, Papa, how many of them are there?" I ask.

"I'm afraid not enough. We've managed to make around four hundred and sixty-two I believe last we counted," says Papa.

"And that's your army?" asks Joey.

"No, that's part of the army. We have the people here I have been working with that's about a thousand or so," says Papa.

"The natives who came with us, I don't how many of them came, but it looks like a fair amount," I say.

"Gray Hare promised us at least eight or nine hundred warriors from the Midwest. He said more may come from other parts of the nation but he couldn't promise they would come," says Julian.

"Gray Hare? You talked to him? Did you see Raine?" I ask.

"No, sorry, I didn't see Raine," says Julian.

"We have the hobos and the Sky Pirates coming too, not sure how many though," says Tom.

"Well we may have an army yet. Come on let me show my other masterpiece," says Papa.

We follow Papa back out of the cave and into the lab. He takes us to a contraption that looks like an engine, sort of, but it's a bit smaller. It's also more round and less complicated than an engine but with lots of gadgets. An odd looking man is working on it and stops when he sees us approach. I say he's odd more out of his mannerisms than his appearance because he's quite handsome for a gentleman his age, I think.

"I have a confession to make," says Papa.

"What is it?" asks.

"This is not all my handiwork. True, I have a lot of input and have organized and managed a great deal but Nikola here is the actual genius. He smuggled himself into America, hoping to find a way to achieve some great things. But the System tried to throw him into a workinhouse, whereupon he shut the entire place down and escaped. Somehow he managed to make his way to us and we have been working in secret for many years. I thought I had some clever ideas, but this is one is an achievement," says Papa.

"What does it do?" asks Tom.

"It is a motor that runs on electricity called AC power," says Nickola.

"What are you going to use it for?" I ask.

"We are going to update the industrial workforce with these. This is a prototype, but with these, motors factories will work much smoother, safer, and more efficient. You'll still need people to run them, but that's another part of the plan," says Papa.

"What plan?" I ask.

"We can't just go and knock out the System without some sort of government to replace it. We also need some way to sustain the people and the commodities. We are putting together a committee of people to work out all the details so that when we are ready to march we will have our ducks in a row," says Papa proudly.

"So you have been doing this for a while, then?" I ask.

"Yes, but in secret, I never realized they were on to me until too late. But all is well now and I have my most top secret weapon ever in store for the battle," says Papa.

"What is it?" I ask.

"You will soon find out," says Papa.

"We have a lot of planning to do, I guess, and we need to get Mr. Clark in on this too," I say.

"Come on then, let's get a meeting of the minds together. Nikola, do you mind finishing up here while I take care of this," asks Papa.

"Not a problem, Mr. Steel," says the odd man.

I hasten after Papa, dragging Joey along with me. Joey has kept quiet this whole time which tells me he has no idea what is going on. I probably don't either but I feel the excitement mounting in the air. I feel like something big is about to happen.

CHAPTER 41

Julian, Tom, and Joey leave with Roger back through the tunnel. I follow Papa through the little makeshift village to a cottage off to one side. Inside there are two cots, a table with two chairs, a cook stove, and a pantry. It's far from luxury; in fact it almost seems like a prison.

"Papa, are these people holding you against your will?" I ask.

"No, of course not, why would you think that?" he asks.

"Captain Dux said there were people who would want to take you hostage and make you work for them," I say.

"So you met the Sky Riders, did you?" he asks, laughing.

"Yes, they saved my life, a man named Bisket tried to kill me and get the map from me," I say.

"Bisque`, you met him too, then?" Papa asks, very serious.

"Yes, but I think he's dead now. I had to shoot him with Mr. Clark's snake venom gun," I say.

"I'm sorry you had to shoot a man, Abby. You're too young to have to defend yourself against the likes of him or anyone else for that matter. It's my fault you got in to all this trouble. I know the System is after you now. I'm not sure where to begin and we don't have a lot of time to discuss all this at the moment. I want you to know that all this is happening for a good reason," he says.

"I know, Papa; I know the System is wrong. I've seen a lot of bad things because of the System and if those inventions of yours will help, then I'm all in," I say.

"That's my girl. Our main problem is I believe we have run out of time. I thought we would have more time to complete some more soldiers and for Nikola to master the motor," he says.

"But why do you think we're out of time, Papa?" I ask.

"Because they found out about me and tried to get at me through you and Granny. The fact that you have been on the run all this time bothers me. You could have been killed. They have been chasing you and following you at the same time. I'm almost certain they were hoping you would lead them right to me," says Papa.

"Oh no! I didn't mean to, Papa! Do you think they followed me?" I ask.

"Maybe not precisely here, but they know I'm close and that's too close for me. No the time has come, we must strike before all our plans are foiled," says Papa.

"Do you mean the revolution?" I ask.

"Yes, I'm afraid we must proceed ahead of schedule," he says.

"My friends, well you met the boys, but Lyza, Freckles and Charlotte, you haven't met them yet. But they all believe in this revolution, Papa. They are all here to help," I say.

"Come here and sit down a moment," says Papa. He motions to the two chairs at the table.

I sit down at the table, feeling a little nervous, afraid of what Papa is about to tell me, his voice sounds so serious. He sits down across from me and takes a deep breath and lets it out slowly before he begins to speak. Papa has always done this when he has something important to say.

"It warms my heart that you have such good and loyal friends that have seen you through these hard times. You're going to need them before the end of this," he says.

"I know it's going to be hard, Papa, but it's for the better and the good of all the people. I also realize it's going to be dangerous too," I say.

"I know you do Little Sis, but there's more to it than that," he says.

"What do you mean, Papa?" I ask.

"Remember I told you I have a secret weapon I had been waiting on?" he asks.

"Yes, Papa," I say.

"You're the secret weapon," he says. A nervous smile plays upon his lips for a moment, and then he looks at me in all seriousness as if reading my reaction.

"What do you mean, Papa?" I ask, unsure if I really want to know.

"I need to tell you about your mother," he says.

"My mother?" I ask.

"She's alive," he says.

"Okay, so?" I say. Geeze, that's not fair. So my mother is alive, but she left me in a boxcar.

"You remember the reason I never married? The woman I once loved all those years ago, she didn't die. She's your mother. But she fell in love with another man and ran away from me before we were to be married," says Papa.

"Papa, don't tell me this, not now," I say.

"You need to know. They came to see me when they hit hard

times and I refused them. The Crushers came for them but she hid you away. I think she knew, or at least maybe she had hoped, that I would find you," says Papa.

"It doesn't matter, Papa, you're still my papa," I say.

"I know," he says. He nods his head. "But you need to know about your grandfather," says Papa.

"My grandfather, aren't you skipping someone like my father?" I ask.

"Your father is no longer alive," says Papa.

"Oh," is all I can think to say.

"That is only part of what you need to know. I'm sorry you didn't get to know your real papa. He was a good man, but I'm afraid doomed from the moment he married your mother. Anyone below her stature would have been, including me," says Papa.

"I don't understand what you're saying, Papa," I say. I see something in his eyes, an emotion I'm not sure how to register.

"Listen, I'm sure by now you've seen the name Grugen in your travels. Mr. Grugen owns a good bit of the mines and the workinhouses," he says.

"Yes I noticed that and a hobo lady once gave me a piece of paper with the name written on it. I didn't understand what it meant," I say.

"Of course not, but she apparently knew about you. Do you remember what she looked like?" he asks.

"Not really, she had a German accent and I wondered about that," I say.

"Yes well it was Grugen who put a stop to immigration. He is the key to the whole use of American citizens as the workers bees to better America. Grugen convinced the government party not to let any more people into America. He would have them believe that immigrants corrupted our way of life, our System," he says.

"So who is this Grugen?" I ask. Then I get it. It hits me like a freight train.

"Grugen is your grandfather. He is your mother's father. I'm not clear on the details of how your father died, if it had been a real accident or not. I do know that Grugen took your mother back into the fold of the family after your father died. I don't believe he knows anything about you or who you are, and that makes you an absolute gem. You are the secret weapon because your mother will never let anything happen to you. Once she finds out that you are alive and well, then we may just have a bargaining tool to get in," says Papa.

"Is that why you kept me all these years, Papa?" I ask.

"Oh no, dear child, you are as precious to me as if you were my own. I would never in a million years intentionally put you in harm's way. I'm angry with myself for letting any of this happen to you. Granny and I love you dearly, AB'Gale," he says.

"I believe you Papa, I love you too. All that doesn't matter to me, but if you think there is some way I can help then I will, Papa," I say.

I stand up and walk over to him giving him a big hug. He hugs me back and when we pull apart I can see tears welling up in his eyes.

"That's my girl. I knew you would understand. Now let's go make some plans and build us a better world, shall we?" he asks. He stands up and grabs some papers off the table and motions me to follow him.

We go back outside and down the path to a large open tent filled with tables and chairs and dirt floor. It's cold and windy outside but here the hillside and the buildings block the wind. It looks like a common area and where everyone goes to eat. On one side is a large cooking area set up with serving tables and water buckets for dish washing. Dutch ovens and fryers are stacked along one end of the table.

"This is the best place to have any sort of a meeting where enough people can get together," says Papa.

No sooner does he say that I hear voices and turn to see people streaming in, led by Roger. Lyza, Freckles, and Charlotte see me and run to my side. I think to introduce them to Papa but already he is introducing himself to other people. I see men I recognize from the hobo jungle. Several natives have come too. A man steps out of the crowd and I recognize him right away as the Sky Pirate, Cinder. I look around wondering if Mandy Moon is here too.

"I'll have to introduce you to Papa later, I guess," I say.

"It's okay, we're so glad you finally found him," says Freckles.

"Yeah, a happy ending, you got your papa and you got your beau," says Charlotte.

"Geeze, Charlotte, are you forgetting we are about to go to war?" asks Lyza.

"Really? We're going to war?" asks Charlotte.

"It looks that way. Papa has been working on some machines to help," I say.

"Jeepers," says Charlotte.

"What, like a weapon?" asks Lyza.

"Well yes, I guess they are," I say.

"Why don't we find some seats in the tent before they're all gone, and find out what's going on," suggests Freckles.

"Good idea," I say.

We all agree and head into the tent. The seats are starting

to fill up but we happen to find some near the back. Now and then I catch someone staring at me as if they know me, or of me. Sometimes I smile and sometimes I ignore them and pretend I don't see them staring.

"Well, we have a lot of people here, that's alright I suppose. We all have an interest in this whether you're leading or fighting or both. We have a cause to fight for, and it's our freedom," says Papa.

The crowd cheers and agrees at this. Papa stands before them not on a pedestal, or in any way above them, but at their level and in front. Sometimes while he talks he walks among the people, looking them in the eye as if speaking one on one with that person.

"Some of you have been here a while, getting prepared for the fight. You are already recruited but wondering what we're up to in that big old building there," says Papa, pointing the direction of his lab. The crowd laughs.

"Some of you just got here, aching for a fight because enough is enough. This is no way to treat your citizens. You can't just take from them whenever you want," says Papa. The crowd is jeering now, angry and agreeing with Papa.

"Now we have several inventions and plans we are going to use and one of them we will use to run this new government once we have put it into place. No more workinhouses and no more mandatory oldies homes. Everybody will have work to do and everybody will get paid for it. We are going to march right into the heart of the System and throw those tyrants out. In their place we will vote in a council to help govern our society in a fair and organized manner. Each state will vote for their representative, and each representative will sit on the council.

We will rule ourselves and be our own people. We will open trade with other countries, selling what we make to them instead of just turning it around for profit to the rich here. We will send our children to school and not make them work in mines and cotton fields. We will make America stand for something special," says Papa.

The crowd claps and cheers, hooting and hollering until I feel for sure the canyon walls will fall. I looked over at my friends and smile. That's my papa up there, and he is gonna change the world.

Something flies past me so fast it's like a bug or something, but it catches my attention. No sooner do I notice this then I hear the sound. A loud crack. Not like thunder but like a snap of a whip but with more of an echo and bass to it. It takes me a moment to recognize the sound, but by the time I figure it out Papa is down on the ground in a pool of blood.

CHAPTER 42

$\mathcal{P}$eople are rushing toward Papa while other people rush away from the scene. A small group chase after the shooter who is weaving his way through the crowd.

I feel numb all over and the whole thing feels so surreal. I think Papa just got shot and the man running did it. 'Someone stop him,' I think to myself. I turn toward Papa, running, pushing my way through the crowd.

Papa is on the floor and there's blood everywhere on his leg, but I can't tell exactly where it's coming from. Two people are trying to stop the blood from flowing but it keeps coming. I just found my papa and now someone has shot him. This can't be happening.

"Papa," I say. I kneel next to him. He reaches out and takes my hand.

"Abby, you need to keep it going, don't stop," he says.

"Hush, Papa. Don't worry about that now, I'll take care of it," I say. I feel the tears welling up in my eyes. He can't be dying, he just can't.

I watch as some men lift Papa and carry him to his shack. I

start to go in but I am pushed back outside by Roger.

"Stay out here. We'll call you if something changes," he says.

"But is there at least a doctor or a nurse?" I ask.

"I'm the doctor, and there are plenty of people in there to help me. Just let me do my work, okay?" he asks.

I nod my head and step back from the door watching it close. I stand there a moment staring at the door not knowing what to do when I feel someone take my hand. I look over and see Freckles. Someone else takes my other hand and it's Joey. Julian and Tom show up with some stools and chairs and set them up just outside the door. Then they go back and drag a table over after I sit down. Lyza and Charlotte bring some tea out and we sit and we wait.

While we wait I tell them all what Papa told me about my mother and father and grandfather. It occurs to me that Papa hadn't told me their names though. I wonder why? He could at least tell me my mother's name.

"So you're the secret weapon. I don't see how that's going to help any," says Lyza.

"Me neither. I guess maybe when we march our army into the System headquarters they're gonna say, 'Oh by the way we got the grandchild of Mr. Grugen here. We know you didn't know about her but she wants to talk to you about changing the entire government system.' They'll say, 'Oh hey great sounds good let's do it,'" I say.

"That's funny," Charlotte laughs.

"Yeah Abby, everything will be peppermints and popsicles now," says Freckles.

We all look at Freckles for a moment and then bust out laughing because what she just said makes no sense at all.

Sometimes a good laugh makes you feel better and that one sure made me feel better.

"Hey, what's that up there?" asks Tom pointing to the sky.

We all look up and there are five small dots way up in the sky. They seem to be moving pretty fast but not like birds or anything natural. As they grow larger I realize they are dirigibles of a sort, but none like the Sky Riders.

"They're flying machines but they have wings like birds," says Charlotte.

"Wow, look at all the colors and designs," says Freckles

"They're not designs, they're painted to look like actual wings so the whole thing looks like a giant bird," says Lyza.

"Are they foe or friend?" asks Julian.

"I have no idea. Wait, I got it," I say. I still have Papa's spy glass strapped to me. I take it out and open it and look through it adjusting the glass until I can see.

"They're natives!" I exclaim.

"Let me see, please?" asks Charlotte.

I hand her the spyglass and she looks through it.

"They are! My, what a strange contraption. Oh look, I see Raine!" she says, excited. She hands the glass to Freckles.

Freckles takes the spy glass and looks through it.

"Where? I don't see her," she says.

"Look at the one to the far right," says Charlotte.

While everyone takes turns looking through Papa's spyglass, I watch the crew climb the ladders to the landings. The landings are high above built along the cliff just for dirigibles and hot air balloons. They have at least twenty of these built along the canyon which I hadn't notice before. I saw the ones with vessels already tethered but now I notice more of these landings. I guess they expected an entire fleet. These people have been planning this for a long time and now it seems that it might actually be happening at last.

The door opens to Papa's shack and Dr. Roger Willow steps out, wiping his hands on a towel. He looks tired and I try to read his face but I can't. He starts to walk over to me and then stops as he notices the vessels coming too. He smiles and then comes to me.

"Your Papa is going to be all right. I'm afraid we had to amputate the lower half of his leg though. The bullet shattered a lot of the bone but that wasn't the worst part," he says.

"What worst part?" I ask.

"There is some kind of poison on the bullet. Even if we could mend the bone the poison has gotten into his bloodstream and would have killed him had we let it get much farther. We managed to cut his leg off in time so not enough of the poison got to his heart to kill him. He will be a little sick for a while," says Roger.

"Poison?" I ask.

"Yes. Have they caught that fellow yet?" he asks.

"I haven't heard anything," I say.

"They will, I'm sure of it. In the meantime your papa will need lots of rest," says Roger.

"How will Papa be able to fight like that or finish his projects?" I ask.

"Don't you worry about that. I'm about to put my top men on the project," he says.

I watch him walk away, wondering what he's talking about. I get up and go inside and see Papa lying on the cot asleep. Most everyone has left the room except for a couple of people still cleaning up. After they leave Joey comes inside and shuts the door.

"Where did everyone go?" I ask.

"They all went to meet Raine and the natives," he says.

"Oh yeah, I forgot," I say.

"Mr. Clark has made camp on the other side of the shack if you need him. He says he'll come and look in on your papa in a little while and see if there is anything he can do," says Joey.

"Okay," I say. I feel a little numb right now, maybe tired and worried, but I don't want to sleep.

"Do you want me to leave?" he asks.

"No, please stay and wait with me until Papa wakes," I say.

"Sure Abby, if you lie down and get some sleep. I'll watch over your papa," he says.

"Okay, sure Joey," I say.

I lie down on the other cot across the room and close my eyes. I don't think I can sleep even if I wanted to. There is so much going on in my head. I mean I knew Papa wasn't my real father, but to find out that my mother is still alive and that she is the daughter of the mastermind behind the System. It's almost sickening. On the other hand it's kind of ironic that I should be part of the plan to bring it all down. In the process maybe I will even get my mother back.

If I get my mother back suppose there is the possibility that Papa and she are still in love? What then? Wow what a thought. They could get married and I could have a whole family. I wonder how Granny feels about my mother.

I'm glad to know my mother didn't leave me because she didn't want me. She didn't leave me in a box for some random person to find. She left me to protect me. She left me in the hope that Bishop Steel would find me and raise me to be his own. She must know I'm alive then.

I will just have to go find her and let her know I'm alive. Maybe her father is holding her hostage and won't let her leave. I can help her escape and she can come live with Papa, Granny and me. She can help us fight the System because she will know the inside secrets.

I must have fallen asleep because I wake up to Joey gently shaking me.

"Hey Abby girl, it morning and your papa is awake," he say.

I jump up right away and rush to Papa's bedside. Roger is standing on the other side of the bed talking with him. He sees me and winks.

"Papa, are you okay?" I ask.

"Yes, I'm right as rain but half a leg short," he says.

"Oh Papa don't joke like that. It's not funny," I say.

"Sometimes child, you have to laugh at things like this when you have managed to beat off the grim reaper," he says.

"You will be up and about in no time. I've got the boys making you a fine leg of oak and leather. It will be the envy of every pirate," says Roger.

"Sounds fine, Roger. I can't wait. Maybe you could add a little something to it like a weapon or something," says Papa.

"Now Bishop, I'm not the tinkerer you are. You'll have to come up with that one on your own," says Roger.

"I believe I have an idea," says Papa.

"Gracious, Abby, keep an eye on him. I've got to go. I have other patients of a sort," he says.

"Is someone sick?" I ask.

"Not exactly. They caught the man who shot your papa. A man called Bisque` and they want to question him," says Roger.

"I know that man. He tried to kill me. I thought I killed him!" I exclaim.

"Did you do that to his face?" asks Roger.

"What's wrong with his face?" I ask.

"Well it's sort of melted and deformed and kind of rotting away," he says.

"Snake venom and acid. I shot him with Mr. Clark's snake venom gun," I say.

"Hmm, could be a useful weapon with a little tweaking, I will have to talk to this Mr. Clark," says Papa.

"Oh hush, Papa. You need to rest," I say.

"Anyway, I have to go make sure they don't kill him while getting the information out of him. Let me know if you need anything, Bishop," says Roger. He leaves, donning his hat as he goes.

I look around and see that Joey has left too and so Papa and I are alone. That's good so we can talk for a little bit. I have some questions I hope he will answer especially the first one.

"Papa, you didn't tell me my mother's name," I say.

"Josephine, her name is Josephine. The most beautiful woman in the world," he says.

"What about my father? What was his name?" I ask.

"Arthur, Arthur Steel," says Papa.

It takes me a moment to realize that he just gave me the name of a man who has the same last name as ours. Wait a minute!

"Papa, is he related to you?" I ask.

"Yes, Arthur was my younger brother," says Papa.

"So you're really my uncle then?" I ask.

"I guess so," he says quietly.

"It doesn't matter; you're my papa anyway, right?" I ask.

"If you still want me as your papa after all these secrets," he says.

"You don't have any more do you?" I ask.

"Just one," he says.

"Well then you better come clean," I say.

"That young man of yours wants to marry you," says papa.

"What?" I ask.

"Joey and I had a nice long chat this morning while you were sleeping. I told him whatever you wanted to do is fine with me as long as you waited until you were eighteen," says Papa.

"Are you serious? He asked for my hand, Papa?" I ask.

"Yes, but I said I'm old fashioned and I would like for you to wait at least until you're eighteen," says Papa.

"Of course I'll wait, Papa," I say.

"But that's our secret. You can't tell him I told you," says Papa.

"Oh I won't, he needs to ask me proper," I say.

"That's my girl. Now I wonder if you wouldn't mind fetching me something to eat. I'm famished," he says.

"Of course I don't mind," I say.

I leave Papa and step outside into the fresh mountain air. I take a deep refreshing breath of the wonderful pine air. Making my way to the common tent, it's odd that only yesterday everything seemed so awful and today things feel so much better. I see all my friends sitting at a table eating. Charlotte sees me and motions me to join them.

Charlotte is sitting next to a handsome young man I've not met before. Freckles and Lyza are talking and laughing with Raine of all people. Tom, Joey, and Julian seem to be in a deep discussion with Gray Hare and Mr. Bo. They all seem to be getting along and having a good time.

I know it won't always be like this especially if we are going to be revolting against the government. There is going to be hard times ahead of us. But we have each other and as long as we stick together and be there for each other I think we're going to be okay. Papa will be up and walking soon and we'll get the automatons ready for battle. The System has no idea what's coming, but we do. There is something in the air and it feels like hope.

CHAPTER 43

Detective Walker contemplates out the window from the hospital bed. His silence is broken by the sound of footsteps approaching from the hall. A knock at the door brings him out of his thoughts.

"Come in," he says.

Two men dressed in the System uniform enter the room. One remains at the door, standing at attention like a toy soldier. The other approaches Detective Walker's bedside. He does not salute or give salutations.

"Detective Walker?" the soldier asks.

"Yes that's me," says Detective Walker.

"Are you ill, sir?" asks the soldier.

"A cracked rib is all. I am on the mend," says Detective Walker.

"You are to report to military duty upon your full recovery and release from the hospital. Here are your orders, sir," says the soldier.

The soldier hands Detective Walker an envelope and waits at attention while he opens it and reads it. Detective Walkers reads the letter twice before looking up at the soldier in disbelief.

"I don't understand, officer. I'm a detective, not a soldier," says Detective Walker.

"It is not my place to decipher your orders, sir, I am only here to deliver them and to make sure you understand them and will comply," says the soldier.

"Is there anyone I can talk to, perhaps your superior officer or someone in rank who I can discuss this with?" asks Detective Walker.

"No sir, not at this time. When you report to duty you may speak with your superior officer regarding your orders at that time. Will you comply, sir?" asks the soldier. "Do I have a choice?" asks Detective Walker.

"Yes sir, you do. I am to escort you to the prison immediately if you are unwilling to comply," says the soldier.

"Then I don't have a choice, really. Yes, sir, I will comply," says Detective Walker.

"Very good, sir. A car will come in the morning to pick you," says the soldier.

"I thought you said once I am on the mend I would report to duty?" asks Detective Walker.

"Yes sir, in the meantime you will be escorted to the military hospital where they will attend to you until you are able to report to your duty," says the solider.

"Of course. Fine then, I'll be ready," says Detective Walker.

The solder nods an affirmative, turns and leaves with the other soldier at his heels. They both walk very precisely and mechanically as if machines themselves. If not for the serious letter, Detective Walker would find this amusing.

He stares down at the letter and reads it again to be sure what he read is correct. After all, his medication might make his eyes and mind play tricks on him.

By Order of the System Council and by reason of your failure to perform your duties as a detective in apprehending notorious criminals, you will report to the military base at Fort Smith, Arkansas where you will begin your training as a military soldier. Your career as a System Detective is at end. Your office has been evacuated and sorted. Your personal belongings, as appropriate, will be shipped to your new location. Any deviance from this Order will be considered treason and you will be tried and court marshalled immediately as a sympathizer and dealt with appropriately.
Signed,
System Detail Assignment Department Counsel

A sympathizer, really? After all he had gone through to find the girl and her father. How could they do this? He is not a sympathizer. He had her in his grasp and was taking her in. He had a hot trail to the father; he almost had the Steels. How could the System believe he was a sympathizer? He remembered clearly that the natives attacked them and stole the girl from him.

The two men with him would attest to that, even in court. Even as they waited for help after the accident they discussed the incident and the two men clearly stated there were natives shooting arrows at them. There were arrows in the tires. Clearly they had been attacked.

A nurse came in, breaking his train of thought. She was the prettier of the two that had been taking care of him, though older but not married. She wore the System blue and white medical uniform and had her blonde hair pulled back in a large bun. He wondered how long it went if she were to let it down.

"How is my handsome patient today?" she asks.

"Much better, I think," he says.

"I saw that you had visitors. I guess this means you will be leaving me soon," she says.

"I'm afraid so, duty calls," he says, trying to put on a smile.

"Oh, all the handsome ones leave me and I get stuck with the old, ugly, and married," she says.

"I'm sorry. Maybe you should be a nurse at the military hospital, perhaps you would meet a handsome solider there," says Detective Walker.

"That's an idea I haven't considered," she says.

"Can you tell me how the two gentlemen are that came in with me?" he asks.

"The two what? You mean the two dead guys?" she asks.

"What do you mean dead guys? No they brought me in with two SPO when we were in the accident. They were in the front of the vehicle. I rode in the back. They had a few cuts and bruises, I think one might have had a broken wrist but they were far from dead. I assure you," says Detective Walker.

"I'm sorry, sir; you must have been in shock. Both of those men were dead. You are the only survivor. You're lucky that girl and her army didn't kill you," she says.

"Army? There is no army, just a few natives who shot the tires out with arrows," says Detective Walker.

"That's not how I heard it. The paper says an army of System rebels shot the tires out and attacked you. Apparently it is debated on as to whether or not you assisted them. You didn't, did you?" she asks.

"Certainly not, why would I do that?" he asks.

"I don't know, but that's what the System reported. That you were under investigation about it," says the nurse.

"Oh, I don't remember talking to any System questioners. Were they here?" asks Detective Walker.

"I don't know. They weren't here on my watch. I'm sure the System knows what they are doing. I'll be back to check on you in an hour or so," she says.

He watches as she leaves the room and stares at the door a moment longer. He wonders what is going on. There had been no army and those men were nowhere near death. How could they be dead? A thought occurs to him, but it's so impossible that he can hardly let himself believe it but he dares. Detective Walker turns and stares out the window and wonders if AB'Gale Steel is right and that the System is all wrong.

****

Josephine Grugen stands on the sidewalk, unmoving. Her forgotten parasol falls to her side as a light breeze begins to pick up blowing loose strands of red hair about her face. Pink lace soaks up dirt and mud at the bottom of her dress as it blows into the gutter unchecked. Still she stands, unmoving, staring at the poster pasted on the wall.

Could it be? She thinks and wonders to herself as she gazes at the hand-drawn black and white poster of a young girl. The likeness is so uncanny that she cannot take her eyes from it. Below the name reads Abigail Steel.

Quickly she looks around and seeing no one about or paying her any mind, she reaches out and rips the poster from the wall. Carefully she folds it and places it in the purse hanging from her wrist. She would read what is says later. Right now she has an appointment with the dressmaker for her wedding gown.

Yet as she walks briskly to the shop her mind is in a flurry of thoughts. Could that child be her daughter? Is she in trouble? Did Bishop actually find the baby she left so long ago in the pile of cotton in the train yard? Her heart leaps into her throat at the thought of it. What if it were her, what if? Does she know about her mother and father, or had Bishop kept it a secret all these years.

So many things go through her mind but most of all, she wonders: What if?

ACKNOWLEDGEMENTS

I would like to thank my husband Matt and daughters Kristina and Amanda for their support and wild ideas. Thank you to my mother Sylvia and my entire family in the west for their encouragement and support. Also, thank you to my uncle Gordon for being one of the father figures in my life.

I would also like to thank and acknowledge the following people for their assistance in either promoting, being a sounding board, giving me ideas, supporting and assisting with research and being a friend: My cousins Cal Harris and Geoff Harris; The Clockwork Community; Cannon Trawets and Airship 67; George Holland, I never get tired of talking with you; Karl Williams, fantastic conversations and many more to come I hope; Larry Kenney, because without Lion-O and the ThnuderCats where would I be today; Michael Glorioso, because it's nice to be remembered when someone goes to another country; Tim Gatewood, you are always so supportive of the arts; my writer's group The Clinton Ink-Slingers but especially J. Moffett Walker, who has been a great mentor.

My thanks to my publisher Stephen Zimmer for believing in me; and my editor Amanda DeBord for putting up with me; and my artist Anne who is amazing.

A big thank you to my readers and the many people who speak to me at conventions and book signings and for their assistance in helping me continue with this story, you know who you are and this is for you.

.

ABOUT THE AUTHOR

A California native born in Hollywood, J.L. Mulvihill has made Mississippi her home for the past seventeen years. Her debut novel was the young adult title The Lost Daughter of Easa, an engaging fantasy novel bordering on science-fiction with a dash of Steampunk, published through Dark Oak Press in 2011. The sequel to this novel is presently in the works.

Her most recent novel, The Boxcar Baby of the Steel Roots series, was released in July 2013 through Seventh Star Press. Steel Roots is a young adult series based in the Steampunk genre and engages the reader into a train hopping heart stopping adventure across America.

She is also the co-editor of Southern Haunts; The Spirits That Walk Among Us which includes a short story of her own called Bath 10, and a fictional thriller involving a real haunted place. Her poem, The Demon of the Old Natchez Trace, debuts in Southern Haunts part 2, Devils in the Darkness.

J.L. also has several short fiction pieces in publication, is very active with the writing community, and is the events coordinator for the

Mississippi Chapter of Imagicopter known as the Magnolia-Tower. She is also a member of the Society of Children's Book Writers and Illustrators (SCBWI), Gulf Coast Writers Association (GCWA), The Mississippi Writers Guild (MWG), as well as the Clinton Ink-Slingers Writing Group.

J.L. continues to write fantasy, steampunk, and poetry and essays inspired by her life in the South. You can find some of her short stories at

Dark Oak Press www.darkoakpress.com

as well as

Seventh Star Press www.seventhstarpress.com

and at her websites:

www.elsielind.com

jlsbooks.blogspot.com/

home.comcast.net/~mulvijen/site

Check out the following pages
to see more from

All Seventh Star Press titles available in
print and an array of specially priced eBook
formats.

Visit www.seventhstarpress.com for further
information

Connect with Seventh Star Press at
www.seventhstarpress.com
seventhstarpress.blogspot.com
www.facebook.com/seventhstarpress
www.twitter.com/7thstarpress

Transcend Reality!

An Anthology of Animal Companions from Editor Scott Sandridge! Available in print and eBook!

Hero's Best Friend
Softcover ISBN: 978-1-937929-51-0
eBook ISBN: 978-1-937929-52-7

How far would Gandalf have gotten without Shadowfax? Where would the Vault Dweller be without Dogmeat? And could the Beastmaster been the Beastmaster without his fuzzy allies? Animal companions are more than just sidekicks. Animals can be heroes, too! Found within are twenty stories of heroic action that focuses on the furries and scalies who have long been the unsung heroes pulling their foolish human buddies out of the fire, and often at great sacrifice-from authors both established and new, including Frank Creed, S. H. Roddey, and Steven S. Long. Whether you're a fan of Epic Fantasy, Sword & Sorcery, Science Fiction, or just animal stories in general, this is the anthology for you! So sit back, kick your feet up, and find out what it truly means to be the *Hero's Best Friend*.

16 Tales of the Paranormal and Ghostly from editors Alexander S. Brown and J.L. Mulvihill!

Softcover ISBN: 978-1-937929-12-1

eBook ISBN: 978-1-937929-14-5

From the shadowed realms of the paranormal comes 16 chilling tales that dwell in the South and South West. From 16 authors, learn of haunted homes, buildings, landmarks and roads where restless entities from beyond the grave desire acknowledgement amongst the living. Become acquainted with the aftermath of an eclipse that awakens the dead in a Memphis cemetery, see what horrors dwell in the woods at Hell's Gate, learn the dark secrets of Sidney's Cotton, and dare to travel down Ghost Road. These and many other tales are sure to keep you awake as you are introduced to what makes the South and South West so unique.... History and GHOSTS!!!!! So, sit back, dim the lights and prepare yourself to face the spirits that walk among us.

Begin the Adventures of Blue Shaefer in *Haunting Blue* from R.J. Sullivan!

Softcover ISBN: 978-1-941706-05-3

eBook ISBN: 978-1-941706-06-0

"She discovered the town's biggest secret..... now there's hell to pay!"

Punk, blue-haired "Blue" Shaefer, is at odds with her workaholic single mother. Raised as a city girl in a suburb of Indianapolis, Blue must abandon the life she knows when her unfeeling mother moves them to a dreadful small town. Blue befriends the only student willing to talk to her: computer nerd "Chip" Farren.

Chip knows the connection between the rickety pirate boat ride at the local amusement park and the missing money from an infamous bank heist the townspeople still talk about. When Blue helps him recover the treasure, they awaken a vengeful ghost who'll stop at nothing--not even murder--to prevent them from exposing the truth behind his evil deeds.

Haunting Blue is Book One of the Adventures of Blue Shaefer

YA Fantasy From Jackie Gamber!
The highly-acclaimed Leland Dragon Series from Jackie
Gamber! Strong character-driven YA Fantasy for those who
enjoy authors such as Christopher Paolini.

Softcover ISBN: 9780983108672

eBook ISBN: 9780983108696

Softcover ISBN: 9781937929893

eBook ISBN: 9781937929817

Softcover ISBN: 9781937929404

eBook ISBN: 9781937929435

From Bram Stoker Award-winning Editor Michael Knost!

Softcover ISBN:

978-1-937929-61-9

eBook ISBN:

978-1-937929-62-6

Writers Workshop of Science Fiction and Fantasy is a collection of essays and interviews by and with many of the movers-and-shakers in the industry. Each contributor covers the specific element of craft he or she excels in. Expect to find varying perspectives and viewpoints, which is why you many find differing opinions on any particular subject.

This is, after all, a collection of advice from professional storytellers. And no two writers have made it to the stage via the same journey-each has made his or her own path to success. And that's one of the strengths of this book. The reader is afforded the luxury of discovering various approaches and then is allowed to choose what works best for him or her.

Featuring essays and interviews with:

Neil Gaiman, Orson Scott Card, Ursula K. Le Guin, Alan Dean Foster, James Gunn, Tim Powers, Harry Turtledove, Larry Niven, Joe Haldeman, Kevin J. Anderson, Elizabeth Bear, Jay Lake, Nancy Kress, George Zebrowski, Pamela Sargent, Mike Resnick, Ellen Datlow, James Patrick Kelly, Jo Fletcher, Stanley Schmidt, Gordon Van Gelder, Lou Anders, Peter Crowther, Ann VanderMeer, Joh Joseph Adams, Nick Mamatas, Lucy A. Snyder, Alethea Kontis, Nisi Shawl, Jude-Marie Green, Nayad A. Monroe, G. Cameron Fuller, Jackie Gamber, Amanda DeBord, Max Miller, Jason Sizemore.

Dystoptian Anthology *Perfect Flaw* Now Available!

Softcover ISBN: 978-1-937929-11-4

eBook ISBN: 978-1-937929-13-8

Readers everywhere are invited to experience adventures of a dystopian nature in the anthology Perfect Flaw, from editor Robin Blankenship! Featuring seventeen speculative fiction tales, spanning many genres, Perfect Flaw explores the subject of societies gone wrong. From "utopian" societies masking an underlying controlled state, to stories of people fighting back against repression, in hopes of a better world, the flaws that create a dystopian atmosphere are brought to light. Thought-provoking and entertaining, Perfect Flaw will be a welcome addition to any reader's collection of dystopian literature.

Softcover ISBN: 978-1-937929-47-3

eBook ISBN: 978-1-937929-48-0

The Fey have been with us since the beginning, sometimes to our great joy but often to our detriment. Usually divided (at least by us silly humans) into two courts, the first volume of A Chimerical World focuses on the Seelie Court: the court we humans seem to view as the "good" faeries. But "good" and "evil" are human concepts and as alien to the Fey as their mindsets are to us.

Inside you will find 19 stories that delve into the world of the faeries of the Seelie Court, from authors both established and new, including George S. Walker, Eric Garrison, and Alexandra Christian.

But be warned: these faeries are nothing like Tinker Bell.

Softcover ISBN: 978-1-937929-49-7
eBook ISBN: 978-1-937929-50-3

The Fey have been with us since the beginning, sometimes to our great joy but often to our detriment. Usually divided (at least by us silly humans) into two courts, the second volume of A Chimerical World focuses on the Unseelie Court: the court we humans seem to view as the "evil" faeries. But "good" and "evil" are human concepts and as alien to the Fey as their mindsets are to us.

Inside you will find 19 stories that delve into the world of the faeries of the Unseelie Court, from authors both established and new, including Michael Shimek, Deedee Davies, and Nick Bryan.

But don't be surprised if these faeries decide to play with their food.

Olde School, a new take on the world of fairy tales and folklore from Selah Janel!

Softcover: 978-1-937929-65-7

eBook: 978-1-937929-67-1

Kingdom City has moved into the modern era. Run by a lord mayor and city council (though still under the influence of the High King of The Land), it proudly embraces a blend of progress and tradition. Trolls, ogres, and other Folk walk the streets with humans, but are more likely to be entrepreneurs than cause trouble. Princesses still want to be rescued, but they now frequent online dating services to encourage lords, royals, and politicians to win their favor. The old stories are around, but everyone knows they're just fodder for the next movie franchise. Everyone knows there's no such thing as magic. It's all old superstition and harmless tradition.

Bookish, timid, and more likely to carry a laptop than a weapon, Paddlelump Stonemonger is quickly coming to wish he'd never put a toll bridge over Crescent Ravine. While his success has brought him lots of gold, it's also brought him unwanted attention from the Lord Mayor. Adding to his frustration, Padd's oldest friends give him a hard time when his new maid seems inept at best and conniving at worst. When a shepherd warns Paddlelump of strange noises coming from Thadd Forest, he doesn't think much of it. Unfortunately for him, the history of his land goes back further than anyone can imagine. Before long he'll realize that he should have paid attention to the old tales and carried a club.

Darkness threatens to overwhelm not only Paddlelump, but the entire realm. With a little luck, a strange bird, a feisty waitress, and some sturdy friends, maybe, just maybe, Padd will survive to eat another meal at Trip Trap's diner. It's enough to make the troll want to crawl under his bridge, if he can manage to keep it out of the clutches of greedy politicians.